COCKTAIL TIME

——— ALSO BY P.G. WODEHOUSE ———

Joy in the Morning

Very Good, Jeeves!

Right Ho, Jeeves

The Inimitable Jeeves

Thank You, Jeeves

The Code of the Woosters

Leave It to Psmith

Uncle Fred in the Springtime

Blandings Castle

Heavy Weather

Summer Lightning

Service With a Smile

Uncle Dynamite

Young Men in Spats

COLLECTIONS:

Just Enough Jeeves

A Bounty of Blandings

Utterly Uncle Fred

COCKTAIL TIME

P. G. WODEHOUSE

W. W. Norton & Company
New York · London

First published as a Norton paperback 2013

For information about special discounts for bulk
purchases, please contact W. W. Norton Special Sales
at specialsales@wwnorton.com or 800-233-4830

Manufacturing by Courier Westford
Book design by Judith Abbate
Production manager: Louise Mattarelliano

Library of Congress Cataloging-in-Publication Data

Wodehouse, P. G. (Pelham Grenville), 1881–1975.
Cocktail time / P.G. Wodehouse. — First Norton
paperback [edition]
        pages cm
   ISBN 978-0-393-34560-5 (paperback)
1. Blandings Castle (England : Imaginary place)—
Fiction. 2. Nobility—Fiction. 3. Inheritance and
succession—Fiction. 4. Shropshire (England)—
Fiction. 5. England—Fiction. I. Title.
            PR6045.O53C6 2013
              823'.912—dc23
                                2012040846

W. W. Norton & Company, Inc.
500 Fifth Avenue, New York, N.Y. 10110
www.wwnorton.com

W. W. Norton & Company Ltd.
Castle House, 75/76 Wells Street, London W1T 3QT

1 2 3 4 5 6 7 8 9 0

COCKTAIL
TIME

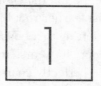

1

THE train of events leading up to the publication of the novel *Cocktail Time*, a volume which, priced at twelve shillings and sixpence, was destined to create considerably more than twelve and a half bobsworth of alarm and despondency in one quarter and another, was set in motion in the smoking-room of the Drones Club in the early afternoon of a Friday in July. An Egg and a Bean were digesting their lunch there over a pot of coffee, when they were joined by Pongo Twistleton and a tall, slim, Guards-officer-looking man some thirty years his senior, who walked with a jaunty step and bore his cigar as if it had been a banner with the strange device Excelsior.

'Yo ho,' said the Egg.

'Yo ho,' said the Bean.

'Yo ho,' said Pongo. 'You know my uncle, Lord Ickenham, don't you?'

'Oh, rather,' said the Egg. 'Yo ho, Lord Ickenham.'

'Yo ho,' said the Bean.

'Yo ho,' said Lord Ickenham. 'In fact, I will go further. Yo frightfully ho,' and it was plain to both Bean and Egg that they were in the presence of one who was sitting on top of the world and who, had he been wearing a hat, would have worn it on the side of his head. He looked, they thought, about as bumps-a-daisy as billy-o.

And, indeed, Lord Ickenham was feeling as bumps-a-daisy as he looked. It was a lovely day, all blue skies and ridges of high pressure extending over the greater part of the United Kingdom south of the Shetland Isles: he had just learned that his godson, Johnny Pearce, had at last succeeded in letting that house of his, Hammer Lodge, which had been lying empty for years, and on the strength of this had become engaged to a perfectly charming girl, always pleasant news for an affectionate godfather: and his wife had allowed him to come up to London for the Eton and Harrow match. For the greater part of the year Lady Ickenham kept him firmly down in the country with a watchful eye on him, a policy wholeheartedly applauded by all who knew him, particularly Pongo.

He seated himself, dodged a lump of sugar which a friendly hand had thrown from a neighbouring table, and beamed on his young friends like a Cheshire cat. It was his considered view that joy reigned supreme. If at this moment the poet Browning had come along and suggested to him that the lark was on the wing, the snail on the thorn, God in His heaven and all right with the world, he would have assented with a cheery 'You put it in a nut-shell, my dear fellow! How right you are!'

'God bless my soul,' he said, 'it really is extraordinary how fit I'm feeling today. Bright eyes, rosy cheeks, and the sap rising strongly in my veins, as I believe the expression is. It's the London air. It always has that effect on me.'

Pongo started violently, not because another lump of sugar had struck him on the side of the head, for in the smoking-room of the Drones one takes these in one's stride, but because he found the words sinister and ominous. From earliest boyhood the loopiness of this uncle had been an open book to him and, grown to man's estate, he had become more than ever convinced that in failing to add him to their membership list such institutions as Colney Hatch and Hanwell were passing up a good thing, and he quailed when he heard him speak of the London air causing the sap to rise strongly in his veins. It seemed to suggest that his relative was planning to express and fulfil himself again, and when Frederick

Altamont Cornwallis Twistleton, fifth Earl of Ickenham, began to express and fulfil himself, strong men—Pongo was one of them—quivered like tuning forks.

'The trouble with Pongo's Uncle Fred,' a thoughtful Crumpet had once observed in this same smoking-room, 'and what, when he is around, makes Pongo blench to the core and call for a couple of quick ones, is that, though well stricken in years, he becomes, on arriving in London, as young as he feels and proceeds to step high, wide and plentiful. It is as though, cooped up in the country all the year round with no way of working it off, he generates, if that's the word I want, a store of loopiness which expends itself with terrific violence on his rare visits to the centre of things. I don't know if you happen to know what the word "excesses" means, but those are what, the moment he sniffs the bracing air of the metropolis, Pongo's Uncle Fred invariably commits. Get Pongo to tell you some time about the day they had together at the dog races.'

Little wonder, then, that as he spoke, the young Twistleton was conscious of a nameless fear. He had been so hoping that it would have been possible to get through today's lunch without the old son of a bachelor perpetrating some major outrage on the public weal. Was this hope to prove an idle one?

It being the opening day of the Eton and Harrow match, the conversation naturally turned to that topic, and the Bean and the Egg, who had received what education they possessed at the Thames-side seminary, were scornful of the opposition's chances. Harrow, they predicted, were in for a sticky week-end and would slink home on the morrow with their ears pinned back.

'Talking of Harrow, by the way,' said the Bean, 'that kid of Barmy Phipps's is with us once more. I saw him in there with Barmy, stoking up on ginger pop and what appeared to be cold steak-and-kidney pie with two veg.'

'You mean Barmy's cousin Egbert from Harrow?'

'That's right. The one who shoots Brazil nuts.'

Lord Ickenham was intrigued. He always welcomed these

opportunities to broaden his mind and bring himself abreast of modern thought. The great advantage of lunching at the Drones, he often said, was that you met such interesting people.

'Shoots Brazil nuts, does he? You stir me strangely. In my time I have shot many things—grouse, pheasants, partridges, tigers, gnus and once, when a boy, an aunt by marriage in the seat of her sensible tweed dress with an airgun—but I have never shot a Brazil nut. The fact that, if I understand you aright, this stripling makes a practice of this form of marksmanship shows once again that it takes all sorts to do the world's work. Not sitting Brazil nuts, I trust?'

It was apparent to the Egg that the old gentleman had missed the gist.

'He shoots things *with* Brazil nuts,' he explained.

'Puts them in his catapult and whangs off at people's hats,' said the Bean, clarifying the thing still further. 'Very seldom misses, either. Practically every nut a hat. We think a lot of him here.'

'Why?'

'Well, it's a great gift.'

'Nonsense,' said Lord Ickenham. 'Kindergarten stuff. The sort of thing one learns at one's mother's knee. It is many years since I owned a catapult and was generally referred to in the sporting world as England's answer to Annie Oakley, but if I had one now I would guarantee to go through the hats of London like a dose of salts. Would this child of whom you speak have the murder weapon on his person, do you suppose?'

'Bound to have,' said the Egg.

'Never travels without it,' said the Bean.

'Then present my compliments to him and ask if I might borrow it for a moment. And bring me a Brazil nut.'

A quick shudder shook Pongo from his upper slopes to the extremities of his clocked socks. The fears he had entertained about the shape of things to come had been realized. Even now, if his words meant what they seemed to mean, his uncle was preparing to be off again on one of those effervescent jaunts of his which had done so much to rock civilization and bleach the hair of his nearest and dearest.

He shuddered, accordingly, and in addition to shuddering uttered a sharp quack of anguish such as might have proceeded from some duck which, sauntering in a reverie beside the duck pond, has inadvertently stubbed its toe on a broken soda-water bottle.

'You spoke, Junior?' said Lord Ickenham courteously.

'No, really, Uncle Fred! I mean, dash it, Uncle Fred! I mean really, Uncle Fred, dash it all!'

'I am not sure that I quite follow you, my boy.'

'Are you going to take a pop at someone's hat?'

'It would, I think, be rash not to. One doesn't often get hold of a catapult. And a point we must not overlook is that, toppers being obligatory at the Eton and Harrow match, the spinneys and coverts today will be full of them, and it is of course the top hat rather than the bowler, the gent's Homburg and the fore-and-aft deerstalker as worn by Sherlock Holmes which is one's primary objective. I expect to secure some fine heads. Ah,' said Lord Ickenham, as the Bean returned, 'so this is the instrument. I would have preferred one with a whippier shaft, but we must not grumble. Yes,' he said, moving to the window, 'I think I shall be able to make do. It is not the catapult, it is the man behind it that matters.'

The first lesson your big game hunter learns, when on safari, is to watch and wait, and Lord Ickenham showed no impatience as the minutes went by and the only human souls that came in sight were a couple of shopgirls and a boy in a cloth cap. He was confident that before long something worthy of his Brazil nut would emerge from the Demosthenes Club, which stands across the street from the Drones. He had often lunched there with his wife's half-brother, Sir Raymond Bastable, the eminent barrister, and he knew the place to be full of splendid specimens. In almost no place in London does the tall silk headgear flourish so luxuriantly.

'Stap my vitals,' he said, enlivening the tedium of waiting with pleasant small-talk, 'it's extraordinary how vividly this brings back to me those dear old tiger-shooting days in Bengal. The same tense expectancy, the same breathless feeling that at any moment something hot may steal out from the undergrowth, lashing its top hat. The only difference is that in Sunny Bengal one was up in a tree with a kid tethered to it to act as an added attraction for the monarch of the jungle. Too late now, I suppose, to tether this young cousin of your friend Barmy Phipps to the railings, but if one of you would step out into the street and bleat a little . . . Ha!'

The door of the Demosthenes had swung open, and there had come down the steps a tall, stout, florid man of middle age who wore his high silk hat like the plumed helmet of Henry of Navarre. He stood on the pavement looking about him for a taxi-cab—with a sort of haughty impatience, as though he had thought that, when he wanted a taxi-cab, ten thousand must have sprung from their ranks to serve him.

'Tiger on skyline,' said the Egg.

'Complete with topper,' said the Bean. 'Draw that bead without delay, is my advice.'

'Just waiting till I can see the whites of his eyes,' said Lord Ickenham.

Pongo, whose air now was that of a man who has had it drawn to his attention that there is a ticking bomb attached to his coat-tails, repeated his stricken-duck impersonation, putting this time even more feeling into it. Only the fact that he had brilliantined them while making his toilet that morning kept his knotted and combined locks from parting and each particular hair from standing on end like quills upon the fretful porpentine.

'For heaven's sake, Uncle Fred!'

'My boy?'

'You can't pot that bird's hat!'

'Can't?' Lord Ickenham's eyebrows rose. 'A strange word to hear on the lips of one of our proud family. Did our representative at King Arthur's Round Table say "Can't" when told off by the front office to go and rescue damsels in distress from two-headed giants? When Henry the Fifth at Harfleur cried "Once more unto the breach, dear friends, once more, or close the wall up with our English dead", was he damped by hearing the voice of a Twistleton in the background saying he didn't think he would be able to manage it? No! The Twistleton in question, subsequently to do well at the battle of Agincourt, snapped into it with his hair in a braid and was the life and soul of the party. But it may be that you are dubious concerning my ability. Does the old skill still linger, you are asking yourself? You need have no anxiety. Anything William Tell could do I can do better.'

'But it's old Bastable.'

Lord Ickenham had not failed to observe this, but the discovery did nothing to weaken his resolution. Though fond of Sir Raymond Bastable, he found much to disapprove of in him. He considered the eminent barrister pompous, arrogant and far too pleased with himself.

Nor in forming this diagnosis was he in error. There may have been men in London who thought more highly of Sir Raymond Bastable than did Sir Raymond Bastable, but they would have been hard to find, and the sense of being someone set apart from and superior to the rest of the world inevitably breeds arrogance. Sir Raymond's attitude toward those about him—his nephew Cosmo, his butler Peasemarch, his partners at bridge, the waiters at the Demosthenes and, in particular, his sister, Phoebe Wisdom, who kept house for him and was reduced by him to a blob of tearful jelly almost daily—was always that of an irritable tribal god who intends to stand no nonsense from his worshippers and is prepared, should the smoked offering fall in any way short of the highest standard, to say it with thunderbolts. To have his top hat knocked off with a Brazil nut would, in Lord Ickenham's opinion, make him a better, deeper, more lovable man.

'Yes, there he spouts,' he said.

'He's Aunt Jane's brother.'

'Half-brother is the more correct term. Still, as the wise old saying goes, half a brother is better than no bread.'

'Aunt Jane will skin you alive, if she finds out.'

'She won't find out. That is the thought that sustains me. But I must not waste time chatting with you, my dear Pongo, much as I always enjoy your conversation. I see a taxi-cab approaching, and if I do not give quick service, my quarry will be gone with the wind. From the way his nostrils are quivering as he sniffs the breeze, I am not sure that he has not already scented me.'

Narrowing his gaze, Lord Ickenham released the guided missile, little knowing, as it sped straight and true to its mark, that he was about to enrich English literature and provide another job of work for a number of deserving printers and compositors.

Yet such was indeed the case. The question of how authors come to write their books is generally one not easily answered. Milton, for instance, asked how he got the idea for *Paradise Lost*, would probably have replied with a vague 'Oh, I don't know, you know. These things sort of pop into one's head, don't you know,' leaving the researcher very much where he was before. But with Sir Raymond Bastable's novel *Cocktail Time* we are on firmer ground. It was directly inspired by the accurate catapultmanship of Pongo Twistleton's Uncle Fred.

Had his aim not been so unerring, had he failed, as he might so well have done, to allow for windage, the book would never have been written.

2

HAVING finished his coffee and accepted the congratulations of friends and well-wishers with a modesty that became him well, the fifth Earl ('Old Sureshot') of Ickenham, accompanied by his nephew Pongo, left the club and hailed a taxi. As the cab rolled off, its destination Lord's cricket ground, Pongo, who had stiffened from head to foot like somebody in the Middle Ages on whom the local wizard had cast a spell, sat staring before him with unseeing eyes.

'What's the matter, my boy?' said Lord Ickenham, regarding him with an uncle's concern. 'You look white and shaken, like a dry martini. Something on your mind or what passes for it?'

Pongo drew a shuddering breath that seemed to come up from the soles of his feet.

'How crazy can you get, Uncle Fred?' he said dully.

Lord Ickenham could not follow him.

'Crazy? I don't understand you. Good heavens,' he said, a bizarre thought occurring to him, 'can it be that you are referring to what took place in the smoking-room just now?'

'Yes, it jolly well can!'

'It struck you as odd that I should have knocked off Raymond Bastable's topper with a Brazil nut?'

'It struck me as about as loopy a proceeding as I ever saw in my puff.'

'My dear boy, that was not loopiness, it was altruism. I was spreading sweetness and light and doing my day's kind act. You don't know Raymond Bastable, do you?'

'Only by sight.'

'He is one of those men of whom one feels instinctively that they *need* a Brazil nut in the topper, for while there is sterling stuff in them, it requires some sudden shock to bring it out. Therapeutic treatment the doctors call it, do they not? I am hoping that the recent nut will have changed his whole mental outlook, causing a revised and improved Raymond Bastable to rise from the ashes of his dead self. Do you know what the trouble is in this world?'

'You ought to. You've started most of it.'

'The trouble in this world,' said Lord Ickenham, ignoring the slur, 'is that so many fellows deteriorate as they grow older. Time, like an ever-rolling stream, bears all their finer qualities away, with the result that the frightfully good chap of twenty-five is changed little by little into the stinker of fifty. Thirty years ago, when he came down from Oxford, where he had been a prominent and popular member of the University rugby football team, Raymond Bastable was as bonhomous a young man as you could have wished to meet. The jovial way he would jump with both feet on the faces of opponents on the football field and the suavity of his deportment when chucked out of the Empire on Boat Race night won all hearts. Beefy, as we used to call him, was a fourteen-stone ray of sunshine in those days. And what is he now? I am still extremely fond of him and always enjoy his society, but I cannot blind myself to the fact that the passing of the years has turned him into what a mutual friend of ours—Elsie Bean, who once held office as housemaid under Sir Aylmer Bostock at Ashenden Manor—would call an overbearing dishpot. It's being at the Bar that's done it, of course.'

'How do you mean?'

'Surely it's obvious. A man can't go on year after year shouting "Chops! Gracious heavens, gentlemen, chops and tomato sauce!"

and telling people that their evidence is a tissue of lies and fabrications without getting above himself. His character changes. He becomes a dishpot. What Beefy needs, of course, is a wife.'

'Ah,' said Pongo, who had recently acquired one. 'Now you're talking. If he had someone like Sally—'

'Or like my own dear Jane. You can't beat the holy state, can you? When you get a wife, I often say, you've got something. It was the worst thing that could have happened to Beefy when Barbara Crowe handed him his hat.'

'Who's Barbara Crowe?'

'The one he let get away.'

'I seem to know the name.'

'I have probably mentioned it to you. I've known her for years. She's the widow of a friend of mine who was killed in a motor accident.'

'Isn't she in the movies?'

'Certainly not. She's a junior partner in Edgar Saxby and Sons, the literary agents. Ever heard of them?'

'No.'

'Well, I don't suppose they have ever heard of you, which evens things up. Yes, Beefy was engaged to her at one time, and then I heard that it was all off. Great pity. She's lovely, she's got a wonderful sense of humour, and her golf handicap is well in single figures. Just the wife for Beefy. In addition to improving his putting, always his weak spot, she would have made him human again. But it was not to be. What did you say?'

'I said "Bad show".'

'And you could scarcely have put it more neatly. It's a tragedy. Still, let's look on the bright side. There's always a silver lining. If things are not all that one could wish on the Bastable front, they're fine in the Johnny Pearce sector. How much did I tell you about Johnny at lunch? I can't remember. Did I mention that your Aunt Jane, exercising her subtle arts, had talked Beefy Bastable into taking a five years lease on that Hammer Lodge place of his?'

'Yes, you told me that.'

'And that he's engaged to a delightful girl? Belinda Farringdon, commonly known as Bunny?'

'Yes.'

'Then you're pretty well up in his affairs, and you will probably agree with me that a bright and prosperous future lies before him. Far different from that which, if your young friends at the Drones are to be believed, confronts the athletes of Harrow-on-the-Hill. But here we are at the Mecca of English cricket,' said Lord Ickenham, suspending his remarks as the cab drew up at the entrance of Lord's. 'Golly!'

'Now what?'

'If only,' said Lord Ickenham, surveying the sea of top hats before him, 'I had my catapult with me!'

They entered the ground, and Pongo, cordially invited to remain at his uncle's side, shied like a startled horse and said he would prefer to be pushing along. It was his settled policy, he explained, never again, if he could avoid it, to be associated with the head of the family in a public spot. Look, he argued, what happened that day at the dog races, and Lord Ickenham agreed that the episode to which he alluded had been in some respects an unfortunate one, though he had always maintained, he said, that a wiser magistrate would have been content with a mere reprimand.

A good deal of walking about and hullo-ing is traditionally done at the Eton and Harrow match, and for some little while after parting from his nephew Lord Ickenham proceeded to saunter hither and thither, meeting old acquaintances and exchanging amiable civilities. Many of these old acquaintances had been contemporaries of his at school, and the fact that most of them looked as if they would never see a hundred and four again was a reminder of the passage of time that depressed him, as far as he was capable of being depressed. It was a relief when he observed approaching him someone who, though stout and florid and wearing a top hat with a dent in it, was at least many years from being senile. He greeted him warmly.

'Beefy, my dear fellow!'

'Ah, Frederick.'

Sir Raymond Bastable spoke absently. His thoughts were elsewhere. He was sufficiently present in spirit to be able to say 'Ah, Frederick,' but his mind was not on his half-brother-in-law. He was thinking of the modern young man. At the moment when Lord Ickenham accosted him, there had just risen before his mental eye a picture of the interior of the Old Bailey, with himself in a wig and silk gown cross-examining with pitiless severity the representative of that sub-species who had knocked his hat off.

When the hat he loved had suddenly parted from its moorings and gone gambolling over the pavement like a lamb in springtime, Sir Raymond Bastable's initial impression that it had been struck by a flying saucer had not lasted long. A clapping of hands and the sound of cheering from across the street drew his attention to the smoking-room window of the Drones Club and he perceived that it framed a sea of happy faces, each split by a six-inch grin. A moment later he had seen lying at his feet a handsome Brazil nut, and all things were made clear to him. What had occurred, it was evident, had been one more exhibition of the brainless hooliganism of the modern young man which all decent people so deplored.

Sir Raymond had never been fond of the modern young man, considering him idiotic, sloppy, disrespectful, inefficient and, generally speaking, a blot on the London scene, and this Brazil-nut sequence put, if one may so express it, the lid on his distaste. It solidified the view he had always held that steps ought to be taken about the modern young man and taken promptly. What steps, he could not at the moment suggest, but if, say, something on the order of the Black Death were shortly to start setting about these young pests and giving them what was coming to them, it would have his full approval. He would hold its coat and cheer it on.

With a powerful effort he removed himself from the Old Bailey.

'So you're here, are you, Frederick?' he said.

'In person,' Lord Ickenham assured him. 'Wonderful, running into you like this. Tell me all your news, my bright and bounding barrister.'

'News?'

'How's everything at home? Phoebe all right?'

'She is quite well.'

'And you?'

'I also am quite well.'

'Splendid. You'll be even better when you're settled in down at Dovetail Hammer. Jane tells me you've taken Johnny Pearce's Hammer Lodge place there.'

'Yes. I shall be moving in shortly. Your godson, isn't he?'

'That's right.'

'I suppose that is why Jane was so insistent on my taking the house.'

'Her motives, I imagine, were mixed. She would, of course, for my sake be anxious to do Johnny a bit of good, but she also had your best interests at heart. She knew Dovetail Hammer was just the place for you. Good fishing, golf within easy reach and excellent fly-swatting to be had in the summer months. You'll be as snug as a bug in a rug there, and you'll find Johnny a pleasant neighbour. He's a capital young fellow.'

'Young?'

'Quite young.'

'Then tell him to keep away from me,' said Sir Raymond tensely. 'If any young man attempts to come near me, I'll set the dog on him.'

Lord Ickenham regarded him with surprise.

'You perplex me, Beefy. Why this bilious attitude toward the younger generation? Doesn't Youth with all its glorious traditions appeal to you?'

'It does not.'

'Why not?'

'Because, if you must know, some young thug knocked off my hat this afternoon.'

'You shock and astound me. With his umbrella?'

'With a Brazil nut.'

'Who was this fiend in human shape?'

'All I know is that he belongs to the Drones Club, which to my lasting regret is situated immediately opposite the Demosthenes. I was standing outside the Demosthenes, waiting for a cab, when something suddenly struck my hat a violent blow, lifting it from my head. I looked down, and saw a Brazil nut. It had obviously been thrown from the room on the ground floor of the Drones Club, for when I looked up the window was full of grinning faces.'

Sir Raymond started. A thought had occurred to him. 'Frederick!'

'Hullo?'

'Frederick!'

'Still here, old man.'

'Frederick, I invited you to lunch with me at the Demosthenes today.'

'And very kind of you it was.'

'You declined because you had a previous engagement to lunch at the Drones Club.'

'Yes. Agony, of course, but I had no option.'

'You did lunch at the Drones Club?'

'Heartily.'

'Did you take your after-luncheon coffee in the smoking-room?'

'I did.'

'Then I put it to you,' said Sir Raymond, pouncing, 'that you must have seen everything that occurred and can identify the individual responsible for the outrage.'

It was plain that Lord Ickenham was impressed by this remorseless reasoning. He stood musing for a space in silence, a frown of concentration on his brow.

'Difficult always to reconstruct a scene,' he said at length, 'but as I close my eyes and think back, I do dimly recall a sort of stir and movement at the window end of the room and a group of young fellows clustered about someone who had . . . yes, by Jove, he had a catapult in his hand.'

'A catapult! Yes, yes, go on.'

'He appeared to be aiming with it at some object across the street, and do you know, Beefy, I am strongly inclined to think that this object may quite possibly have been your hat. To my mind, suspicion seems to point that way.'

'Who was he?'

'He didn't give me his card.'

'But you can describe his appearance.'

'Let me try. I remember a singularly handsome, clean-cut face and on the face a look of ecstasy and exaltation such as Jael, the wife of Heber, must have worn when about to hammer the Brazil nut into the head of Sisera, but . . . no, the mists rise and the vision fades. Too bad.'

'I'd give a hundred pounds to identify the fellow.'

'With a view to instituting reprisals?'

'Exactly.'

'You wouldn't consider just saying "Young blood, young blood" and letting it go at that?'

'I would not.'

'Well, it's for you to decide, of course, but it's rather difficult to see what you can do. You can't write a strong letter to *The Times*.'

'Why not?'

'My dear fellow! It would be fatal. Jane was telling me the other day that you were going to stand for Parliament at . . . where was it? Whitechapel?'

'Bottleton East. Frampton is thinking of retiring, and there will be a by-election there next summer probably. I am expecting the nomination.'

'Well, then, think of the effect of a letter to *The Times* on the electorate. You know what the British voter is like. Let him learn that you have won the Derby or saved a golden-haired child from a burning building, and yours is the name he puts a cross against on his ballot paper, but tell him that somebody has knocked your topper off with a Brazil nut and his confidence in you is shaken. He purses his lips and asks himself if you are the right man to represent him in the mother of Parliaments. I don't defend this attitude, I merely say it exists.'

It was Sir Raymond's turn to muse, and having done so he was forced to admit that there was truth in this. Bottleton East, down Limehouse way, was one of those primitive communities where the native sons, largely recruited from the costermongering and leaning-up-against-the-walls-of-public-houses industries, have a primitive sense of humour and think things funny which are not funny at all. Picturing Bottleton East's probable reaction on learning of the tragedy which had darkened his life, he winced so strongly that his hat fell off and got another dent in it.

'Well,' he said, having picked it up, 'I do not intend to let the matter rest. I shall most certainly do something about it.'

'But what? That is the problem we come up against, is it not? You might . . . no, that wouldn't do. Or . . . no, that wouldn't do, either. I confess I see no daylight. What a pity it is that you're not an author. Then you would be on velvet.'

'I don't understand you. Why?'

'You could have got these views of yours on the younger generation off your chest in a novel. Something on the lines of Evelyn Waugh's *Vile Bodies*—witty, bitter, satirical and calculated to make the younger generation see itself as in a mirror and wish that Brazil nuts had never been invented. But in your case, of course, that is out of the question. You couldn't write a novel if you tried for a hundred years. Well, goodbye, my dear fellow,' said Lord Ickenham, 'I must be moving along. Lot of heavy Hullo-there-how-are-you-old-boy-ages-since-we-met-ing to be done before yonder sun sets. Sorry I could not have been of more help. If anything occurs to me later, I'll let you know.'

He tripped away, and Sir Raymond was conscious of a mounting sense of indignation. He strongly resented that remark about his not being able to write a novel if he tried for a hundred years. Who the devil was Ickenham to say whether he could write a novel or not?

Anything in the nature of a challenge had always been a spur to Sir Raymond Bastable. He was one of those men who take as a personal affront the suggestion that they are not capable of carrying to a successful conclusion any task to which they may see fit to set their hand. Years ago, when a boy at school, he had once eaten seven vanilla ice creams at a sitting because a syndicate of his playmates had betted him he couldn't. It sent him to the sanatorium for three days with frozen gastric juices, but he did it, and the passage of time had in no way diminished this militant spirit.

All through the rest of the day and far into the night he brooded smoulderingly on Lord Ickenham's tactless words, and rose from his bed next morning with his mind made up.

Write a novel?

Of course he could write a novel, and he would. Every man, they say, has one novel in him, and he had the advantage over most commencing authors of being in a state of seething fury. There is nothing like fury for stimulating the pen. Ask Dante. Ask Juvenal.

But though his theme was ready to hand and his rage continued unabated, there were moments, many of them, in the weeks that followed when only the iron Bastable will kept him from giving in and abandoning the project. As early as the middle of Chapter One he had discovered that there is a lot more to this writing business than the casual observer would suppose. Dante could have told him, and so could Juvenal, that it does not come easy. Blood, they would have said, is demanded of the man who sets pen to paper, also sweat and tears.

However, as their fellow poet Swinburne would have reminded them, even the weariest river winds somewhere safe to sea: and came a day when Sir Raymond was able to point at a mass of type-script on his desk, the top sheet of which was inscribed:

COCKTAIL TIME
by
RICHARD BLUNT

and to point at it with pride. His whole soul had gone into *Cocktail Time*—a biting title with its sardonic implication that that was all the younger generation lived for—and he knew it was good. It was an infernal shame, he felt, that circumstances compelled him to hide his identity under a pseudonym.

As, of course, they did. No question about that. It is all very well for your Dantes and your Juvenals to turn out the stuff under their own names, but a man who is hoping for the Conservative nomination at Bottleton East has to be cautious. Literary composition is not entirely barred to those whose ambition it is to carve for themselves a political career, but it has to be the right sort of literary composition—a scholarly Life of Talleyrand, for instance, or a thoughtful study of conditions in the poppet-valve industry. You cannot expect to get far on the road to Downing Street if you come up with something like *Forever Amber*.

And he was forced to admit as he skimmed through its pages, that there was no gainsaying the fact that in both tone and sub-stance *Cocktail Time* had much in common with Miss Winsor's masterpiece. Sex had crept into it in rather large quantities, for while exposing the modern young man he had not spared the modern young woman. His experiences in the divorce court—notably when appearing for the petitioner in the cases of Bingley versus Bingley, Botts and Frobisher and of Fosdick versus Fosdick, Wills, Milburn, O'Brien, ffrench-ffrench, Hazelgrove-Hazelgrove and others—had given him a low opinion of the modern young woman, and he saw no reason why she, too, should not have her share of the thunderbolts.

Yes, he mused, *Cocktail Time* was unquestionably outspoken in one or two spots, particularly Chapter 13. A Raymond Bastable, revealed as the man behind Chapter 13 and in a somewhat lesser degree Chapters 10, 16, 20, 22 and 24, could never hope to receive the nomination for the impending election at Bottleton East. A prudish Conservative Committee would reject him with a shudder and seek for their candidate elsewhere.

3

Into the early vicissitudes of Sir Raymond's brain-child it is not necessary to go in any great detail, for it had much the same experiences as any other first novel. He sent it from an accommodation address to Pope and Potter, and it came back. He sent it to Simms and Shotter, and it came back; to Melville and Monks, and it came back; to Popgood and Grooly, Bissett and Bassett, Ye Panache Presse and half a dozen other firms, and it came back again. It might have been a boomerang or one of those cats which, transferred from Surbiton to Glasgow, show up in Surbiton three months later, a little dusty and footsore but full of the East-West-home's-best spirit. Why it should eventually have found journey's end in the offices of Alfred Tomkins Ltd one cannot say, but it did, and they published it in the spring, with a jacket featuring a young man with a monocle in his right eye doing the rock 'n roll with a young woman in her step-ins.

After that, as is customary on these occasions, nothing much happened. It has been well said that an author who expects results from a first novel is in a position similar to that of a man who drops a rose petal down the Grand Canyon of Arizona and listens for the echo. The book had a rather limited press. The *Peebles Courier* called it not unpromising, the *Basingstoke Journal* thought it not uninteresting, and the *Times Literary Supplement* told its readers that it was published by Alfred Tomkins Ltd and contained 243 pp, but apart from that it received no critical attention. The younger generation at whom it was aimed, if they had known of its existence, would have said in their uncouth way that it had laid an egg.

But Fame was merely crouching for the spring, simply waiting in the wings, as it were, for the cue which would bring it bounding on stage to drape the chaplet about the brow of its favoured son. At two minutes past five one Tuesday afternoon the venerable Bishop of Stortford, entering the room where his daughter Kathleen sat, found her engrossed in what he presumed to be a work of devotion but which proved on closer inspection to be a novel entitled *Cocktail Time*. Peeping over her shoulder, he was able to read a paragraph or two. She had got, it should be mentioned, to the middle of Chapter 13. At 5.5 sharp he was wrenching the volume from her grasp, at 5.6 tottering from the room, at 5.10 in his study scrutinizing Chapter 13 to see if he had really seen what he had thought he had seen.

He had.

At 12.15 on the following Sunday he was in the pulpit of the church of St Jude the Resilient, Eaton Square, delivering a sermon on the text 'He that touches pitch shall be defiled' (Ecclesiasticus 13-1) which had the fashionable congregation rolling in the aisles and tearing up the pews. The burden of his address was a denunciation of the novel *Cocktail Time* in the course of which he described it as obscene, immoral, shocking, impure, corrupt, shameless, graceless and depraved, and all over the sacred edifice you could see eager men jotting the name down on their shirt cuffs, scarcely able to wait to add it to their library list.

In these days when practically anything from Guildford undertaker bitten in leg by Pekinese to Ronald Plumtree (II) falling off his bicycle in Walthamstow High Street can make the front page of the popular press as a big feature story with headlines of a size formerly reserved for announcing the opening of a world war, it was not to be expected that such an event would pass unnoticed. The popular press did it proud, and there was joy that morning in the offices of Alfred Tomkins Ltd. Just as all American publishers hope that if they are good and lead upright lives, their books will be banned in Boston, so do all English publishers pray that theirs will be denounced from the pulpit by a bishop. Full statistics are not to hand, but it is estimated by competent judges that a good bishop, denouncing from the pulpit with the right organ note in his voice, can add between ten and fifteen thousand to the sales.

Mr Prestwick, the senior partner, read the *Express*, the *Mail* and the *Mirror* in the train coming from his Esher home, and within five minutes of his arrival at the office was on the telephone to Ebenezer Flapton and Sons, printers of Worcester and London, urging Ebenezer and the boys to drop everything and start rushing out a large new edition. *Cocktail Time*, which Alfred Tomkins Ltd had been looking on all this while as just another of the stones the builder had refused, was plainly about to become the head stone of the corner.

But there was no corresponding joy in the heart of Sir Raymond Bastable as he paced the lawn of Hammer Lodge. Ever since he had read his morning paper at the breakfast table, his eyes had been glassy, his mind in a ferment.

To anyone who paces the lawn of Hammer Lodge, that desirable residence replete with every modern comfort, a wide choice of scenic beauties is available. He can look to the left and find his eye roving over green pasture land and picturesque woods, or he can look to the right and get an excellent view of the park of Hammer Hall with its lake and noble trees and beyond it the house itself, a lovely legacy from Elizabethan days. He can also, if it is a Monday, Wednesday or Friday, look in front of him and see a jobbing gardener leaning on a spade in a sort of trance in the kitchen garden. There is, in short, no stint.

But Sir Raymond saw none of these attractive sights or, if he did, saw them as through a glass darkly. His whole attention was riveted on the morrow and what it was going to bring forth. In writing *Cocktail Time*, he had had a malevolent hope that he would be starting something, but he had never expected to start anything of these dimensions, and the thought that chilled him to the very spinal marrow was this. Would that pseudonym of his be an adequate safeguard?

If there is one thing the popular press of today is, it is nosey. It tracks down, it ferrets out. Richard Blunt becomes front page news, and it is not long before it is asking itself who is this Richard Blunt? It wants photographs of him smoking a pipe or being kind to the dog and interviews with him telling the world what his favourite breakfast cereal is and what he thinks of the modern girl. It institutes enquiries and discovers that nobody has ever seen the gifted Blunt and that his only address is a sweets-and-tobacco shop in a side street near Waterloo station, and before you know where you are headlines have begun to appear. As it might be:

LITERARY MYSTERY

or

PHANTOM AUTHOR

or possibly

DICK, WHERE ART THOU?

and from that to exposure is but a step. At this very moment, Sir Raymond felt, a dozen reporters must be sniffing on his trail, and the contemplation of the appalling mess in which he had landed himself made him writhe like an Ouled Nail stomach-dancer.

He was still busily writhing when the voice of Peasemarch, his butler, spoke softly at his side. Albert Peasemarch always spoke softly when addressing Sir Raymond Bastable. He knew what was good for him. It is no pleasure to a butler to be thundered at and asked if he imagines himself to be a barrow boy calling attention to his blood oranges.

'I beg your pardon, Sir Raymond.'

The author of *Cocktail Time* came slowly out of the uneasy dream in which he had been sustaining the role of the stag at bay.

'Eh?'

'It is Madam, sir. I think you should come.'

'Come? What do you mean? Come where?'

'To Madam's room, sir. I am afraid she is not well. I was passing her door a moment ago, and I heard her sobbing. As if her heart would break,' said Peasemarch, who liked to get these things right.

A wave of exasperation and self-pity flooded Sir Raymond's tortured soul. Phoebe, he was thinking, *would* start sobbing at a time like this, when he needed to devote every little grey cell in his brain to the problem of how to elude those infernal reporters. For an instant he was inclined to counter with a firm refusal to go within a mile of Madam's room. He had just been deriving a faint consolation from the thought that, she having breakfasted in bed and he being about to take train and spend the day in London, he would not have to meet her till late tonight, by which time, he hoped, his agitation would be less noticeable. Phoebe, seeing him now, would infallibly ask what was the matter, and when he assured her that nothing was the matter would say 'But what *is* the matter, dear?' and carry on from there.

Then kindlier feelings prevailed, or possibly it was just the curiosity and urge to probe first causes which we all experience when told that someone is crying as if her heart would break. He accompanied Peasemarch back to the house and found his sister sitting up in bed, dabbing at her eyes with a liquid something that looked as if it might have been at one time a pocket handkerchief.

Except that her ears did not stick up and that she went about on two legs instead of four, Phoebe Wisdom was extraordinarily like a white rabbit, a resemblance which was heightened at the moment by the white dressing jacket she was wearing and the fact that much weeping had made her nose and eyes pink. As Sir Raymond closed the door behind him, she uttered a loud gurgling sob which crashed through his disordered nervous system like an expanding bullet, and his manner when he spoke was brusque rather than sympathetic.

'What on earth's the matter?' he demanded.

Another sob shook the stricken woman, and she said something that sounded like 'Cosh him'.

'I beg your pardon?' said Sir Raymond, clenching his hands till the knuckles stood out white under the strain, like the hero of an old-fashioned novel. He was telling himself that he must be calm, calm.

'Cossie!' said his sister, becoming clearer.

'Oh, Cosmo? What about him?'

'He says he's going to shoot himself.'

Sir Raymond was in favour of this. Cosmo Wisdom, the fruit of the unfortunate marriage Phoebe had made twenty-seven years ago, long before he had become influential and important enough to stop her, was a young man he disliked even more than he disliked most young men in these days when the species had deteriorated so lamentably. Algernon Wisdom, Cosmo's father, had at one time sold secondhand cars, at another been vaguely connected with the motion pictures, and had occasionally acted as agent for such commodities as the Magic Pen-Pencil and the Monumento Mouse Trap, but during the greater part of his futile career had been what he euphemistically described as 'between jobs', and Cosmo took after him. He, too, was frequently between jobs. He was one of those young men, with whom almost all families seem to be afflicted, who are in a constant state of having to have something done about them. 'We must do something about poor Cossie,' were words frequently on his mother's lips, and Sir Raymond would say in the unpleasant voice which he used when addressing hostile witnesses that he had no desire to be unduly inquisitive, but would she mind telling him what precisely she meant by the pronoun 'we'.

The most recent attempt on his part to do something about poor Cossie had been to secure him a post in the export and import firm of Boots and Brewer of St Mary Axe, and the letter his sister was reducing to pulp announced, he presumed, that Boots and Brewer had realized that the only way of making a success of importing and exporting was to get rid of him.

'What has he been doing?' he asked.

'What, dear?'

Sir Raymond took a turn about the room. He found it helped a little.

'Why have Boots and Brewer dismissed him? They have, I take it?'

'He doesn't say so. He just says he wants two hundred pounds.'

'He does, does he?'

'And I haven't *got* two hundred pounds.'

'Very fortunate. You won't be tempted to throw it down the drain.'

'What, dear?'

'Letting Cosmo have it would be tantamount to that. Don't give him a penny.'

'He doesn't want a penny, he wants two hundred pounds.'

'Let him want.'

'But he'll shoot himself.'

'Not a hope,' said Sir Raymond, with a wistful little sigh as the bright picture the words had conjured up faded. 'If he tries, he'll be sure to miss. For heaven's sake stop worrying. All that letter means is that he thinks he may get a tenner out of you.'

'He says two hundred pounds.'

'They always say two hundred pounds. It's common form.'

'What, dear?'

'Phoebe, in the name of everything infernal, *must* you put your head on one side like a canary and say "What, dear?" every time

I speak to you? It's enough to madden a saint. Well, I can't stand here talking. I shall miss my train. Take an aspirin.'

'What, dear?'

'Take an aspirin. Take two aspirins. Take three,' said Sir Raymond vehemently, and whirled off like a tornado to the car which was waiting to convey him to the station.

4

OF the several appointments he had in London that day the first was lunch with Lord Ickenham at the Demosthenes Club. Arriving there, he found the place its old peaceful self, the smoking-room full of the usual living corpses lying back in armchairs and giving their minds a rest. He eyed them with distaste, resenting this universal calm at a time when he himself was feeling like a character in a Greek tragedy pursued by the Furies. Though he would have said, if you had asked him, that far too much fuss was made about being pursued by Furies. The time to start worrying was when you were pursued by reporters. Curse their notebooks and pencils and damn their soft hats and raincoats. He could see them in his mind's eye, dozens of them, creeping about like leopards and getting nosier every moment.

His guest was late, and to while away the time of waiting he went to the centre table and picked up a paper. One glance at its front page, and he had dropped it as if it had bitten him and was tottering to the nearest chair. It was not often that he indulged in alcoholic stimulant before lunch, but he felt compelled now to order a double dry martini. What he had seen on that front page had made him feel quite faint.

He had just finished it when Lord Ickenham was shown in, all apologies.

'My dear old Beefy, you must be feeling like Mariana at the

moated grange. Sorry I'm so late. I started walking here in plenty of time, but I met Barbara in Bond Street.'

'Who?'

'Barbara Crowe.'

'Oh?'

'We got talking. She asked after you.'

'Oh?'

'Affectionately, I thought.'

'Oh?'

Lord Ickenham regarded him disapprovingly.

'It's no good saying "Oh?" in that tone of voice, Beefy, as if you didn't care a damn. You know perfectly well that one word of encouragement from her, and you would be at her side, rolling over on your back with all your paws in the air.'

'Well, really, Frederick!'

'You think I am showing a little too much interest in your private affairs?'

'If you like to put it that way.'

'I'm fond of you, Beefy, stuffed shirt though you have become after a promising youth and young manhood. I wish you well, and want to see you happy.'

'Very good of you. Cocktail?'

'If you'll join me.'

'I have had one.'

'Have another.'

'I think I will. Phoebe upset me this morning. Her son Cosmo appears to have been getting into trouble again. You know him?'

'Just sufficiently well to duck down a side street when I see him coming.'

'He is trying to borrow two hundred pounds.'

'You don't say? Big operator, eh? Will he get it?'

'Not from me.'

'Is Phoebe distressed?'

'Very.'

'And I suppose you yelled at her. That's your great defect, Beefy. You bark and boom and bellow at people. Not at me, for my austere dignity restrains you, but at the world in general. Used you to bellow at Barbara?'

'Shall we change—'

'I'll bet you did, and it was that that made her break off the engagement. But from the way she was speaking of you just now, I got the impression that your stock was still high with her and you've only to stop avoiding her and never seeing her to start things going again. For heaven's sake, what's a broken engagement? Jane broke ours six times. Why don't you look her up and take her out to lunch and make a fuss of her. Show yourself in a good light. Dance before her. Ask her riddles.'

'If you don't mind, Frederick, I really would prefer to change the subject.'

'Do simple conjuring tricks. Sing love songs accompanied on the guitar. And, just to show her you're not such a fool as you look, tell her that you are the author of the best-selling novel, *Cocktail Time*. That'll impress her.'

It is very rarely that the smoking-room of a club in the West End of London suddenly springs into spasmodic life, with its walls, its windows, its chairs, its tables, its members and its waiters pirouetting to and fro as if Arthur Murray had taught them dancing in a hurry, but that was what the smoking-room of the Demosthenes seemed to Sir Raymond Bastable to be doing now. It swayed and shimmied about him like something rehearsed for weeks by a choreographer, and it was through a sort of mist that he stared pallidly at his companion, his eyes wide, his lower jaw drooping, perspiration starting out on his forehead as if he were sitting in the hot room of a Turkish bath.

'What . . . what do you mean?' he gulped.

Lord Ickenham, usually so genial, betrayed a little impatience. His voice, as he spoke, was sharp.

'Now come, Beefy. You aren't going to say you didn't? My dear fellow, to anyone who knows you as I do, it's obvious. At least three scenes in the thing are almost literal transcriptions of stories you've told me yourself. You've used the Brazil nut episode. And apart from the internal evidence we have the statement of Jane.'

'Jane?'

'She came to London one day on a shopping binge and thought it would be the half-sisterly thing to do to look you up and slap you on the back, so she called at your house. You were out, but Pease-march let her in and parked her in the study. After nosing about awhile, she started, as women will, to tidy your desk, and shoved away at the back of one of the drawers was a brown paper par-cel from the publishing house of Simms and Shotter, despatched by them to Richard Blunt at some address which has escaped my memory. She mentioned this to me on her return. So you may as well come clean, Beefy. Denial is useless. You are this Blunt of whom we hear so much, are you not?'

A hollow groan escaped Sir Raymond.

'Yes. I am.'

'Well, I don't see what you're groaning about. With all this pub-licity you ought to make a packet, and if there's one thing in the world that's right up your street, it's money. You love the stuff.'

'But, Frederick, suppose it comes out? You haven't told anyone?'

'My dear fellow, why would I? I assumed from your having used a pseudonym that you wanted it kept dark.'

'And Jane?'

'Oh, Jane's forgotten all about it ages ago. It just happened to stick in my mind because I remembered saying something to you once about writing a novel. But what does it matter if it comes out?'

'Good heavens, it would mean the end of any hope I have of a political career.'

'Well, why do you want a political career? Have you ever been in the House of Commons and taken a good square look at the inmates? As weird a gaggle of freaks and sub-humans as was ever collected in one spot. I wouldn't mix with them for any money you could offer me.'

'Those are not my views. I have set my heart on getting that nomination for Bottleton East, Frederick. And there isn't a chance that they will give it to me, if it's in all the papers that I wrote a book like *Cocktail Time*.'

'Why should it be in all the papers?'

'These reporters. They find things out.'

'Oh? Yes, I see.'

Lord Ickenham was silent for some moments. From the frown of concentration on his forehead he appeared to be exercising that ingenious brain of his.

'Yes,' he said, 'they do find things out. I suppose that's what worried Bacon.'

'Bacon?'

'And made him, according to the Baconians, get hold of Shakespeare and slip him a little something to say he had written the plays. After knocking off a couple of them, he got cold feet. "Come, come, Francis," he said to himself, "this won't do at all. Let it become known that you go in for this sort of thing, and they'll be looking around for another Chancellor of the Exchequer before you can say What-ho. You must find some needy young fellow who for a consideration will consent to take the rap." And he went out and fixed it up with Shakespeare.'

Sir Raymond sat up with a convulsive jerk, spilling his glass. For the first time since breakfast that morning he seemed to see dimly, like the lights of a public-house shining through a London fog, a ray of hope.

'Don't you know any needy young fellows, Beefy? Why, of course you do. One springs immediately to the mind. Your nephew Cosmo.'

'Good God!'

'You say he wants two hundred pounds. Give it him, and tell him he can stick to all the royalties on the book, and the thing's in the bag. You'll find him just as willing and eager to co-operate as Shakespeare was.'

Sir Raymond breathed deeply. The ray of hope had become a blaze. Across the room he could see old Howard Saxby, the Demosthenes Club's leading gargoyle, talking—probably about bird-watching, a pursuit to which he was greatly addicted—to Sir Roderick Glossop, the brain specialist, who was usually ranked as the institution's Number Two gargoyle, and it seemed to him that he had never beheld anything so attractive as the spectacle they presented.

'Frederick,' he said, 'you have solved everything. It's a wonderful idea. I don't know how to thank you . . . Yes?'

A waiter had materialized at his side, one of the waiters who a short while before had been dancing the shimmy with the walls, the tables and the chairs.

'A gentleman to see you, sir.'

As far as was possible in his seated position, Sir Raymond himself did a modified form of the shimmy. A reporter? Already?

'Who is he?' he asked pallidly.

'A Mr Cosmo Wisdom, sir.'

'What!'

'Beefy,' said Lord Ickenham, raising his glass congratulatorially, 'it's all over but the shouting. The hour has produced the man.'

5

I T was in uplifted mood and with buoyant step that Sir Raymond
a few moments later entered the small smoking-room, which
was where visitors at the Demosthenes were deposited. He found
his nephew huddled in a chair, nervously sucking the knob of his
umbrella, and once again experienced the quick twinge of
resentment which always came to him when they met. A social
blot who was so constantly having to have something done about
him had, in his opinion, no right to be so beautifully dressed.
Solomon in all his glory might have had a slight edge on Cosmo
Wisdom, but it would have been a near thing. Sir Raymond also
objected to his beady eyes and his little black moustache.

'Good morning,' he said.

'Oh—er—hullo,' said Cosmo, standing on one leg.

'You wished to see me?'

'Er—yes,' said Cosmo, standing on the other leg.

'Well, here I am.'

'Quite,' said Cosmo, shifting back to the first leg. He was only
too well aware that there he was.

It was as the result of a telephone conversation with his mother
that the young man had ventured into the Demosthenes Club this
morning. Phoebe, sobbingly regretting her inability to produce
more than fifteen shillings and threepence of the two hundred
pounds he required, had made a constructive suggestion. 'Why

don't you ask your uncle, dear?' she had said, and Cosmo, though he would greatly have preferred to enter the cage of a sleeping tiger and stir it up with a short stick, had seen that this was the only way. A *tête-à-tête* with Sir Raymond Bastable always made him feel as if he were being disembowelled by a clumsy novice who had learned his job through a correspondence school, but when you are up against it for a sum like two hundred pounds it is necessary to sink personal prejudices and go to the man who has got two hundred pounds. Charm of manner, after all, is not everything.

So now, having taken one more refreshing suck at the umbrella knob, he stiffened the sinews, summoned up the blood and said:

'Er—uncle.'

'Yes?'

'Er—uncle, I don't want to bother you, but I wonder if you could . . . if you could manage . . . if you could see your way to letting me have . . .'

'What?'

'Eh?'

Sir Raymond adopted the second of the two manners that got him so disliked by witnesses in court, the heavily sarcastic.

'Let me refresh your memory, my dear Cosmo. After expressing a kindly fear that you might be bothering me—an idle fear, for you are not bothering me in the least—you went on to say "I wonder if you could . . . if you could manage . . . if you could see your way to letting me have . . ." and there you paused, apparently overcome with emotion. Naturally, my curiosity aroused, I ask "What?" meaning by the question, what is it you are hoping that I shall be able to see my way to letting you have? Can it be that your visit has something to do with the letter I found your mother bedewing with her tears this morning?'

'Er—yes.'

'She was somewhat incoherent, but I was able to gather from her that you need two hundred pounds.'

Actually, Cosmo needed two hundred and fifty, but he could

not bring himself to name the sum. And anyway, though his book-maker, to whom he owed two hundred, must be paid immediately, his friend Gordon Carlisle, to whom he was in debt for the remain-der, would surely be willing to wait for his money.

'Er—yes. You see—'

Sir Raymond was now enjoying himself thoroughly. He reached for his coat-tails as if they had been those of a silk gown and gave a sidelong glance at an invisible jury, indicating to them that they had better listen carefully to this, because it was going to be good.

'With the deepest respect,' he said, 'you are in error. I do not see. I am at a loss. Boots and Brewer pay you a good salary, do they not?'

'I wouldn't call it good.'

Sir Raymond shot another glance at the jury.

'You must pardon me, a rude unlettered man, if by inadvertence I have selected an adjective that fails to meet your critical approval. One is not a Flaubert. I have always considered your emolument—shall we say, adequate.'

'But it isn't. I keep running short. If I don't get two hundred quid today, I don't know what I shall do. I'm half inclined to end it all.'

'So your mother was telling me. An excellent idea, in my opin-ion, and one that you should consider seriously. But she, I believe, does not see eye to eye with me on that point, so as I have a great fondness for her in spite of her habit of putting her head on one side and saying "What, dear?" I am prepared to save you from mak-ing the last supreme sacrifice.'

Cosmo came up from the depths. It was always difficult to understand what his relative was talking about, but there had been something in that last remark that sounded promising.

'You mean—?'

'Two hundred pounds is a lot of money, but it is just possible that I might be able to manage it. What do you want it for?'

'I owe it to a bookie, and he—er—he's making himself rather unpleasant.'

'I can readily imagine it. Bookies are apt to get cross on occasion. Well, I think I can help you out.'

'Oh, uncle!'

'On certain conditions. Let us speak for a while of current literature. Have you read any good books lately, Cosmo? This novel *Cocktail Time*, for instance?'

'The thing there was all that in the *Express* about this morning?'

'Precisely.'

'No, I haven't read it yet, but I'm going to. It sounds hot stuff. Nobody seems to know who wrote it.'

'I wrote it.'

This was so obviously a whimsical jest that Cosmo felt it only civil to smile. He did so, and was asked by his uncle not to grin like a half-witted ape.

'I wrote it, I repeat. I assume that you can understand words of one syllable.'

Cosmo gaped. His hand, as always in moments of surprise and bewilderment, flew to his upper lip.

'That moustache of yours looks like a streak of ink,' said Sir Raymond malevolently. 'Stop fondling it and listen to me. I wrote *Cocktail Time*. Is your weak mind able to grasp that?'

'Oh, rather. Oh, quite. But—'

'But what?'

'Er—why?'

'Never mind why.'

'Well, I'll be damned!'

'And so shall I, if it ever comes out.'

'Is it as bad as all that?'

'It is not bad at all. It is frank and outspoken, but as a work of fiction it is excellent,' said Sir Raymond, pausing to wonder if it was worth while to quote the opinions of the *Peebles Courier* and the *Basingstoke Journal*. He decided that they would be wasted on his present audience. 'It is not, however, the sort of book which a man in my position is expected to write. If those reporters find out that I did write it, my political career will be ruined.'

'It's a bit near the knuckle, you mean?'

'Exactly.'

Cosmo nodded intelligently. The thing was beginning to make sense to him.

'I see.'

'I supposed you would. Now, the thought that immediately flashes into your mind, of course, is that you are in a position on parting from me to hurry off and sell this information to the gutter press for what it will fetch, and I have no doubt that you would leap to the task. But it would be a short-sighted policy. You can do better for yourself than that. Announce that you are the author of *Cocktail Time*—'

'Eh?'

'I want you to give it out that it was you who wrote the book.'

'But I never wrote anything in my life.'

'Yes, you did. You wrote *Cocktail Time*. I think I can make it clear even to an intelligence like yours that our interests in this matter are identical. We both benefit from what I have proposed. I regain my peace of mind, and you get your two hundred pounds.'

'You'll really give it me?'

'I will.'

'Coo!'

'And in addition you may convert to your own use such royalties as may accrue from the book.'

'Coo!' said Cosmo again, and was urged by his uncle to make up his mind whether he was a man or a pigeon.

'These,' said Sir Raymond, 'in light of the publicity it is receiving, should be considerable. My contract calls for ten per cent of the published price, and after all this fuss in the papers I should imagine that the thing might sell—well, let us be conservative—say ten thousand copies, which would work out—I am no mathematician, but I suppose it would work out at between six and seven hundred pounds.'

Cosmo blinked as if something had struck him between the eyes.

'Six and seven hundred?'

'Probably more.'

'And I get it?'

'You get it.'

'Coo!' said Cosmo, and this time the ejaculation passed without rebuke.

'I gather,' said Sir Raymond, 'from your manner that you are willing to co-operate. Excellent. Everything can be quite simply arranged. I would suggest a letter to each of the papers which have commented on the affair, hotly contesting the bishop's views, which you consider uncalled for, intemperate and unjust, and revealing yourself as Richard Blunt. If you will come to the writing-room, I will draft out something that will meet the case.'

And having done so, Sir Raymond returned to the smoking-room to tell Lord Ickenham that the thing, as he had predicted it would be, was in the bag.

6

As might have been expected, the announcement, appearing in the papers two days later, that Cosmo Wisdom was the author of the novel *Cocktail Time*, now at the height of its notoriety, did not pass unnoticed. One of the first to notice it was J. P. Boots of Boots and Brewer, and it was the work of an instant for him, on arriving at his office in St Mary Axe, to summon the young man to his presence and inform him that his services, such as they were, would no longer be required. Import and export merchants, whether of St Mary Axe or elsewhere, have the reputation of the firm to think of and cannot afford to retain in their entourage employees capable of writing Chapter 13 of that work. J. P. Boots did not in so many words bid Cosmo go and sin no more, but this was implied in his manner.

It was, however, only this importer and exporter who struck the jarring note. Elsewhere the reactions were uniformly pleasant. Alfred Tomkins Ltd wrote Cosmo an affectionate letter, telling him to come up and see them some time, and an equally affectionate letter came from Howard Saxby of Edgar Saxby and Sons, the literary agents, recommending him to place his affairs in the hands of the Saxby organization (offices in London, New York and Hollywood). This Cosmo, feeling that the situation in which he had been placed was one of those where a fellow needs a friend, decided to do, though wincing a little at the thought of that ten per cent commission.

Two little girls, Ava Rackstraw, aged ten, and Lana Cootes (12) wrote asking for his autograph, saying that he had long been their favourite author and they had read all his books. He was invited to address the Herne Hill Literary Society on 'Some Aspects of the Modern Novel'. Six unpublished authors sent him their unpublished works with a request for a detailed criticism. And Ivor Llewellyn, president of the Superba-Llewellyn motion picture company of Hollywood, about to return to California after a visit to London, told his secretary to go out and buy a copy of the book for him to read on the plane. Mr Llewellyn was always on the lookout for material which, if he could ease it past the Johnston office, would excite the clientele, and *Cocktail Time*, from what everyone was saying about it, seemed likely to be just the sort of thing he wanted.

And, finally, Mrs Gordon Carlisle, breakfasting in the sitting-room of the flat which she shared with her husband, opened her morning paper, looked at page one, started, said something that sounded like 'Cheese!' and lifting her attractive head shouted 'Hey, Oily!'

'Yes, sweetie?'

'Cummere,' said Mrs Carlisle, and there entered from the bedroom a tall, slender, almost excessively gentlemanly man in a flowered dressing-gown, who might have been the son of some noble house or a Latin-American professional dancer.

Actually, he was neither. He was a confidence trick artist whose virtuosity won him considerable respect in the dubious circles in which he moved. American by birth and residence, he had brought his wife to Europe on a pleasure trip. After years of strenuous work he proposed to take a sabbatical, though of course if something really good came up, he was always prepared to get back into harness again. The Carlisles did not spare themselves.

'Yay?' he said, hoping that his loved one had not summoned

him to tell him he must wear his thick woollies. She had a way of doing so when the English summer was on the chilly side, and they tickled him. ''Smatter, sweetie?'

'Want to show you somef'n.'

Gertrude ('Sweetie') Carlisle was a strapping young woman with bold hazel eyes and a determined chin. These eyes were now flashing, and the chin protruded. It was plain that what she had read had stirred her.

'Listen, Oily. Didn't you tell me you won fifty pounds from a guy named Cosmo Wisdom the other night?'

Mr Carlisle nodded. It was the sombre nod of a man reluctant to be reminded of a sad experience.

'I did, yes. But he didn't pay me. He turned out to be one of these forty-dollar-a-week city clerks. The woods are full of them over here. They fool you by dressing like dukes, and when it's too late you find they're office boys or something. That's what you get for coming to a strange country. It would never have happened back home.'

'What did you do?'

'I didn't do anything.'

'I'd have busted him one.'

Mr Carlisle could well believe it. Impulsiveness and a sturdy belief in direct action were the leading features of his mate's interesting character. Some time had passed since the incident occurred and the bump had gone down now, but there still remained green in his memory the occasion when a fancied misdemeanour on his part had led her to hit him on the back of the head with a large vase containing gladioli. It had, in his opinion, spoiled the honeymoon.

'Well, too late to do anything now,' he said moodily. 'Just got to write it off as a bad debt.'

'Bad debt nothing. He was playing you for a sucker.'

Mr Carlisle started. His *amour-propre* was wounded.

'A sucker? *Me*?'

'Certainly he was. He was holding out on you. Read this.'

'Read what?'

'This.'

'Which?'

'This stuff in the paper here about him having written this book they're all talking about. He's got oodles of money. It's a best seller.'

Mr Carlisle took the paper, scanned it and said 'Well, I'll be darned!' Gentlemanliness was his aim in life, for he had found it his best professional asset, and he seldom used any stronger expletive.

'Looks like you're right.'

'Sure, I'm right.'

'Unless,' said Oily, struck by a damping thought, 'it's some other Cosmo Wisdom.'

His wife scoffed at the theory. Even in England, she reasoned, there couldn't be two men with a name like that.

'Where does he live, this guy?'

'Down Chelsea way. One of those side streets off the King's Road.'

'Then have a bite of breakfast and go see him.'

'I will.'

'Don't come back without those fifty smackers.'

'I won't.'

'Get tough.'

'You betcher.'

'And wear your thick woollies.'

'Oh, sweetie! Must I?'

'Certainly you must. There's a nasty east wind.'

'But they make me want to scratch.'

'Well, go ahead, then. They can't jail you for scratching.'

'Oh, hell!' said Oily.

It was not a word he often employed, but it seemed to him that the circumstances justified it.

• • •

It was getting on for lunch time when he returned to the little nest, and there was nothing in his face to indicate whether his mission had had a happy ending or the reverse. The better to succeed in his chosen career, Oily Carlisle had trained his features to a uniform impassivity which often caused his wife annoyance. Though recognizing the professional value of a dead pan, she wished that he would not carry it into the life of the home.

'Well?' she said.

'Rustle me up an old-fashioned, will you, sweetie?' said Oily. 'My tongue's hanging out.'

Mrs Carlisle rustled him up an old-fashioned, and having done so said 'Well?' again.

'Did you see him?'

'I saw him.'

'What did he say?'

'Plenty.'

'Did you get the fifty?'

'No. Matter of fact, I lent him another twenty.'

'For heaven's sake!'

'But I got something a darned sight better than fifty pounds.'

'What do you mean?'

'I'll tell you.'

In Oily's demeanour as he took another sip of his cocktail and prepared to speak there was a suggestion of that Ancient Mariner of whom the poet Coleridge wrote. Like him, he knew he had a good story to relate, and he did not intend to hurry it.

'Yes, I saw him, and I said I'd been expecting to hear from him before this, because wasn't there a little matter of a hundred and fifty dollars or so he owed me, and he said Yes, that was right, and I said it would be righter, if he'd come through with it, and he said he hadn't got it.'

'The nerve!'

Oily took in the last drops of his old-fashioned, lit a cigarette and put his feet on the table.

'And he couldn't raise it, he said. Oh, no? I said. How about this book of yours you can't pick up a paper without seeing all that stuff about it? I said. The money must be pouring in like a tidal wave, I said.'

'What did he say to that?'

'Said it wasn't any such thing. These publishers pay up twice a year, he said, and it would be months before he could touch. I said Well, why didn't he get something from them in advance, and he said he'd just been trying to and they'd told him it would be foreign to their policy to anticipate the customary half-yearly statement.'

'Do what?'

'They wouldn't bite. Said he'd have to wait.'

'So what did you say?'

'I said "Too bad".'

A bitter sneer marred the beauty of Gertrude Carlisle's face.

'Got all fierce, didn't you? Scared the pants off him, I shouldn't wonder.'

'I said "Too bad",' proceeded Oily equably, 'and I said "Sweetie will be vexed", I said, and he said "Who's Sweetie?" and I said "Mrs Carlisle". And when Sweetie's vexed, I said, she generally hits people over the head with a bottle. And I told him about you and me and the vase.'

'Oh, honey, we've forgotten all that.'

'I haven't. Forgiven, yes. Forgotten, no. I can remember, just the same as if it had been yesterday, how it feels to get hit on the back of the head with a vase containing gladioli, and I described the symptoms to him. He turned greenish.'

'And then?'

'Then I came away.'

Mrs Carlisle's lips had closed in a tight line, and there was a sombre glow in her fine eyes. Her air was that of a woman thinking in terms of bottles and making a mental note to set aside the next one that became empty.

'What's this guy's address?'

'Why?'

'I thought I'd call around and say Hello.'

'You won't need to. Relax, sweetie. You ain't heard nothing yet. When I told you I came away, I ought to have said I started to come away, because he called me back. Seemed worried, I thought. He was gulping quite a good deal.'

'I'll gulp him!'

'And then he came clean and spilled the whole works. You know what he said? He said he didn't write that book at all.'

'And you believed him?'

'Sure I believed him, after I'd heard the rest of it. He said his uncle wrote it. His uncle's a guy called Sir Raymond Bastable. Big lawyer and going in for politics and knew that if it came out that he had written this *Cocktail Time* thing, he'd be ruined.'

'Why?'

'Seems in England you can't mix writing that sort of book with standing for parliament, which is what he's set on. So he got our Mr Wisdom to say he'd done it. Well, I needn't tell you what I said to myself when I heard that.'

'Yes, you need. What did you say to yourself?'

'I said "Here's where I touch the big money."'

'I don't get it.'

Oily smiled an indulgent smile.

'Look, sweetie. Use your bean. You're this Bastable character. You write a book, and it's too hot to handle, so you get your nephew to take the rap, and the papers run a big story about it's him that wrote it. All straight so far?'

'Sure, but—'

'Well, what do you do when you get a letter from the nephew saying he's been thinking it over and his conscience won't let him go on with the ramp, so he's going to tell the world it wasn't him who done it, it was you? Here's what you do—you pay up. You say "How much do you want, to keep this under your hat?" And you get charged as much as the traffic will bear.'

Mrs Carlisle's eyes widened. Her lips parted. She might have known, she was feeling, that she could have trusted her Oily. Gazing at him reverently, she expressed her emotion in a quick 'Gosh!'

'But will he do it?'

'Will who do what?'

'This Wisdom fellow. Will he write the letter?'

'He's done it. I've got it right here in my pocket. I said I'd mail it for him. I explained the idea, and he saw it at once. Very enthusiastic he was. He said his uncle's got all the money in the world—you know what they pay these big lawyers—and there isn't a chance that he won't cough up prac'lly anything.'

'Protection money.'

'That's right, protection money. So I dictated the letter and brought it away with me. That's when I loaned him that twenty pounds. He said he wanted to celebrate. Now what?' asked Oily, noting that a cloud had passed over the face of the moon of his delight.

'I was only feeling what a pity it is you'll have to split with him. You will, I guess?'

'That's what he guesses, too, but, ask me, he's guessing wrong. I'm taking the letter to this Bastable after lunch—he's living in the country at a place called Dovetail Hammer—and I shall want the money right down on the counter. Well, of course, it's just possible I may decide to give Wisdom his half of it, but I doubt it, sweetie, I doubt it very much indeed.'

'Oily,' said Mrs Carlisle, her eyes shining with a soft light, 'there's no one like you. You're wonderful.'

'I'm pretty good,' agreed Mr Carlisle modestly.

7

THE 3.26, Oily decided, having consulted the railway guide, was the train to take to Dovetail Hammer. It would, he pointed out, give them nice time for lunch at the Ritz and Gertie, all enthusiasm, begged him to lead her to it. Too often in her past luncheon had had to be a thing of sandwiches and dill pickles on the home premises, and she was a girl who, like the fifth Earl of Ickenham, enjoyed stepping high, wide and plentiful.

It was at about the moment when they were sipping their coffee and Oily had lighted a seven-and-sixpenny cigar that Lord Ickenham, who had been taking the mid-day meal with his nephew Pongo at the Drones preparatory to going and visiting his godson at Hammer Hall, looked out of the smoking-room window at the Demosthenes across the way and heaved a sigh.

'Boo!' said Pongo.

'I beg your pardon?'

'Just trying to scare you. Said to be good for hiccups.'

'It would take a lot more than that to scare an intrepid man like me. Chilled Steel Ickenham they used to call me in the old regiment. And, anyway, that was not a hiccup, it was a sigh.'

'Why were you sighing?'

'Because I felt a pang. No, sorry, three pangs. What caused one of them was the thought that, going off to stay with Johnny, I shall be deprived for quite a time of your society and those pleasant and instructive afternoons we have so often had together. It would have been delightful to have remained in London, seeing the sights with you.'

'You don't see any ruddy sights with *me*. I know you when you're seeing sights.'

'My second pang—Pang B you might call it—was occasioned by looking across the street at the Demosthenes Club, for it brought my semi-brother-in-law, Beefy Bastable, to my mind. I found myself thinking of something that happened last summer. You have probably forgotten the incident, but about a year ago, seated in this window, I shot his topper off with a Brazil nut.'

'Gosh!'

'Ah, I see you remember. Well, I had hoped that the experience would have proved a turning point in his life, making him a gentler, kinder Beefy, a sweeter, softer Bastable, more patient with and tolerant of his sister Phoebe. I was too sanguine.'

'Isn't he patient with and tolerant of his sister Phoebe?'

'Far from it. My well-meant effort appears to have had no effect whatsoever. According to Peasemarch, his butler, with whom I correspond, his manner toward her is still reminiscent of that of Captain Bligh of the *Bounty* displeased with the behaviour of one of the personnel of the fo'c'stle. Of course, he could make out a case for himself, I suppose. Phoebe, poor lost soul, has a way of putting her head on one side like a canary and saying "What, dear?" when spoken to which must be very annoying to a man accustomed to having one and all hang upon his lightest word. It is when she has done this some six or seven times in the course of a breakfast or luncheon that, according to Peasemarch, he shoots up to the ceiling in a sheet of flame and starts setting about her regardless of her age and sex. Yes, I can see his side of the thing, but it must be very bad for his blood pressure and far from pleasant for all concerned. Peasemarch says it wrings his heart to listen with his ear to the keyhole. You don't know Bert Peasemarch, do you?

'No.'

'Splendid chap. About as much brain as you could put comfortably into an aspirin bottle, but what are brains if the heart be of gold? I first met him when he was a steward on the Cunard-White Star. Later, he came into some house property and left the sea and settled down in a village near Ickenham. Then, if you remember, war broke out and there was all that bother about the invasion of England, and I joined the Home Guard, and whom should I find standing shoulder to shoulder with me but Bert Peasemarch. We saw it through together, sitting up all night at times, chilled to the bone, but with our upper lips as stiff as our hip joints. Well, two men don't go through all that without becoming buddies. I grew to love Bert like a brother, and he grew to love me like a brother. Two brothers in all. I got him his job with Beefy.'

'I thought you said he came into house property.'

'Quite a bit of it, I understand.'

'Then why did he want to buttle?'

'Ennui, my dear boy, the ennui that always attacks all these fellows who retire in their prime. He missed the brave tang of the old stewarding days. Years of life on the ocean wave had left him ill-fitted to sit on his fat trouser seat and do nothing. Well, a steward is practically a butler, so I advised him to make a career of that. My Coggs down at Ickenham coached him, and when Coggs said the time was ripe, I unloaded him on Beefy.'

'How did he get on with him?'

'I think he found him something of a trial. But that was before Beefy moved to the country. Who knows that living in the country will not improve him out of all knowledge. The quiet rural life does have a wonderful effect on people. Take me. There are times, I admit, when being cooped up at Ickenham makes me feel like a caged skylark, though not of course looking like one, but there is no question that it has been the making of me. I attribute to it the fact that I have become the steady, sensible, perhaps rather stodgy man I am today. I beg your pardon?'

'Eh?'

'I thought you spoke.'

'I said "Ha!" if you call that speaking.'

'Why did you say "Ha!"?'

'Because I felt like saying "Ha!" No objection to me saying "Ha," is there?'

'None whatever. This is Liberty Hall.'

'Thanks. Well, I can't see it.'

'See what?'

'All this about old Bastable becoming a different man. According to you, he still bites pieces out of his sister.'

'Merely because he is always coming up to London and bullying witnesses in court. This makes his progress slower than one could wish. But I am confident that the magic of Dovetail Hammer will eventually work. Give him time. It isn't easy for leopards to change their spots.'

'Do they want to?'

'I couldn't say. I know so few leopards. But I think Beefy will improve. If Barbara Crowe hadn't returned him to store, he would already have become a reformed character. I am convinced that, married to her, he would today be the lovable Beefy of thirty years ago, for she wouldn't have stood that Captain Bligh stuff for a minute. Too bad the union blew a fuse, but how sadly often that happens. When you get to my age, my dear Pongo, you will realize that what's wrong with the world is that there are far too many sundered hearts in it. I've noticed it again and again. It takes so little to set a couple of hearts asunder. That's why I'm worried about Johnny.'

'Isn't he all right?'

'Far from it.'

'Doesn't he like being married?'

'He isn't married. That's the whole trouble. He's been engaged to Bunny Farringdon for more than a year, but not a move on his part to set those wedding bells ringing out in the little village church. She speaks to him of buying two of everything for her trousseau and begs him to let her have the green light, but all she gets is a "Some other time". It gives me a pang.'

'Pang C?'

'Pang, as you say, C. Good heavens,' said Lord Ickenham, looking at his watch. 'Is it as late as that? I must rush. I'm catching the 3.26.'

'But half a second. Tell me more about this. Isn't she getting fed up?'

'Distinctly so. I was having lunch with her yesterday, and the impression I received was that she was becoming as mad as a wet hen. Any day now I expect to see in *The Times* an announcement that the wedding arranged between Jonathan Twistleton Pearce of Hammer Hall, Dovetail Hammer, Berks, and Belinda Farringdon of Plunkett Mews, Onslow Square, South Kensington, will not take place.'

'What do you think's at the bottom of it? Money? Johnny's pretty hard up, of course.'

'Not too well fixed, I agree. The cross he has to bear is that Hammer Hall is one of those betwixt-and-between stately homes of England, so large that it costs the dickens of a lot to keep up but not large enough to lure the populace into packing sandwiches and hard-boiled eggs and coming in charabancs to inspect it at half-a-crown a head. Still, what with running it as a guest-house and selling an occasional piece of furniture and writing those suspense novels of his, he should be in a position to get married if he wants to. Especially now that he is getting quite a satisfactory rent from Beefy for the Lodge. I don't think money is the trouble.'

Pongo drew thoughtfully at his cigarette. A possible solution of the mystery had occurred to him. Devoted to his Sally, he personally would not have looked at another female—no, not even if she had come leaping at him in the nude out of a pie at a bachelor party, but he was aware that there were other, less admirable men who were inclined to flit like butterflies from flower to flower and to run their lives more on the lines of Don Juan and Casanova. Could it be that his old friend Jonathan Pearce was one of these?

'I don't often get together with Johnny these days,' he said. 'It must be well over a year since I saw him last. How is he as of even date?'

'Quite robust, I believe.'

'I mean in the way of staunchness and steadfastness. It just struck me that the reason he's jibbing at jumping off the dock might be that he's met someone else down at Dovetail Hammer.'

'Do you know Dovetail Hammer?'

'Never been there.'

'I thought you hadn't, or you would not have made a fatuous suggestion like that. It isn't a place where you meet someone else. There's the vicar's daughter, who is engaged to the curate, and the doctor's daughter, betrothed to a chap who's planting coffee in Kenya, and that, except for Phoebe and Johnny's old nurse, Nannie Bruce, exhausts the female population. It's not possible for his heart to have strayed.'

'Well, something must have happened.'

'Unquestionably.'

'You'd better talk to him.'

'I intend to, like a Dutch godfather. We can't have this playing fast and loose with a young girl's affections. Letting the side down, is the way I look at it. And now, young Pongo, stand out of my way, or I'll roll over you like a Juggernaut. If I miss that train, there isn't another till five-forty.'

8

UNLESS your destination is within comfortable walking distance—the Blue Boar, let us say, or the Beetle and Wedge, both of which are just across the street from the station—the great thing to do on alighting from the train at Dovetail Hammer is to nip out quick and make sure of getting the station cab. (There is only one—Arthur Popworth, proprietor.)

Lord Ickenham, who had been there before and knew the ropes, did this. The afternoon was now warm, and he had no desire to trudge the mile to the Hall carrying a suitcase. He had just bespoken Mr Popworth's services and was about to enter the vehicle, when there emerged from the station a gentlemanly figure crying 'Hey, taxi!' and registering chagrin on perceiving that he had been forestalled. Oily Carlisle had lingered on the platform seeking from a porter with no roof to his mouth information as to where Sir Raymond Bastable was to be found.

Lord Ickenham, always the soul of consideration, turned back and beamed with his customary geniality. He did not particularly like Oily's looks, but he was humane.

'If you are going my way, sir,' he said, 'I shall be delighted to give you a lift.'

'Awfully kind of you, sir,' said Oily in the Oxford accent which he had been at some pains to cultivate for professional purposes. 'I want a place called Hammer Hall.'

'My own objective. Are you staying there?'

'No—I'm—'

'I thought you might be. It's a guest-house now.'

'Is that so? No, I'm returning to town. Just run down to see a man on business. Hammer Lodge the porter said the name of his house was, and it's somewhere near the Hall.'

'Just before you get there. I'll drop you.'

'Frightfully kind of you.'

'Not at all, not at all. It all comes under the head of spreading sweetness and light.'

The cab made a noise like an explosion in a boiler factory and began to move. There was a momentary silence in its interior, occupied by Lord Ickenham in wondering what business this dubious character, whose fishiness his practised eye had detected at a glance, could have to conduct with Beefy; by Oily in massaging the small of his back. For a long time now the heavy underclothing on which his loved one had insisted had been irking him.

'Warm day,' said Lord Ickenham at length.

'I'll say,' said Oily. 'And can you beat it?' he went on, having reached the stage of exasperation when a man has to have a confidant, no matter who he be. 'My wife made me wear my thick woollies.'

'You shock me profoundly. Why was that?'

'Said there was a nasty east wind.'

'I hadn't noticed it.'

'Me, neither.'

'You have a sensitive skin?'

'Yes, I have. Very.'

'I suspected that that was the reason why you were behaving like a one-armed paperhanger with the hives. Watching you at work, I was reminded of the young lady of Natchez, whose clothes were all tatters and patches. In alluding to which, she would say, "Well, Ah itch, and wherever Ah itches, Ah scratches." If you wish to undress, pay no attention to me. And Mr Popworth, I know, is a married man and will take the broad view.'

A feeling of irritation, the spiritual equivalent of the one he was feeling in the small of the back, began to grip Oily. He found his companion's manner frivolous and unsympathetic and was conscious of an urge to retaliate in some way, to punish this scoffer for his untimely gaiety, to wipe, in a word, that silly smile off his face. And most fortunately he possessed the means to do so. In his vest pocket there nestled a ring made of what looked like gold, in which was set a large red stone that looked like a ruby. It seemed the moment to produce it.

Oily Carlisle had not always been a man at the top of his profession, selling stock in non-existent copper mines to the highest in the land and putting through deals that ran into five figures. He had started at the bottom of the ladder as the genial young fellow who had found a ruby ring in the street and was anxious to sell it, the darned thing being of no use to him, and a touch of sentiment led him to carry on his person always this symbol of his beginnings. He regarded it as a sort of charm or luck piece.

Fingering it now, he said:

'Take a look at this.'

Lord Ickenham did so, and felt a pleasurable glow stealing over him. His, in the years before he had succeeded to the title and was an impecunious younger son scratching for a living in New York, Arizona and elsewhere, had been a varied and interesting career, in the course of which he had encountered a considerable number of what are technically known as lumberers, and he had always obtained a great deal of spiritual uplift from their society. To meet once again an optimist who—unless he was sadly wronging this sleek and shiny fellow-traveller—hoped to sell him a ruby ring he had found in the street carried him back to those good old days and would have restored his youth, had his youth needed restoring.

'My word!' he said admiringly. 'That looks valuable. How much did you give for that?'

'Well, I'll tell you,' said Oily. 'It's rather an odd story. You're not a lawyer, by any chance, are you, sir?'

Lord Ickenham said he was not.

'Why I asked was, I was walking along Piccadilly this morning, and saw this lying on the side-walk, and I thought you might be able to tell me if findings are keepings in a case like that.'

'Speaking as a layman, I should say most certainly.'

'You really think so?'

'I do indeed. The advice I always give to young men starting out in life and finding ruby rings in the street is "Grab the money and run for the train." You want to sell it, I suppose?'

'If it's not against the law. I wouldn't want to do anything that wasn't right.'

'Of course not. Naturally. About how much were you thinking of charging?'

Oily, too, had now begun to feel a pleasurable glow. This was pretty elementary stuff, of course, and he knew he ought to have been a little ashamed of himself for stooping to it, but it was giving him something of a nostalgic thrill to be back in the days when he had been a young fellow starting to break into the game.

'That's where I can't seem to make up my mind,' he said. 'If it's genuine, I suppose it's worth a hundred pounds or so, but how's one to tell?'

'Oh, I'm sure it's genuine. Look at that ruby. Very red.'

'That's true.'

'And the gold. Very yellow.'

'That's true, too.'

'I think you would be perfectly justified in asking a hundred pounds for this ring.'

'You do?'

'Fully that.'

'Would you buy it for a hundred pounds?'

'Like a shot.'

'Then—'

'But', proceeded Lord Ickenham, 'for the fact that as a pur-
chaser of ruby rings from chance-met strangers I am unfortunately
situated. Some time ago my wife, who is a woman who believes in
a strong, centralized government, decided to take over the family
finances and administer them herself, leaving me just that little bit
of spending money which a man requires for tobacco, self-respect,
golf balls and so on. So I have to watch the pennies. My limit is
a shilling. If you would care to settle for that, you have found a
customer. Or, as this warm friendship has sprung up between us,
shall we say eighteen pence?'

Oily was too much the gentleman to use bad language, but the
look he gave his companion was not at all the sort of look he ought
to have directed at anyone with whom he had formed a warm
friendship.

'You make me sick,' he said, speaking the words from between
clenched teeth with no trace of an Oxford accent.

It was in jovial mood that some moments later, having dropped
the stowaway outside Hammer Lodge, Lord Ickenham stepped
from the station cab at the door of Hammer Hall. He was genu-
inely grateful to his recent buddy for having given him five minutes
of clean, wholesome entertainment, free from all this modern sug-
gestiveness, and he wished him luck if he was planning to sell that
ring to Beefy.

The ordinary visitor to the ancestral home of the Pearces, arriving at the front door, stands on the top step and presses the bell, and
when nothing happens presses it again, but these formalities are not
for godfathers. Lord Ickenham walked right in, noting as he passed
through the spacious entrance hall how clean, though shabby,
everything was. Nannie Bruce's work, he presumed, with a little
assistance, no doubt, from some strong-young-girl-from-the-village.

Externally unchanged in the four hundred years during which
it had housed the family of Pearce, internally, like so many coun-

try mansions of the post-second-world-war period, Hammer Hall showed unmistakable signs of having seen better days. There were gaps on the walls where tapestries had hung, hiatuses along the floor where chests and tables were missing. A console table which was a particular favourite of his, Lord Ickenham observed, had folded its tents like the Arabs and silently stolen away since his last visit, and he was sorry to see that that hideous imitation walnut cabinet, a survival from Victorian days, had not gone the same way, for it had always offended his educated eye and he had often begged his godson to get rid of it.

He sighed a little, and with a fourth pang added to the three he had mentioned to Pongo made his way to the room down the passage where Johnny Pearce, when not interrupted by Nannie Bruce, wrote those suspense novels which helped, though not very much, to keep Hammer Hall's head above water.

It was apparent that she had interrupted him now, for the first thing Lord Ickenham heard as he opened the door was her voice, speaking coldly and sternly.

'I've no patience, Master Jonathan. Oh, good evening, your lordship.'

Nannie Bruce, a tall, gangling light-heavyweight with a suggestion in her appearance of a private in the Grenadiers dressed up to play the title role in *Charley's Aunt*, was one of those doggedly faithful retainers who adhere to almost all old families like barnacles to the hulls of ships. As what she called a slip of a girl, though it was difficult, seeing her now, to believe that she had ever had a girlish sliphood, she had come to Hammer Hall to act as nurse to the infant Johnny. By the time he went off to his first school and the need for her services might have been supposed to have ceased, the idea of dispensing with them had become an idle dream. She was as much a fixture as the stone lions on the gates or the funny smell in the attic.

'You are in your old room, your lordship,' she said. 'I'll be going and seeing to it. So I'll be glad if you would kindly speak to her, Master Jonathan.'

'She does her best, Nannie.'

'And a poor best it is. She's a gaby, that one. Verily, as a jewel of gold in a swine's snout is a woman which is without discretion. That's what Ecclesiastes wrote in the good book, Master Jonathan,' said Miss Bruce, 'and he was right.'

The door closed behind her, and Johnny Pearce, a personable young man with a pleasant but worried face, sat jabbing moodily with his pen at the sheet of paper on which he had been writing of Inspector Jervis, a fictional character to whom he was greatly addicted. Lord Ickenham eyed him with concern. If vultures were not gnawing at his godson's bosom, he was feeling, he did not know a vulture-gnawed bosom when he saw one. Only the thought that Belinda Farringdon was having similar vulture-trouble and that he had come here to talk to Johnny about it like a Dutch godfather restrained him from condoling and sympathizing.

'What was all that?' he asked.

'The same old thing. Another row with the cook.'

'She has them frequently?'

'All the time.'

'Has the cook given notice?'

'Not yet, but she will. Cooks never stay here more than about five minutes. They can't stand Nannie.'

'She is a bit testing, I suppose, though a useful person to have around if you want to brush up your Ecclesiastes. However, it is not of Nannie and cooks and Ecclesiastes that I wish to speak,' said Lord Ickenham, getting down to it. 'Far more urgent matters are toward. I saw Bunny yesterday.'

'Oh, did you?'

'Gave her lunch. Smoked salmon, *poulet en casserole* and a fruit salad. She toyed with them in the order named. In fact, the word "toyed" overstates it. She pushed her plate away untasted.'

'Good Lord! Isn't she well?'

'Physically, yes, but spiritually considerably below par. It's in the soul that it catches her. She is fretting and chafing because you keep postponing the happy day. Why the devil don't you marry the girl, Johnny?'

'I can't!'

'Of course you can. Better men than you have got married. Myself for one. Nor have I ever regretted it. I'm not saying I enjoyed the actual ceremony. I had the feeling, as I knelt at the altar, that the eyes of everybody in the ringside pews were riveted on the soles of my boots, and it bathed me in confusion. I have a foot as shapely as the next man and my boots were made to order by the best booterers in London, but the illusion that I was wearing a pair of those things people go hunting fish under water in was very strong. That, however, was but a passing *malaise* and the thought that in about another brace of shakes the dearest girl in the world would be mine bucked me up like a week at Bognor Regis. Honestly, Johnny, you ought to nerve yourself and go through it. It only needs will power. You're breaking that pen,' said Lord Ickenham, 'and what is far, far worse, you are breaking the heart of a sweet blue-eyed girl with hair the colour of ripe corn. You should have seen her yesterday. I am a strong man, not easily shaken, but as I watched her recoiling from that *poulet en casserole*, as if it had been something dished up by the Borgias, my eyes were wet with unshed tears. I blush for you, Johnny, and am surprised and hurt that you seem incapable of blushing for yourself. To think that any godson of mine can go about the place giving the woman who has placed her trust in him the sleeve across the windpipe like this makes me realize that godsons are not what they were.'

'You don't understand.'

'Nor does B. Farringdon.'

'I'm in a hell of a jam.'

Johnny Pearce quivered as he spoke, and passed a feverish pen over his brow. The sternness of Lord Ickenham's demeanour softened a little. It had become evident to him that he was the godfather of a toad beneath the harrow, and one has to make allowances for toads so situated.

'Tell me the whole story in your own words, omitting no detail, however slight,' he said. 'Why can't you get married? You haven't got some incurable disease, have you?'

'That's just it. I have.'

'Good heavens! What?'

'Nannie Bruce.'

It seemed to Lord Ickenham that the toad raising a haggard face to his was a toad who spoke in riddles, and he said so.

'What on earth do you mean?'

'Have you ever had a faithful old nurse who stuck to you like a limpet?'

'Never. My personal attendants generally left at the end of the first month, glad to see the last of me. They let me go and presently called the rest of the watch together and thanked God they were rid of a knave. But what have faithful old nurses got to do with it? I don't follow you.'

'It's perfectly simple. Nannie Bruce has been here for twenty-five years—damn it, it's nearer twenty-seven—and she has become the boss of the show. She runs the place. Well, do you suppose that, if I get married, she's going to step meekly down and hand over to my wife? Not a hope.'

'Nonsense.'

'It isn't nonsense. You saw her in action just now. A perfectly good cook melting away like snow on a mountain side, and why? Because Nannie will insist on butting in all the time and criticizing. And it would be the same with Bunny. Nannie would make life impossible for her in a million ways. I'd call her high-spirited, wouldn't you?'

'Nannie?'

'Bunny.'

'Oh, Bunny. Yes, very high-spirited.'

'Well, then. Is she going to enjoy being interfered with and ordered around, told not to do it that way, do it this way, treated as a sort of half-witted underling? And her sniff. You know the way she sniffs.'

'Bunny?'

'Nannie.'

'Oh, Nannie. Yes, she does sniff.'

'And that hissing noise she makes, like a wet thumb drawn across the top of a hot stove. It would drive a young bride potty. And there's another thing,' said Johnny, vigorously plying the pen. 'Do you realize that every single discreditable episode in my past is filed away in Nannie's memory? She could and would tell Bunny things about me which in time would be bound to sap her love. How long could a wife go on looking on her husband as a king among men after hearing an eye-witness's account of his getting jerked before a tribunal and fined three week's pocket money for throwing rocks at the kitchen window or a blow-by-blow description of the time he was sick at his birthday party through eating too much almond cake? In about two ticks I should sink to the level of a fifth-rate power. Yes, I know. You're going to say why don't I get rid of her?'

'Exactly,' said Lord Ickenham, who was. It seemed to his alert mind the logical solution.

'How can I? I can't throw her out on her—'

'Please, Johnny! There are gentlemen present.'

'Ear.'

'Oh—ear. Sorry. But couldn't you pension her off?'

'What with?'

'Surely she would not want a fortune. A couple of quid or so a week . . .'

'I know exactly what she wants. Five hundred pounds.'

'In a lump sum?'

'Cash down.'

'It seems unusual. I should have thought a weekly dole . . .'

A sort of frozen calm descended on Johnny Pearce, the calm of despair.

'Let me tell you my story, omitting, as you say, no detail, however slight. I did offer her a weekly dole.'

'And she refused?'

'No, she accepted. That was when I felt justified in proposing to Bunny. I ought to have told you, by the way, that she's engaged to the policeman.'

'Bunny?'

'Nannie.'

'Oh, Nannie. What policeman would that be?'

'The one in the village. There's only one. His name's McMurdo.'

'Short-sighted chap?'

'Not that I know of. Why?'

'I was only thinking that it would be very difficult to be attracted to Nannie Bruce while seeing her steadily and seeing her whole. However, that is neither here nor there. Policemen are paid to take these risks. Proceed with your narrative.'

'Where was I?'

'You had just offered her a weekly sum, and she had accepted it. Which sounds to me like the happy ending, though obviously for some reason it was not. What came unstuck?'

'McMurdo won a football pool last winter. Five hundred pounds.'

'And why was that a disaster?' asked Lord Ickenham, for his godson had made this announcement in a hollow voice and was looking as if his was the head upon which all the ends of the world had come. 'I could do with winning a football pool myself. Wasn't Nannie pleased?'

'No, she wasn't. Her pride was touched, and she said she wasn't going to marry any man who had five hundred quid salted away unless she had the same amount herself. She said her aunt Emily had no money and married a man with a goodish bit of it and he treated her like an orphan child. She had to go to him for everything. If she wanted a new hat, he'd say hadn't he bought her a hat only five or six years ago and get off nasty cracks about women who seemed to think they'd married into the Rothschild family. None of that for her, Nannie said.'

'But, dash it, my dear Johnny, the two cases are entirely different. Musing on Emily, one draws in the breath sharply and drops a silent tear, but Nannie, with a weekly income, wouldn't be in her position at all. She would be able to make whatever kind of splash seemed fit to her. Didn't you point that out to the fatheaded woman?'

'Of course I did, but do you think it's possible to make Nannie see reason, once her mind's made up? Either she had five hundred pounds, or all bets were off. That was final. And that's how matters stand today,' said Johnny.

He dug the pen into Inspector Jervis's latest bit of dialogue once more and resumed.

'I thought I saw a way of straightening things out. It meant taking a chance, but it was no moment for prudence and caution. Did you read that last book of mine, *Inspector Jervis at Bay*?'

'Well, what with one thing and another, trying to catch up with my Proust and Kafka and all that—'

'Don't apologize. The British Isles are stiff with people who didn't read it. You see them on every side. But there were enough who did to enable me to make a hundred and eleven pounds six and threepence out of it.'

'Nice going.'

'So I took the hundred and put it on an outsider in the Derby. Ballymore.'

'My unhappy lad! Beaten by Moke the Second after a photo finish.'

'Yes, if it had had a longer nose, my troubles would have been at an end.'

'And you have no other means of raising that five hundred?'

'Not that I can see.'

'How about the furniture?'

'I've come to the end of the things I'm allowed to sell. All the rest are heirlooms, except the fake walnut cabinet, of course, Great-Uncle Walter's gift to Hammer Hall.'

'That eyesore!'

'I can sell that without getting slapped into gaol. I'm putting it up for auction soon. It might fetch a fiver.'

'From somebody astigmatic.'

'But, as you are about to point out, that would still leave me short four hundred and ninety-five. Oh, hell! Have you ever robbed a bank, Uncle Fred?'

'Not that I can recall. Why?'

'I was just thinking that that might be the simplest way out. But, with my luck, if I bust the Bank of England, I'd find they hadn't got five hundred quid in the safe. Still, there's always one consolation.'

'What's that?'

'It'll be all the same in a hundred years. And now, if you don't mind buzzing off and leaving me, I'll be getting back to Inspector Jervis.'

'Yes, it's time that I was moving. The Big Chief said I was on no account to fail to go and pay my respects to Beefy Bastable, and I want to have a chat with my old friend Albert Peasemarch. Lots of thread-picking-up to be done. I shall be back in an hour or so and shall then be wholly at your disposal.'

'Not that there's a damn thing you can do.'

'It is always rash to say that about an Ickenham. We are not easily baffled. I agree that your problem undoubtedly presents certain features of interest, but I am confident that after turning it over in my mind I shall be able to find a formula.'

'You and your formulas!'

'All right, me and my formulas. But wait. That is all I say—wait.'

And with a wave of the hand and a kindly warning to his godson not to take any wooden nickels, Lord Ickenham tilted his hat slightly to one side and set off across the park to Hammer Lodge.

9

THERE was a thoughtful frown on Lord Ickenham's brow and a pensive look in his eye as he skirted the lake, on the other side of which the grounds of Hammer Lodge lay. A cow was paddling in the shallows, and normally he would have paused to throw a bit of stick at it, but now he hurried on, too preoccupied to do the civil thing.

He was concerned about Johnny. His story would have made it plain to a far less intelligent godfather that the lad was in a spot. He was not on intimate terms with Nannie Bruce, but he was sufficiently acquainted with her personality to recognize the impossibility, once her mind was made up, of persuading her to change it. If Nannie Bruce wanted five hundred pounds cash down, she would get five hundred pounds cash down, or no wedding bells for Officer McMurdo. And as Johnny did not possess five hundred pounds, the situation had all the earmarks of an impasse. It is not too much to say that, though his hat was on the side of his head and his walk as jaunty as ever, Lord Ickenham, as he rang the front door bell of Hammer Lodge and was admitted by his friend Albert Peasemarch, was mourning in spirit.

Butlers come in three sizes—the large, the small, and the medium. Albert Peasemarch was one of the smalls. Short and somewhat overweight for his height, he had a round, moonlike face, in which were set, like currants in a suet dumpling, two brown eyes. A captious critic, seeing, as captious critics do, only the dark side, would have commented on the entire absence from these eyes of anything like a gleam of human intelligence: but to anyone non-captious this would have been amply compensated for by their kindliness and honesty. His circle of friends, while passing him over when they wanted someone to explain the Einstein Theory to them, knew that, if they were in trouble, they could rely on his help. True, this help almost invariably made things worse than they had been, for if there was a way of getting everything muddled up, he got it, but his intentions were excellent and his heart in the right place.

His face, usually disciplined to a professional impassivity, melted into a smile of welcome as he recognized the visitor.

'Oh, good evening, m'lord.'

'Hullo, Bert. You're looking very roguish. Is the old folk at home?'

'Sir Raymond is in his study, m'lord, but a gentleman is with him at the moment—a Mr Carlisle.'

'I know the chap you mean. He's probably trying to sell him a ruby ring. Well, then, if the big shot is tied up in conference, we've nice time for a spot of port in your pantry, and very agreeable it will be after a hot and dirty journey. You haven't run short of port?'

'Oh, no, m'lord. If you will step this way, m'lord.'

'California, as you might say, here I come. This,' said Lord Ickenham some moments later, 'is the real stuff. The poet probably had it in mind when he spoke of the port of heaven. "If the Dons sight Devon, I'll quit the port of heaven an' drum them up the Channel as we drummed them long ago." Sir Henry Newbolt. Drake's Drum. Are you familiar with Drake's Drum? But of course you are. What am I thinking of? I've heard you sing it a dozen times round the old camp fire in our Home Guard days.'

'I was always rather partial to Drake's Drum, m'lord.'

'And how you belted the stuffing out of it! It was like hearing a Siberian wolf-hound in full cry after a Siberian wolf. I remember thinking at the time how odd it is that small men nearly always have loud, deep voices. I believe midgets invariably sing bass. Very strange. Nature's law of compensation, no doubt.'

'Very possibly, m'lord.'

Lord Ickenham, who had been about to sip, lowered his glass with a reproachful shake of the head.

'Now listen, Bert. This "M'lord" stuff. I've been meaning to speak to you about it. I'm a Lord, yes, no argument about that, but you don't have to keep rubbing it in all the time. It's no good kidding ourselves. We know what lords are. Anachronistic parasites on the body of the state, is the kindest thing you can say of them. Well, a sensitive man doesn't like to be reminded every half second that he is one of the untouchables, liable at any moment to be strung up on a lamp post or to have his blood flowing in streams down Park Lane. Couldn't you substitute something matier and less wounding to my feelings?'

'I could hardly call your lordship "Ickenham".'

'I was thinking of "Freddie".'

'Oh, no, m'lord.'

'Then how about "old man" or "cully"?'

'Certainly not, m'lord. If your lordship would not object to "Mr I"?'

'The ideal solution. Well, Bert, how are things in the home now? Not much improvement, I gather from your letters. Our mutual friend still a little terse with the flesh and blood, eh?'

'It is not for me to criticize Sir Raymond.'

'Don't come the heavy butler over me, Bert. This meeting is tiled. You may speak freely.'

'Then I must say that I consider that he treats Madam very badly, indeed.'

'Bellows at her?'

'Almost daily, Mr I.'

'They will bring their court manner into private life, these barristers. I was in court once and heard Beefy cross-examining a meek little man who looked like Bill the Lizard in *Alice in Wonderland*. I forget what the actual words were, but the fellow piped up with some perfectly harmless remark, and Beefy fixed him with a glittering eye and thundered "Come, come, sir, don't attempt to browbeat *me!*" And he's still like that in the home, is he?'

'More so now than ever before. Madam is distressed because Mr Cosmo has written this book there is so much talk about. She disapproves of its moral tone. This makes her cry a good deal.'

'And he ticks her off?'

'Most violently. Her tears appear to exasperate him. I sometimes feel I can't bear it any longer.'

'Why don't you hand in your portfolio?'

'And leave her? I couldn't.'

Lord Ickenham looked at him keenly. His host's face, usually, like Oily Carlisle's, an expressionless mask, was working with an odd violence that made him seem much more the Home Guardsman of years ago than the butler of today.

'Hullo!' he said. 'What's this?'

Albert Peasemarch remained for a moment in the process of what is commonly known as struggling for utterance. Finding speech at length, he said in a low, hoarse voice very different from the one he employed when rendering Drake's Drum:

'I love her, Mr I.'

It always took a great deal to surprise Lord Ickenham. Where another man, hearing this cry from the heart, might have leaped in his chair and upset his glass of port, he merely directed at the speaker a look full of sympathy and understanding. His personal feeling that loving Phoebe Wisdom was a thing beyond the scope of the most determined Romeo he concealed. It could, apparently, be done.

'My poor old Bert,' he said. 'Tell me all. When did you feel this coming on?'

A dreamy look came into Albert Peasemarch's eye, the look of one who tenderly relives the past.

'It was our rheumatism that first brought us together,' he said, his voice trembling a little.

Lord Ickenham cocked an enquiring eyebrow.

'I'm not sure I quite got that. Rheumatism, did you say?'

'Madam suffers from it in the left shoulder, and I have it in the right leg, and we fell into the habit of discussing it. Every morning Madam would say "And how is your rheumatism, Peasemarch?" and I would tell her, and I would say "How is *your* rheumatism, madam?" and she would tell *me*. And so it went on.'

'I see. Swapping gossip from the lazar house. Yes, I understand. Naturally, if you tell a woman day after day about the funny burning feeling in your right leg, and she tells you about the curious shooting sensation in her left shoulder, it forms a bond.'

'And then last winter . . .'

'Yes—?'

A reverent note crept into Albert Peasemarch's voice. 'Last winter I had influenza. Madam nursed me throughout my illness.'

'Smoothed your pillow? Brought you cooling drinks?'

'And read Agatha Christie to me. And something came right over me, Mr I, and I knew that it was love.'

Lord Ickenham was silent for some moments, sipping his port and turning this revelation over in his mind. It still puzzled him that anyone could have had the divine spark touched off in him by Phoebe Wisdom. In a vague way, though he knew her to be more than a decade younger than himself, he had always regarded her as many years his senior. She looked, he considered, about eighty. But presumably she did not look eighty to Albert Peasemarch, and, even if she did, a woman who for years had kept house for Beefy Bastable was surely entitled to look a hundred.

His heart went out to Albert Peasemarch. Dashed unpleasant it must be, he was feeling, for a butler to fall in love with the chatelaine of the establishment. Having to say 'Yes, madam,' 'Very good, madam,' 'The carriage waits, madam' and all that sort of thing, when every fibre of his being was urging him to tell her that she was the tree on which the fruit of his life hung and that for her sake he would pluck the stars from the sky, or whatever it is that butlers say when moved by the fire within. A state of affairs, Lord Ickenham thought, which would give him personally the pip. He resolved to do all that in him lay—and on these occasions there was always quite a lot that in him lay—to push the thing along and bring sweetness and light into these two at present sundered lives.

'Taken any steps about it?' he asked.

'Oh, no, m'lord, I mean Mr I. It wouldn't be proper.'

'This is no time to mess about, being proper,' said Lord Ickenham bluffly. 'Can't get anywhere if you don't take steps.'

'What do you advise, Mr I?'

'That's more the tone. I don't suppose there's a man alive better equipped to advise you than I am. I'm a specialist at this sort of thing. The couples I've brought together in my time, if placed end to end, not that I suppose one could do it, of course, would reach from Piccadilly Circus to well beyond Hyde Park Corner. You don't know Bill Oakshott, do you? He was one of my clients, my nephew Pongo another. And there was the pink chap down at Mitching Hill, I've forgotten his name, and Polly Pott and Horace Davenport and Elsie Bean the housemaid, oh, and dozens more. With me behind him, the most diffident wooer can get the proudest beauty to sign on the dotted line. In your case, the relationship between you and the adored object being somewhat unusual, one will have to go rather carefully. The Ickenham system, for instance, might seem a little abrupt.'

'The Ickenham system, Mr I?'

'I call it that. Just giving you the bare outlines, you stride up to the subject, grab her by the wrist, clasp her to your bosom and shower burning kisses on her upturned face. You don't have to say much—just "My mate!" or something of that sort, and, of course, in grabbing by the wrist, don't behave as if you were handling a delicate piece of china. Grip firmly and waggle her about a bit. It seldom fails, and I usually recommend it, but in your case, as

I say, it might be better to edge into the thing more gradually. I think that as a starter you should bring her flowers every day, wet with the morning dew. And when I say "bring", I don't mean hand them over as if you were delivering a parcel from the stores. Put them secretly in her room. No message. An anonymous gift from a mystery worshipper. That will pique her curiosity. "Hullo!" she will say to herself. "What's all this in aid of?" and at a suitable moment you reveal that they came from you, and it knocks her base over apex. Wait!' said Lord Ickenham. A thought had come like a full-blown rose, flushing his brow. 'I'm seeing deeper into this thing. Isn't there a language of flowers? I'm sure I've read about it some-where. I mean, you send a girl nasturtiums or lobelias or whatever it may be, and it signifies "There is one who adores you respect-fully from afar" or "Watch out, here comes Albert!" or something. You've heard of that?'

'Oh, yes, indeed. There are books on the subject.'

'Get one, and make of it a constant companion.' Lord Ickenham mused for a moment. 'Is there anything else? Ah, yes. The dog. Has she a dog?'

'A cocker spaniel, Mr I, called Benjy.'

'Conciliate that dog, Bert. Omit no word or act that will lead to a *rapprochement* between yourself and it. The kindly chirrup. The friendly bone. The constant pat on the head or ribs, according to the direction in which your tastes lie. There is no surer way to a woman's heart than to get in solid with her dog.'

He broke off. Through the window of the pantry he had seen a gentlemanly figure pass by.

'The boss's conference has concluded,' he said, rising. 'I'd bet-ter go and pass the time of day. You won't forget, Bert? An atmo-sphere of the utmost cordiality where the dog Benjy is concerned, and the daily gift of flowers.'

'Yes, Mr I.'

'Every morning without fail. It's bound to work. Inevitably the little daily dose will have its effect,' said Lord Ickenham, and went along the passage to the study where, he presumed, Sir Raymond Bastable would still be—gloating, possibly, over the ruby ring he had purchased.

His manner was even more preoccupied than it had been when he ignored the paddling cow. So many problems had presented themselves, coming up one after the other. It was never his habit to grumble and make a fuss when this happened, but he did some-times, as now, feel that the life work he had set himself of spread-ing sweetness and light—or, as some preferred to put it, meddling in other people's business—was almost more than any man could be expected to undertake singlehanded. In addition to that of his godson Johnny, he now had Albert Peasemarch's tangled love life to worry about, and to promote a union between a butler and the sister of his employer is in itself a whole-time task, calling for all that one has of resolution and ingenuity. And there was, further-more, the matter of the reformation of Beefy Bastable, whose atti-tude toward his sister Phoebe, so like that of a snapping turtle suffering from ulcers, he was determined to correct.

A full programme.

Still, 'Tails up, Ickenham. Remember your triumphs in the past,' he was saying to himself. This was not the first time in his career that the going had been sticky.

He was right about Sir Raymond being in the study, but wrong about the ruby ring. His half-brother-in-law was sitting huddled in a chair with his head between his hands, his air that of a man who, strolling along a country lane thinking of this and that, has caught an unexpected automobile in the small of the back, and his outward appearance mirrored perfectly the emotions within. At about three-fifteen on a November afternoon at Oxford, when the University rugby football team were playing Cardiff, a Welshman with a head constructed apparently of ivory or one of the harder metals had once butted Sir Raymond Bastable in the solar plexus, giving him the illusion that the world had suddenly come to an end and judgment day set in with unusual severity. It had happened a matter of thirty years ago, but the episode had never faded from his memory, and until this evening he had always looked on it as the high spot of his life.

Some five minutes previously, when Oily Carlisle, producing Cosmo Wisdom's letter, had revealed its contents and gone off to give him, as he explained, time to think it over, it had been eclipsed.

10

LORD Ickenham came into the room, concern in every hair of his
raised eyebrows. Many men in his place, beholding this poor bit
of human wreckage, would have said to themselves 'Oh, my gosh,
another toad beneath the harrow' and ducked out quickly to avoid
having to listen to the hard luck story which such toads are always
so ready to tell, but to the altruistic peer it never occurred to adopt
such a course. His was a big heart, and when he saw a toad not
only beneath the harrow but apparently suffering from the effects
of one of those gas explosions in London street which slay six, he
did not remember an appointment for which he was already late
but stuck around and prepared to do whatever lay in his power to
alleviate the sufferer's distress.

'Beefy!' he cried. 'My dear old bird, what on earth's the matter?
You look like a devastated area.'

It took Sir Raymond some little time to tell him what the matter
was, for he had much to say on the subject of the black-hearted vil-
lainy of his nephew Cosmo and also a number of pungent remarks
to make about Oily Carlisle. As he concluded the recital of their
skulduggery, his audience, which he had held spellbound, clicked
its tongue. It shocked Lord Ickenham to think that humanity could
sink to such depths, and he blamed himself for having allowed this
new development to catch him unprepared.

'We should have foreseen this,' he said. 'We should have told ourselves that it was madness to place our confidence in anyone like young Cosmo, a twister compared with whom corkscrews are straight and spiral staircases the shortest line between two points. Seeing that little black moustache of his, we should have refused him the nomination and sought elsewhere for a co-worker. "Never put anything on paper, my boy," my old father used to say to me, "and never trust a man with a small black moustache." And you, my poor Beefy, have done both.'

Sir Raymond's reply was somewhat muffled, for he was having trouble with his vocal cords, but Lord Ickenham understood him to say that it was all his, Lord Ickenham's, fault.

'You suggested him.'

'Surely not? Yes, by Jove, you're right. I was sitting here, you were sitting there, lapping up martinis like a vacuum cleaner, and I said . . . Yes, it all comes back to me. I'm sorry.'

'What's the use of that?'

'Remorse is always useful, Beefy. It stimulates the brain. It has set mine working like a buzz-saw, and already a plan of action is beginning to present itself. You say this fellow went off? Where did he go?'

'How the devil do I know where he went?'

'I ask because I happen to be aware that he has a sensitive skin and is undergoing considerable discomfort because his wife made him put on his winter woollies this morning. I thought he might be in the garden somewhere, stripped to the buff in order to scratch with more authority, in which case his coat would be on the ground or hung from some handy bough, and I could have stolen up, not letting a twig snap beneath my feet, and gone through his pockets. But I doubt if he is the sort of man to be careless with a coat containing important documents. I shall have to try the other plan I spoke of, the one I said was beginning to present itself. Since you last heard from me, I have shaped it out, complete to the last button, and it will, I am convinced, bring home the bacon. You're sure he's coming back?'

'Of course he's coming back, curse him!'

'Through those French windows, no doubt. He would hardly ring the front door bell and have himself announced again. It would confuse Albert Peasemarch and make him fret. All right, Beefy, receive him courteously, ask after his sensitive skin and keep him engaged in conversation till I am with you again.'

'Where are you going?'

'Never mind. When the fields are white with daisies, I'll return,' said Lord Ickenham, and withdrew through the door a minute or so before Oily Carlisle came in through the French windows.

It could scarcely be said that Sir Raymond received Mr Carlisle courteously, unless it is courteous to glare at someone like a basilisk and call him a slimy blackmailer, nor did he enquire after his skin or engage him in conversation. What talk ensued was done by Oily, who was in excellent spirits and plainly feeling that all was for the best in this best of all possible worlds. Cosmo's letter, nestling in his inside coat pocket, made a little crackling sound as he patted it, and it was music to his ears. There was a brisk cheerfulness in his manner as he started talking prices that gashed his companion like a knife.

He had just outlined the tariff and was suggesting that if Sir Raymond would bring out his cheque book and take pen in hand, the whole thing could be cleaned up promptly, neatly and to everybody's satisfaction, when there came to him a sudden doubt as to the world being, as he had supposed, the best of all possible. The door opened, and Albert Peasemarch appeared.

'Inspector Jervis,' he announced, and with an uneasy feeling in his interior, as if he had recently swallowed a heaping tablespoonful of butterflies, Oily recognized, in the tall, slim figure that entered, his fellow-traveller from the station. And noting that his eyes, so genial in the cab, were now hard and his lips, once smiling, tight and set, he quailed visibly. He remembered a palmist at Coney Island once telling him, in return for fifty cents, that a strange man would cross his path and that of this strange man he would do well to beware, but not even the thought that it looked as if he were going to get value for his half dollar was enough to cheer him.

If Lord Ickenham's eyes were hard and his lips set, it was because that was how he saw the role he had undertaken. There were gaps in his knowledge of his godson's literary work, but he had read enough of it to know that when Inspector Jervis found himself in the presence of the criminal classes, he did not beam at them. The eyes hard, the lips set, the voice crisp and official—that was how he envisaged Inspector Jervis.

'Sir Raymond Bastable?' he said. 'Good evening, Sir Raymond, I am from the Yard.'

And looked every inch of it, he was feeling complacently. He was a man who in his time had played many parts, and he took a pride in playing them right. It was his modest boast that there was nothing in existence, except possibly a circus dwarf, owing to his height, or Gina Lollobrigida, owing to her individual shape, which he could not at any moment and without rehearsal depict with complete success. In a single afternoon at The Cedars, Mafeking Road, in the suburb of Mitching Hill, on the occasion when he had befriended the pink chap to whom he had alluded in his talk with Albert Peasemarch, he had portrayed not only an official from the bird shop, come to clip the claws of the resident parrot, but Mr Roddis, owner of The Cedars, and a Mr J. G. Bulstrode, one of the neighbours, and had been disappointed that he was given no opportunity of impersonating the parrot, which he was convinced he would have done on broad, artistic lines.

Oily continued to quail. Not so good, he was saying to himself, not so good. He had never been fond of inspectors, and the time when their society made the smallest appeal to him was when they popped up just as he was concluding an important deal. He did not like the way this one was looking at him and, when he spoke, he liked what he said even less.

'Turn out your pockets,' said Lord Ickenham curtly.

'Eh?'

'And don't say "Eh?" I have been watching this man closely,' said Lord Ickenham, turning to Sir Raymond, whose eyes were bulging like a snail's, 'since I saw him on the station platform in London. His furtive behaviour excited my suspicions. "Picking pockets right and left, that chap," I said to myself. "Helping himself to wallets and what not from all and sundry."'

Oily started, and a hot flush suffused his forehead. His professional pride was piqued. In no section of the community are class distinctions more rigid than among those who make a dishonest living by crime. The burglar looks down on the stick-up man, the stick-up man on the humbler practitioner who steals milk cans. Accuse a high-up confidence artist of petty larceny, and you bring out all the snob in him.

'And when I shared a cab with him to Hammer Hall and discovered on alighting that I was short a cigarette case, a tie pin, a packet of throat pastilles and a fountain pen, I knew that my suspicions had been well founded. Come on, my man, what are we waiting for?'

Oily was still gasping.

'Are you saying I picked pockets? You're crazy. I wouldn't know how.'

'Nonsense. It's perfectly simple. You just dip. It's no use pleading inability. If Peter Piper,' said Lord Ickenham, who on these occasions was always a little inclined to let his tongue run away with him, 'could pick a peck of pickled peppers, I see no reason why you should not be capable of picking a peck of pickled pockets. Has the fellow been left alone in here?' he asked Sir Raymond, who blinked and said he had not.

'Ah? Then he will have had no opportunity of trousering any of your little knick-knacks, even if he still had room for them. But let us see what he has got. It should be worth more than a casual glance.'

'Yes,' said Sir Raymond, at last abreast. He was always rather a slow thinker when not engaged in his profession. 'Turn out your pockets, my man.'

Oily wavered, uncertain what to do for the best. If he had been calmer, it might have struck him that this was a most peculiar inspector, in speech and manner quite unlike the inspectors with whom his professional activities had brought him into contact in his native country, and his suspicions, too, might have been excited. But he was greatly agitated and feeling far from his usual calm self. And perhaps, he was thinking, all English inspectors were like this. He had never met one socially. His acquaintance with Scotland Yard was a purely literary one, the fruit of his reading of the whodunits to which he was greatly addicted.

It was possibly the fact that Sir Raymond was between him and the window that decided him. The Beefy Bastable who had recently celebrated his fifty-second birthday was no longer the lissom athlete of thirty years ago, but he was still an exceedingly tough-looking customer, not lightly to be engaged in physical combat by one who specialized in the persuasive word rather than violence. Drinking in his impressive bulk, Oily reached a decision. Slowly, with a sad sigh as he thought how different it all would have been if his Gertie had been there with her vase of gladioli, he emptied his pockets.

Lord Ickenham appeared surprised at the meagreness of their contents.

'He seems to have cached the swag somewhere, no doubt in a secret spot marked with a cross,' he said. 'But, hullo! What's this? A letter addressed to you, Sir Raymond.'

'You don't say?'

'Written, I should deduce from a superficial glance, by a man with a small black moustache.'

'Well, well.'

'Just what I was going to say myself.'

'Most extraordinary!'

'Very. Will you press a charge against this man for swiping it?'

'I think not.'

'You don't want to see him in a dungeon with dripping walls, getting gnawed to the bone by rats? You string along with the Bard of Avon about the quality of mercy not being strained? Very well. It's up to you, of course. All right, Mr Carlisle, you may go.'

It was at this moment, when everything appeared, as Oily would have put it, to have been cleaned up neatly and to everybody's satisfaction, that the door opened again and Mrs Phoebe Wisdom pottered in, looking so like a white rabbit that the first impulse of any lover of animals would have been to offer her a lettuce.

'Raymond, dear,' she said, 'have you seen my pig?'

For the past half-hour Sir Raymond Bastable had been under a considerable strain, and though relief at the success of his half-brother-in-law's intervention had lessened this, he was still feeling its effects. This sudden introduction of the pig motif seemed to take him into a nightmare world where nothing made sense, and for a moment everything went blank. Swaying a little on his base, he said in a low whisper:

'Your pig?'

'The little gold pig from my charm bracelet. It has dropped off, and I can't find it anywhere. Well, Frederick, how nice to see you after all this time. Peasemarch told me you were here. When did you arrive?'

'I came on the 3.26 train. I'm staying with my godson, Johnny Pearce, at the Hall. You don't look too well, Phoebe. What's the trouble? Not enough yeast?'

'It's this book of Cossie's, Frederick. I can't imagine how he came to write such a book. A bishop denouncing it!'

'Bishops will be bishops.'

'I went up to London yesterday to see him and tell him how upset I was, but he wasn't there.'

'Somewhere else, perhaps?' Lord Ickenham suggested.

Oily had been listening to these exchanges with growing bewilderment. From the first he had thought this Inspector an odd Inspector, but only now was it borne in on him how very odd he was.

'Say, who *is* this guy?' he demanded.

'Hasn't my brother introduced you?' said Phoebe. 'He is my half-sister's husband, Lord Ickenham. *You* haven't seen my pig, have you, Frederick?'

'Phoebe,' said Sir Raymond, 'get out!'

'What, dear?'

'Get out!'

'But I was going to look for my pig.'

'Never mind your pig. Get OUT!' bellowed Sir Raymond in the voice that had so often brought plaster down from the ceiling of the Old Bailey and caused nervous court officials to swallow their chewing gum.

Phoebe withdrew, sobbing softly and looking like a white rabbit that has had bad news from home, and Oily confronted Lord Ickenham. His face was stern, but there was a song in his heart, as there always is in the hearts of men who see defeat turn into victory.

'So!' he said.

'So what?' said Lord Ickenham.

'I'm afraid you're in a lot of trouble.'

'I am? Why is that?'

'For impersonating an officer. Impersonating an officer is a very serious offence.'

'But, my dear fellow, when did I ever impersonate an officer? Wouldn't dream of doing such a thing.'

'The butler announced you as Inspector Jervis.'

'What the butler said is not evidence. Am I to be blamed because a butler tries to be funny? That was just a little private joke we have together.'

'You said you were from the Yard.'

'I referred to the yard outside the kitchen door. I was smoking a cigarette there.'

'You made me turn out my pockets.'

'*Made* you? I *asked* you to, and you very civilly did.'

'Give me that letter.'

'But it is addressed to Sir Raymond Bastable. It belongs to him.'

'Yes,' boomed Sir Raymond, intervening in the debate, 'it belongs to me, and when you talk of serious offences, you foul excrescence, let me remind you that interfering with the mails is one of them. Give me that letter, Frederick.'

Lord Ickenham, who had been edging to the door, paused with his fingers on the handle.

'No, Beefy,' he said. 'Not yet. You must earn this letter.'

'What!'

'I can speak freely before Mr Carlisle, for I could see from the way he winced that your manner toward your sister Phoebe just now distressed him deeply. I, too, have long been wounded by your manner toward your sister Phoebe, Beefy, considering it to resemble far too closely that of one of the less attractive fauna in the Book of Revelations. Correct this attitude. Turn on that brotherly charm. Coo to her like a cushat dove. Take her up to London for dinner and a theatre from time to time, and when addressing her bear in mind that the voice with the smile wins and that you are not an Oriental potentate dissatisfied with the efficiency of an Ethiopian slave. If I learn from Albert Peasemarch, who will be watching you closely, that there has been a marked and substantial improvement, you shall have this letter. Meanwhile, I am going to keep it and hold it over you like the sword of . . . who was the chap? . . . no, it's gone. Forget my own name next,' said Lord Ickenham, annoyed, and went out, shutting the door behind him.

A moment later, it opened again, and his head appeared.

'Damocles,' he said. 'Sword of Damocles.'

The door closed.

11

O N a sunny morning precisely two weeks after Lord Ickenham had
adjusted the sword of Damocles over the head of Sir Raymond
Bastable, completely spoiling the latter's day and causing him to
entertain toward the sweetness-and-light specialist thoughts of a
kind that no one ought to have entertained toward a brother-in-
law, even a half one, the door of Brixton prison in the suburbs of
London was opened by a uniformed gentleman with a large key,
and a young man in a form-fitting navy blue suit emerged. Cosmo
Wisdom, his debt to Society paid, was in circulation once more.
He was thinner and paler than when last seen, and the first act of
the beauty-loving authorities had been to remove his moustache.
This, however, was not so great a boon to pedestrians and traffic
as it might seem, for he was resolved, now that he was in a position
to do so, to grow it again.

The Law of Great Britain is a smoothly functioning automatic
machine, providing prison sentences to suit all tastes. You put your
crime in the slot, and out comes the appropriate penalty—seven
years, as it might be, for embezzling trust funds, six months for
carving up a business competitor with a razor, and for being drunk
and disorderly and while in that condition assaulting the police
fourteen days without the option of a fine. Cosmo had drawn the
last of these.

When Oily Carlisle in a moment of unwonted generosity had

lent Cosmo twenty pounds, the latter, it may be remembered, receiving these pennies from heaven, had expressed his intention of celebrating. He had done so only too heartily. The thought of the good red gold which would soon be gushing like a geyser from the coffers of his Uncle Raymond had given wings to his feet as he started on his way along the primrose path. There was a sound of revelry by night and, one thing leading to another, in what seemed almost no time at all he was kicking Police Constable Styles of the C division, whose manner when he was trying to steal his helmet had offended him, rather severely in the stomach. Whistles blew, colleagues of the injured officer rallied to the spot, and presently stern-faced men were leading Cosmo off to the local hoosegow with gyves upon his wrists.

It was not a case, in the opinion of the magistrate at Bosher Street police court next morning, which could be met by the mere imposition of a fine. Only the jug, the whole jug and nothing but the jug would show the piefaced young son of a what-not where he got off, he said, though he phrased it a little differently, and he seemed chagrined at not being able to dish out more than those fourteen days. The impression he gave was that if he had been a free agent with no book of the rules to hamper him, Cosmo would have been lucky to escape what is known to the Chinese as the Death Of A Thousand Cuts. You could see that he was thinking that they manage these things better in China, and P.C. Styles, whose stomach was still paining him, thought the same.

The first act of your ex-convict on coming out into the great world after graduating from the Alma Mater is to buy a packet of cigarettes, his second to purchase a morning paper, his third to go and get the substantial lunch of which he has been dreaming ever since he clocked in. During the past two weeks Cosmo, rubbing along on the wholesome but rather meagre prison fare, had given a good deal of thought to the square meal he would have on getting out, and after considering the claims of Barribault's, Mario's, Claridge's, and the Savoy, had decided to give his custom to Simpson's in the Strand, being well aware that at no establishment in London are the meals squarer. As he hastened thither, with the picture rising before him of those white-coated carvers wheeling around their massive joints, his mouth watered and a fanatic gleam came into his eyes, as if he had been a python which has just heard the dinner bell. It was one of those warm summer days when most people find their thoughts turning to cold salmon and cucumber salad, but what he wanted was roast beef, smoking hot, with York-shire pudding and floury potatoes on the side, followed by some-thing along the lines of roly-poly pudding and Stilton cheese.

The paper he had bought was the *Daily Gazette*, and he glanced at it in the intervals of shovelling nourishing food into himself like a stevedore loading a grain ship. *Cocktail Time*, he noted with a touch of disapproval, had been dislodged from the front page by a big feature story about a twelve-year-old school-boy who had shaved all his hair off in order to look like Yul Brynner, but it came into its own on page four with a large black headline which read:

FRANK, FORTHRIGHT, FEARLESS
BEGINNING FRIDAY

and beneath this the announcement that *Cocktail Time* was about to appear in the *Daily Gazette* as a serial. 'The sensational novel by Richard Blunt,' said the announcement, adding that this was the pseudonym of Cosmo Wisdom, a prominent young man about town who is, of course, the nephew of the well-known Queen's Counsel, Sir Raymond Bastable.

The roast beef, roly-poly pudding and Stilton cheese had done much to bring Cosmo into a cheerful frame of mind, and the man-ner in which this manifesto was worded completed the good work. For obviously, if in the eyes of the *Daily Gazette* he was still the author of *Cocktail Time*, it could only mean that his Uncle Ray-mond, reading that letter, had prudently decided to play for safety and pay the price of secrecy and silence. No doubt, Cosmo felt, there was a communication to that effect waiting at his rooms in Budge Street, Chelsea, and his only regret was that the pangs of hunger had made it impossible for him to go there and read it before making up leeway at Simpson's.

So far, so good. But after he had been gloating happily for some little time over the picture of Uncle Raymond at his desk, pen in hand and writing golden figures in his cheque book, the sunshine was suddenly blotted from his life. It had just occurred to him to speculate on the possible activities of his friend Gordon Carlisle during his enforced absence, and this train of thought was a chilling one. Suppose his friend Gordon Carlisle—shown by his every action to be a man who thought on his feet and did it now—had taken that letter in person to Uncle Raymond, disclosed its contents, got cash down for it and was already on his way back to America, his pockets full of Uncle Raymond's gold. It was fortunate for Cosmo that he had already consumed his roly-poly pudding, for, had he not, it would have turned to ashes in his mouth.

But in envisaging Gordon Carlisle leaning on the rail of an ocean liner, watching porpoises and totting up his ill-gotten gains, he had allowed imagination to mislead him. Oily was not on his way to America. He was at this moment in the process of rising from a table on the opposite side of Chez Simpson, where he had been lunching with his wife Gertie. And though, like Cosmo, he had lunched well, his heart was heavy. There, said those who saw him to each other, went a luncher who had failed to find the blue bird.

Cosmo's inexplicable disappearance had tried Gordon Carlisle sorely. It was holding up everything. Scarcely five minutes after leaving Hammer Lodge his astute brain had grasped what must be done to stabilize the situation, but the scheme he had in mind could not be put into operation without the assistance of Cosmo, and Cosmo had vanished. Every day for the past two weeks Oily had called at Budge Street, hoping for news, and every day he had been sent empty away by a landlady who made no secret of the fact that she was sick of the sight of him. He was in much the same position as a General who, with his strategic plans all polished and ready to be carried out, finds that his army has gone off somewhere, leaving no address.

It is not to be wondered at, therefore, that when, as he made for the door, he heard a voice utter his name and, turning, found himself gazing into the face of the man he had sought so long, his heart leaped up as if he had beheld a rainbow in the sky. Rather more so, in fact, for, unlike the poet Wordsworth, he had never cared much for rainbows.

'Carlisle!' cried Cosmo exuberantly. He was blaming himself for having wronged this man in thought, and remorse lent to his voice something of the warmth which a shepherd exhibits when he sees a lost sheep reporting for duty. 'Sit down, my dear old chap, sit down!'

His dear old chap sat down, but he did so in a reserved and distant manner that showed how deeply he was stirred. Wrath had taken the place of joy in Oily's bosom. Thinking of the strain to which he had been subjected in the last fourteen days, he could not readily forgive. The eye which he fixed on Cosmo was the eye of a man who intends to demand an explanation.

'Mrs Carlisle,' he said curtly, indicating his companion. 'This is the Wisdom guy, sweetie.'

'It is, is it?' said Gertie. Her teeth made a little clicking sound, and as she looked at Cosmo, she, too, seemed to bring a chill into the summer day.

The austerity of their demeanour passed unnoticed by Cosmo. His cordiality and effervescence continued undiminished.

'So here you are!' he said. 'Well?'

Oily had to remember that he was a gentleman before he could trust himself to speak. Words which he had learned in early boyhood were jostling each other in his mind. He turned to his wife.

'He says "Well?"'

'I heard him,' said Gertie grimly.

'"Well?" He sits there and says "Well?" Can you beat it?'

'He's got his nerve,' Gertie agreed. 'He's certainly there with the crust, all right. Listen, you. Where the heck have you been all this time?'

It was an embarrassing question. One likes to have one's little secrets.

'Oh—er—away,' said Cosmo evasively.

• The words had the worst effect on his companions. Already cold and austere, they became colder and austerer, and so marked was their displeasure that he was at last forced to realize that he was not among friends. There was a bottle on the table, and a quick shiver ran down his spine as he observed Mrs Carlisle's hand stray absently in its direction. Knowing what a magnetic attraction bottles had for this woman, when cross, he decided that the moment had come to be frank, forthright and fearless.

'As a matter of fact, I've been in prison.'

'What!'

'Yes. I went on a toot and kicked a policeman, and they gave me fourteen days without the option. I got out this morning.'

A magical change came over the Carlisles, Mr and Mrs. An instant before stern and hostile, they looked at him now with the sympathetic eyes of a Mr and Mrs who understood all. The claims of prison are paramount.

'Oh, so that was it!' said Oily. 'I see. I couldn't think what had become of you, but if you were in the cooler . . .'

'How are they over here?' asked Gertie.

'Eh?'

'The coolers.'

'Oh, the coolers. Not too good.'

'Much the same as back home, I guess. Prison's all right for a visit, I always say, but I wouldn't live there if you gave me the place. Well, too bad they pulled you in, but you're here now, so let's not waste any more time. Give him the over-all picture, Oily.'

'Right away, sweetie. Things have gone and got a mite gummed up, Wisdom. You know a guy called Ickenham?'

'Lord Ickenham? Yes. He married my uncle's half-sister. What about him?'

Oily did not believe in breaking things gently.

'He's got that letter.'

Cosmo, as Police Constable Styles had done two weeks previously, made an odd, gurgling sound like water going down a waste pipe.

'My letter?'

'Yay.'

'Old Ickenham has?'

'Yup.'

'But I don't understand.'

'You will.'

Gordon Carlisle's narrative of the happenings at Hammer Lodge was a lengthy one, and long before it had finished Cosmo's jaw had dropped to its fullest extent. He had got the over-all picture, and his spirits were as low as his jaw.

'But what do we do?' he said hoarsely, seeing no ray of light among the clouds.

'Oh, now that I've contacted you, everything's nice and smooth.'

'Nice?'

'Yay.'

'Smooth?'

'Yup.'

'I don't see it,' said Cosmo.

Oily gave a gentlemanly little chuckle.

'Pretty clear, I'd have said. Fairly simple, seems to me. You just write your uncle another letter, saying you've been thinking it over some more and still feel the same way about letting everybody know that it was him and not you that wrote the book, and you're going to spill the beans in the next couple of days or so. Won't that make him play ball? Of course it will.'

The hearty lunch with which his rather bewildered gastric juices were doing their best to cope had dulled Cosmo's wits a good deal, but they remained bright enough to enable him to grasp the beauty of the scheme.

'Why, of course! It doesn't matter that Ickenham has got the letter, does it?'

'Not a bit.'

'This second one of mine will do the trick.'

'Sure.'

'I'll go home and write it now.'

'No hurry. I see you've got the *Gazette* there. You've read about the serial?'

'Yes. I suppose Saxby sold it to them. I had a letter from a literary agent called Saxby, asking if he could handle the book, and I thought it was a good idea. I told him he could.'

'Well, the first thing you do is go see him and get the money.'

'And the second,' said Gertie, 'is slip Oily his cut. Seventy smackers, if you remember. You owed him fifty, and he loaned you another twenty. Making seventy in all.'

'That's right. It all comes back to me.'

'And now,' said Gertie, speaking with a certain metallic note in her voice, 'it's coming back to Oily. He'll call around at your place in an hour or so and collect it.'

12

Old Mr Howard Saxby was seated at his desk in his room at the Edgar Saxby literary agency when Cosmo arrived there. He was knitting a sock. He knitted a good deal, he would tell you if you asked him, to keep himself from smoking, adding that he also smoked a good deal to keep himself from knitting. He was a long, thin old gentleman in his middle seventies with a faraway unseeing look in his eye, not unlike that which a dead halibut on a fishmonger's slab gives the pedestrian as he passes. It was a look which caused many of those who met him to feel like disembodied spirits, so manifest was it that they were making absolutely no impression on his retina. Cosmo, full though he was of roast beef, roly-poly pudding and Stilton cheese, had the momentary illusion as he encountered that blank, vague gaze that he was something diaphanous that had been hurriedly put together with ectoplasm.

'Mr Wisdom,' said the girl who had led him into the presence.

'Ah,' said Howard Saxby, and there was a pause of perhaps three minutes, during which his needles clicked busily. 'Wisdom, did she say?'

'Yes. I wrote *Cocktail Time*.'

'You couldn't have done better,' said Mr Saxby cordially. 'How's your wife, Mr Wisdom?'

Cosmo said he had no wife.

COCKTAIL TIME · 101

'Surely?'

'I'm a bachelor.'

'Then Wordsworth was wrong. He said you were married to immortal verse. Excuse me a moment,' murmured Mr Saxby, applying himself to the sock again. 'I'm just turning the heel. Do you knit?'

'No.'

'Sleep does. It knits up the ravelled sleave of care.'

In the Demosthenes Club, where he lunched every day, there was considerable speculation as to whether old Saxby was as pronounced an old lunatic as he appeared to be or merely for some whimsical purpose of his own playing a part. The truth probably came midway between these two contending views. As a boy he had always been inclined to let his mind wander—'needs to concentrate', his school reports had said—and on entering the family business he had cultivated this tendency because he found it brought results. It disconcerts a publisher, talking terms with an agent, when the agent stares fixedly at him for some moments and then asks him if he plays the harp. He becomes nervous, says fifteen per cent when he meant to say ten, and forgets to mention subsidiary rights altogether.

On Cosmo the Saxby manner acted as an irritant. Though meek in the presence of his Uncle Raymond, he had his pride, and resented being treated as if he were some negligible form of insect life that had strayed out from the woodwork. He coughed sharply, and Mr Saxby's head came up with a startled jerk. It was evident that he had supposed himself alone.

'Goodness, you made me jump!' he said. 'Who are you?'

'My name, as I have already told you, is Wisdom.'

'How did you get in?' asked Mr Saxby with a show of interest.

'I was shown in.'

'And stayed in. I see, Tennyson was right. Knowledge comes, but Wisdom lingers. Take a chair.'

'I have.'

'Take another,' said Mr Saxby hospitably. 'Is there,' he asked, struck by a sudden thought, 'something I can do for you?'

'I came about that serial.'

Mr Saxby frowned. A subject had been brought up on which he held strong views.

'When I was a young man,' he said severely, 'there were no cereals. We ate good wholesome porridge for breakfast and throve on it. Then along came these Americans with their Cute Crispies and Crunchy Whoopsies and so forth, and what's the result? Dyspepsia is rife. England riddled with it.'

'The serial in the paper.'

'Putting the beastly stuff in paper makes no difference,' said Mr Saxby, and returned to his sock.

Cosmo swallowed once or twice. The intellectual pressure of the conversation was making him feel a little light-headed.

'I came,' he said, speaking slowly and carefully, 'about that serial story of mine in the *Daily Gazette*.'

Mr Saxby gave a little cry of triumph.

'I've turned the heel! I beg your pardon? What did you say?'

'I came . . . about that serial story of mine . . . in the *Daily Gazette*.'

'You want my opinion of it? I would give it gladly, were it not for the fact that I never read serial stories in newspapers. Years ago I promised my mother I wouldn't, and to that promise I have faithfully adhered. Foolishly sentimental, you will say, pointing out that my mother, who has long been in heaven, would never know, but there it is. One has these rules to live by. And now,' said Mr Saxby, putting his sock away in a drawer and rising, 'I fear I must leave you. I have found your conversation very interesting, most interesting, but at this hour I always take a brisk constitutional. It settles my lunch and allows the digestive processes to work smoothly. If more people took brisk constitutionals after meals, there wouldn't be half the deaths there are, if any.'

COCKTAIL TIME · 103

He left the room, to return a moment later and regard Cosmo
with a vague, benevolent eye.

'Do you play leap-frog?' he asked.

Cosmo, speaking rather shortly, said that he did not.

'You should. Neglect no opportunity to play leap-frog. It is the
best of all games and will never become professionalized. Well,
goodbye, my dear fellow, so glad to have met you. Look in again,
and next time bring your wife.'

For some moments after the old gentleman had shuffled out,
the dizzy feeling, as of being in some strange nightmare world,
which came upon so many people after a *tête-à-tête* with Howard Saxby, had Cosmo strongly in its grip, and he sat motionless,
breathing jerkily from between parted lips. Then torpor gave place
to indignation. As Roget would have put it in his excellent Thesaurus, he was angry, wroth, irate, ireful, up in arms, flushed with passion and in high dudgeon, and he intended to make his presence
felt. He rose, and pressed the bell on Mr Saxby's desk, keeping his
thumb on it so forcefully that the girl who answered the summons
did so in something of the manner of an athlete completing a four-
minute mile, thinking that at last old Mr Saxby must have had the
seizure the office force had been anticipating for years.

'I want to see somebody,' said Cosmo.

Wilting beneath his eye, which was blazing like a searchlight,
the underling panted a little, and said:

'Yes, sir.' Then, for one likes to know these things, 'Who?'

'Anyone, anyone, anyone, anyone!'

'Yes, sir,' said the underling, and withdrew. She went to the
second door down the passage, and knocked. Roget would have
described her as upset, disconcerted, thrown off her centre and
rattled (*colloq*), and employees of the Edgar Saxby literary agency
when thus afflicted always sought out Barbara Crowe, knowing
that they could rely on her for sympathy and constructive counsel.

'Come in,' called a musical voice, a voice like a good brand of

Burgundy made audible. 'Why, hullo, Marlene, you look agitated. What's the matter?'

'There's a gentleman in old Mr Saxby's room who says he wants to see someone.'

'Can't he see old Mr Saxby?'

'He isn't there, Mrs Crowe.'

'Hell's bells!' said Barbara. She knew old Mr Saxby's habits. 'Left the poor gentleman flat, has he? All right, I'll go and soothe him.'

She spoke confidently, and her confidence was justified, for at the very first sight of her Cosmo's righteous indignation sensibly diminished. A moment before, he would gladly have put the entire personnel of the Edgar Saxby literary agency to the sword, but now he was inclined to make an exception in favour of this member of it. Here, he could see at a glance, was a nice change from the sock-knitting old museum piece whose peculiar methods of conducting a business talk had turned his thoughts in the direction of mayhem.

It is probable that almost anyone, even one of the Jukes family with two heads, would have looked good to Cosmo after old Mr Saxby, but in sealing Barbara Crowe with the stamp of his approval he was perfectly justified. Lord Ickenham, speaking of this woman to Pongo, had used the adjective 'lovely'. While not quite that, she was undeniably attractive. Brown eyes, brown hair, just the right sort of nose and a wide, humorous mouth that smiled readily and was smiling now. Her personality, too, had a distinct appeal of its own. There was about her a kindly briskness which seemed to say 'Yes, yes, you have your troubles, I can see you have, but leave everything to me.' Fierce authors who came into the Saxby offices like lions always went out like lambs after talking with Barbara Crowe.

'Good afternoon,' she said. 'Is there something I can do for you? They tell me you have been in conference with old Mr Saxby. Very rash of you. What made you ask for him?'

'He wrote to me. He said he wanted to handle my novel *Cocktail Time*.'

'*Cocktail Time*? Good heavens! Are you Cosmo Wisdom?'

'Yes.'

'I know your uncle. My name is Mrs Crowe.'

Not moving much in his Uncle Raymond's circle, Cosmo had never seen Barbara Crowe, but he knew all about her from his mother, and looking at her now he was amazed that anyone, having succeeded in becoming engaged to her, could have let her get away. It confirmed the opinion he had always held that his Uncle Raymond, though possibly possessed of a certain rude skill in legal matters, was in every other respect the world's champion fathead.

'How is he?' asked Barbara.

'Uncle Raymond? Well, I don't see very much of him, but somebody who met him two weeks ago said he seemed worried.'

'Worried?'

'A bit on the jumpy side.'

A cloud passed over Barbara's cheerful face. As Lord Ickenham had indicated, she had by no means thrust Sir Raymond Bastable from her thoughts.

'He *will* overwork. He isn't ill?'

'Oh, no. Just . . . nervous,' said Cosmo, finding the *mot juste*.

There was a momentary silence. Then Barbara reminded herself that she was a conscientious literary agent and this young man not merely the nephew of the man whom for all his fatheadedness she still loved but an author, and an author plainly in need of having his hand held.

'But you didn't come here to talk about your uncle, did you? You came to discuss business of some sort. I don't suppose you got far with old Mr Saxby? No, I thought not. Was he knitting?'

Cosmo winced. Her question had touched an exposed nerve.

'Yes,' he said coldly. 'A sock.'

'How was it coming along?'

'I understood him to say that he had turned the heel.'

'Good. Always the testing part. Once past the heel, you're home. But except for learning that the sock was going well, you did not get much satisfaction out of him, I imagine. Not many of our clients do. Old Mr Saxby likes to come here still and potter about, though supposed to have retired at about the time when Gutenberg invented the printing press, but he is not what you would call an active cog in the machine. Our only authors who ever see him now are those who mistakenly ask for Howard Saxby. I suppose you did?'

'Yes. That was the name on the letter I got.'

'It should have been signed H.S., junior. Young Mr Howard Saxby is old Mr Howard Saxby's son. He runs things here, with as much assistance as I am able to give him. He's away today, so I am your only resource. What did you come about?'

'That serial in the *Daily Gazette*.'

'Oh, yes. A cheque for that was sent to you more than a week ago. Didn't you get it?'

'I've—er—been away.'

'Oh, I see. Well, it's waiting for you at your rooms. And we're hoping to have more good news for you at any moment. The movie end.'

It had never occurred to Cosmo that there was a movie end.

'You think the book might sell to the pictures?'

'Our man in Hollywood seems sure it will. He's been sending significant cables almost daily. The last one, which arrived yesterday, said . . . Yes?'

The girl Marlene had entered, bearing a russet envelope. She looked nervously at Cosmo, and sidled out. Barbara Crowe opened the envelope, and uttered an exclamation.

'Well, of all the coincidences!'

'Eh?'

'That you should have been here when this came and just when I was starting to tell you about the movie prospects. It's from our man in Hollywood, and . . . better sit down. Oh, you are sitting down. Well, hold on to your chair. He says he has now had a firm offer for the picture rights of *Cocktail Time* from the Superba-Llewellyn studio. Would it interest you to hear what it is?'

It would, Cosmo intimated, interest him exceedingly.

'A hundred and five thousand dollars,' said Barbara.

13

IT was a stunned and dizzy Cosmo Wisdom who some quarter of an hour later tottered from the premises of the Saxby literary agency, hailed a cab and tottered into it. He was feeling very much as his Uncle Raymond had felt on that faraway afternoon at Oxford when he had taken the Welsh forward to his bosom. But whereas Sir Raymond's emotions on that occasion had been of a sombre nature, those of Cosmo, as he drove to Budge Street, Chelsea, can best be described by the adjective ecstatic. It is not easy to drive in a taxi-cab of the 1947 vintage and feel that you are floating on a pink cloud high up in the empyrean, but he did it. And this in spite of the fact that his head was still hurting him quite a good deal.

At the moment when Barbara opened the cable from the man in Hollywood, he had been tilting his chair back, and the convulsive spasm which had resulted when she talked figures had caused him to take a nasty toss, bumping his occipital bone with considerable force on the side of old Mr Saxby's desk. But, placed right end up again with a civil 'Upsy-daisy', he had speedily forgotten physical discomfort in the rapture and what Roget would have called oblectation (*rare*) of listening to her subsequent remarks.

For this offer from the Superba-Llewellyn studio was, it appeared, not an end but a beginning. The man in Hollywood, she assured him, would not rest on his laurels with a complacent 'That's that.' He was, like so many men-in-Hollywood, a live wire who, once started, went from strength to strength. There would now, she said, come the bumping-up process—the mentioning to a rival studio that S-L were offering a hundred and five thousand dollars, the extracting from the rival studio of a bid of a hundred and fifty thousand, the trotting back to the Superba-Llewellyn with this information and . . .

'Well, you get the idea,' said Barbara.

Cosmo did indeed get the idea, and nearly injured his occipital bone again when this woman, a ministering angel if ever he saw one, went on to speak of one of the agency's clients whose latest work the man in Hollywood had just bumped up to three hundred and fifty thousand. True, he was feeling as he drove to Budge Street, he could not count on *Cocktail Time* bringing in quite as much as that, but even two hundred thousand would be well worth having. It is evidence of the heady effect which these chats about Hollywood have on authors that he had now begun to look on Superba-Llewellyn's original offer with a sort of amused contempt. Why this parsimony, he was wondering. Money was made to spend. Had no one ever told the Superba-Llewellyn studio that you can't take it with you?

But in every ointment there is a fly, in every good thing a catch of some sort. Elated though he was, Cosmo could not but remember that he had written a letter—in his own personal handwriting and signed with his own name—specifically disclaiming the authorship of *Cocktail Time*, and that this letter was in the possession of Lord Ickenham. For the moment, that blot on the peerage was withholding its contents from the public, but who could say how long he would continue to do so? Somehow, by some means, he must get the fatal paper into his hands and burn it, thus destroying the only evidence that existed that the book was the work of another.

It was not too difficult to sketch out a tentative plan to this end. From Oily, in the course of his narrative at Simpson's, he had learned that Lord Ickenham was staying at Hammer Hall, where paying guests were taken in. His first move must obviously be to become one of these paying guests. A vital document like that letter would presumably be hidden somewhere in the old buster's room, for where else in a country house could anyone hide anything? Once on the spot, he would sooner or later find an opportunity of searching that room. In the stories which were his favourite reading people were always searching rooms, generally with excellent results.

It was with his spirits high again that he entered No. II Budge Street. In the hall he encountered his landlady, a Mrs Keating, a gloomy woman whom two weeks of daily visits from Oily had rendered gloomier. Oily often had that effect on people.

'Why, hullo!' she said, plainly surprised at this return to the fold. 'Where you been all this time?'

'Away,' said Cosmo, wondering how often he was going to have to answer this question. 'Staying with friends.'

'You didn't take any luggage.'

'They lent me everything.'

'You're looking thinner.'

Cosmo admitted that he had lost a little weight.

'Tuberculosis, I should say,' said Mrs Keating, brightening a little. 'That's what Keating died of. There's a lot of letters in there for you, and there's been a fellow calling asking for you every day these last two weeks. Carmichael or some such name.'

'Carlisle. I've seen him.'

'Seemed to think I've nothing to do but answer the bell. You be wanting dinner tonight?'

'No, I'm going away again. I just looked in to pack.'

'Odd some folks don't seem able to stay put for two minutes on end. It's this modern restless spirit. Gadding about. I've lived here twenty years and never been further than the King's Road, except to Kensal Green, when Keating was laid to his rest. Wasted away to a shadow, he did, and it wasn't two months before we were wearing our blacks. Tuberculosis it was, same as you've got. Where you going this time?'

'Dovetail Hammer in Berkshire. Forward my letters to Hammer Hall.'

'More work,' said Mrs Keating, and went off to the kitchen to attend to whatever it was on the stove that was making the house smell as if a meal were being prepared for a pack of hounds.

Quite a considerable mail awaited Cosmo in his sitting-room. The table was piled with letters. Most of them had been forwarded from Alfred Tomkins, Ltd, and he read them with enjoyment— an author is always glad to hear from the fans—but the one that pleased him most was the one from the Edgar Saxby literary agency containing that cheque. It was one of those fat, substantial cheques, and he enclosed it in an envelope addressed to his bank. After which, feeling that things were making a good start, he went to his bedroom and began packing. He had filled a large suitcase and was standing on the front steps with it, waiting for a taxi, when Oily arrived—without, he was relieved to see, Sweetie, the bottle addict.

The indications of impending departure which met his eye surprised Oily.

'Where are you going?' he asked.

It was a change from being asked where he had been, but Cosmo made his customary answer.

'Away. Thought I'd have a couple of days at Bournemouth.'

'Why Bournemouth?'

'Why not Bournemouth?' said Cosmo rather cleverly, and Oily appeared to see the justice of this.

'Well, I'm glad I caught you,' he said, having expressed the opinion that his young friend might just as well bury himself alive. Oily was the metropolitan type, never at his ease outside big cities. 'What have you done with the letter?'

Cosmo, rehearsing this scene in the privacy of his bedroom, had decided to be nonchalant. It was nonchalantly that he now replied:

'Oh, the letter? I was going to tell you about that. I've changed my mind. I'm not going to write it.'

'What!'

'No. I think I'll let things stay the way they are. Oh, by the way, I owe you some money, don't I? I wrote a cheque. I've got it some-where. Yes, here you are. Taxi!' cried Cosmo, waving.

Oily was still standing stunned among the ruins of his hopes and dreams.

'But—'

'It's no good saying "But,"' said Cosmo briskly, 'if you really want to know, I like being the author of *Cocktail Time*. I enjoy getting all these letters from admirers of my work—'

'What do you mean, your work?'

'Well, Uncle Raymond's work. It's the same thing. And being the author of *Cocktail Time* improves my social standing. To give you an instance, I found a note in there from Georgina, Lady Witherspoon, inviting me to one of her Sunday afternoon teas. It isn't everybody by any means whom Georgina, Lady Witherspoon, invites to her Sunday afternoon teas. She runs a sort of salon, and you have to be somebody of importance to get in. I don't feel like throwing away all that just to collect a few hundred pounds or whatever it may be from Uncle Raymond.' Less, probably, he almost said, than the absurd chicken-feed the Superba-Llewellyn people were offering. 'So there you are. Well, goodbye, Carlisle, it's been nice knowing you. I must be off,' said Cosmo, and was, leaving Oily staring blankly after him and asking himself if these things could really be. Even a high-up confidence artist has to expect disappointments and setbacks, of course, from time to time, but he never learns to enjoy them. In the manner of Gordon Carlisle as half an hour later he entered the presence of his wife Gertie there still lingered a suggestion of Napoleon returning from Moscow.

Gertie, having listened frowningly to the tale he had to tell, expressed the opinion that Cosmo was a low-down double-crossing little rat, which was of course quite true.

'There's oompus-boompus going on,' she said.

'Oompus-boompus, sweetie?'

'Yay. Social standing, did he say?'

'That's what he said.'

Gertie emitted what in a less attractive woman would have been a snort.

'Social standing, my left eyeball! When he left us, he was going to see his agent, wasn't he? Well, it's as clear what's happened as if he'd drawn a diagram. The agent told him there's been a movie offer.'

'Gosh!'

'Sure. And a big one, must have been.'

'I never thought of that. You're dead right. It would explain everything.'

'And he isn't going to any Bournemouth—who the hell goes to Bournemouth?—he's going to this Dovetail-what-is-it place to try to snitch that letter off the Ickenham character, because if he can get it and destroy it, there's nothing in the world to prove he didn't write the book. So what we do is go to Dovetail-and-what-have-you and snitch it before he does.'

'I get you. If we swing it, we'll be sitting pretty.'

'In the catbird seat. There we'll be, in the middle, with the Wisdom character bidding for it and the Bastable character bidding for it, and the sky the limit. And it oughtn't to be so hard to find out where the Ickenham character is keeping the thing. We'll go through his room with a fine-tooth comb, and if it isn't there, we'll know he's got it on him. Then all there is to it is beaning him with a blackjack and hunting around in his pockets, see what I mean?'

Oily saw what she meant. She could hardly have been more lucid. He drew an emotional breath, and even the most short-sighted could have seen the lovelight in his eyes.

'What a comfort you are to me, sweetie!' he said.

'I try to be,' said Gertie virtuously. 'I think a wife oughter.'

14

IT was two days after the vultures had decided to muster at Hammer Hall that a little procession emerged from the front door of Hammer Lodge, the country seat of Sir Raymond Bastable, Q.C. It was headed by Mrs Phoebe Wisdom, who was followed by the local veterinary surgeon, who was followed by Albert Peasemarch. The veterinary surgeon got into his car, spoke a few parting words of encouragement and good cheer, and drove off. He had been in attendance on Mrs Wisdom's cocker spaniel Benjy, who, as cocker spaniels will, had 'picked up something'. Both Phoebe and Albert, having passed the night at the sick bed, were looking in need of rest and repose, but their morale was high, and they gazed at each other tenderly, like two boys of the old brigade who have been standing shoulder to shoulder.

'I don't know how to thank you, Peasemarch,' said Phoebe.

'It was nothing, madam.'

'Mr Spurrell said that if it had not been for you making the poor angel swallow that mustard and water, the worst would have happened.'

It occurred to Albert Peasemarch as a passing thought that the worst could not have been much worse than what had happened when the invalid reacted to the healing draught. It would, he was convinced, remain for ever photographically lined on the tablets

of his memory when a yesterday had faded from its page, just as
the eruption of the Old Faithful geyser in Yellowstone Park lingers
always in the memory of the tourist who sees it.

'I am glad to have given satisfaction, madam,' he said, remem-
bering a good line taught him by Lord Ickenham's Coggs at the
time when he was being coached for the high office he held. And,
thinking of Lord Ickenham, he felt how right the clear-seeing peer
had been in urging him to spare no effort that would lead to a
rapprochement between this cocker spaniel and himself. Unless
he was greatly mistaken there was a new light in Phoebe's eyes as
she gazed at him, the sort of light a knight of King Arthur's Round
Table might have observed in the eyes of a damsel in distress, as
he dusted his hands after dispatching the dragon which had been
causing her annoyance. The vigil of the night had brought them
very close together. He found his thoughts turning in the direction of what his mentor had called the Ickenham System. Had the
moment come for putting this into operation?

He had the drill, he fancied, pretty clear in his mind. How
did it go? Ah, yes. Stride up, grab by wrist, waggle about a bit, say
'My mate!' clasp to bosom and shower burning kisses on upturned
face. All quite simple, and yet he hesitated. And, as always happens when a man hesitates, the moment passed. Before he could
nerve himself to do something constructive, she had begun to
speak of warm milk with a little drop of brandy in it. Mr Spurrell,
the veterinary surgeon, had recommended this.

'Will you heat some up in a saucepan, Peasemarch?'

Albert Peasemarch sighed. To put the Ickenham System into
operation with any hope of success, a man needs something in the
nature of a cue, and cannot hope to give of his best if the saucepan
motif is introduced into the conversation. Romeo himself would
have been discouraged, if early in the balcony scene Juliet had
started talking about saucepans.

'Very good, madam,' he said dully.

'And then you ought to lie down and have a good rest.'

'I was about to suggest the same thing to you, madam.'

'Yes, I am feeling tired. But I want to speak to Lord Ickenham first.'

'I see his lordship is fishing on the lake, madam. Could I take a message?'

'No, thank you very much, Peasemarch. It's something I must say to him personally.'

'Very good, madam,' said Albert Peasemarch, and went off to heat saucepans with the heavy heart of a man conscious of having missed the bus. Possibly there were ringing in his ears the words of James Graham, first Marquis of Montrose:

> *He either fears his fate too much*
> *Or his deserts are small,*
> *That dares not put it to the touch,*
> *To win or lose at all.*

Or, of course, possibly not.

What knitting was to old Mr Saxby, fishing was to Lord Ickenham. He had not yet caught anything, nor was he expecting to, but sitting in a punt, watching a bobbing float, with the white clouds drifting across the blue sky above him and a gentle breeze from the west playing about his temples, helped him to think, and happenings at Hammer Hall of late had given him much to think about. The recent muster of the vultures had not escaped his notice, and, even had it done so, the fact that his room had been twice ransacked in the past two days would have drawn it to his attention. Rooms do not ransack themselves. There has to be a motivating force behind the process, and if there are vultures on the premises, one knows where to look for suspects.

Except for the nuisance of having to tidy up after these vultures, their arrival had pleased rather than perturbed Lord Ickenham. He was a man who always liked to have plenty happening around him, and he found the incursion of Cosmo Wisdom, closely followed by that of Gordon Carlisle and wife, a pleasant break in what was at the moment a dull visit. Enjoying the company of his fellows, he was finding himself distinctly short of it at Hammer Hall. He could scarcely, after what had occurred, hobnob with Beefy Bastable; Albert Peasemarch was hard to get hold of; and Johnny Pearce, racked with anxiety about his Belinda, had been for the last week a total loss as a companion.

So on the whole, he reflected, it was probably no bad thing to have a vulture or two about the home. They livened things up. What puzzled him about this current consignment was the problem of what had brought them to Hammer Hall and why, being there, they had ransacked his room. They were apparently searching eagerly for that letter of young Cosmo's, but he could imagine no reason for them to consider it of any value. Like Oily, he had seen immediately that Cosmo could quite easily write another, which would have precisely the same effect as the first. Eccentric blighters, these vultures, he told himself.

Another thing that perplexed him was that they seemed to be on such distant terms with one another. There was no mistaking the coolness that existed between Mr and Mrs Carlisle on the one side and Cosmo Wisdom on the other. One expects vultures, when they muster, to be a chummy bunch, always exchanging notes and ideas and working together for the good of the show. But every time Gordon Carlisle's eye rested on Cosmo, it rested with distaste, and if Cosmo passed Gordon Carlisle in the hall, he did so without appearing to see him. Very curious.

He was roused from these meditations by hearing his name called, and perceived Phoebe standing on the shore. Reluctantly, for he would have preferred to be alone, he drew in his line and rowed to land. Disembarking and seeing her at close quarters, he was a good deal shocked by her appearance. It reminded him of that of women he had seen at Le Touquet groping their way out into the morning air after an all-night session at the Casino.

'My dear Phoebe,' he exclaimed, 'you appear to be coming apart at the seams somewhat, if you don't mind me being personal. Not your bonny self at all. What's happened?'

'I was up all night with Benjy, Frederick. The poor darling was terribly ill. He picked up something.'

'Good Lord, I'm sorry to hear that. Is he all right now?'

'Yes, thanks to Peasemarch. He was wonderful. But I came to talk about something else, Frederick.'

'Anything you wish, my dear. Had you any particular topic in mind?' said Lord Ickenham, hoping that she had not come to resume yesterday's conversation about her son Cosmo and how thin he looked and how odd it was that, visiting Dovetail Hammer, he should be staying at the Hall and not with his mother at the Lodge. He could hardly explain that Cosmo was at the Hall because he wanted to be on the spot, to ransack people's rooms.

'It's about Raymond, Frederick.'

'Oh, Beefy?' said Lord Ickenham, relieved.

'I'm dreadfully worried about him.'

'Don't tell me he has picked up something?'

'I think he is going off his head.'

'Oh, come!'

'Well, there is insanity in the family, you know. George Winstanley ended his days in an asylum.'

'I'm not so well up on George as I ought to be. Who was he?'

'He was in the Foreign Office. He married my mother's second cousin Alice.'

'And went off his onion?'

'He had to be certified. He thought he was Stalin's nephew.'

'He wasn't, of course?'

'No, but it made it very awkward for everybody. He was always sending secret official papers over to Russia.'

'I see. Well, I doubt if the pottiness of a second cousin by marriage is hereditary,' said Lord Ickenham consolingly. 'I don't think you need have any anxiety about Beefy. What gives you the idea that he has not got all his marbles?'

'His what?'

'Why do you think he is *non compos*?'

'It's the way he's behaving.'

'Tell me all.'

Phoebe brushed away the tears that came so readily to her eyes.

'Well, you know how . . . what shall I say . . . how *impatient* dear Raymond has always been with me. It was the same when we were children. He has always had such a keen brain, and I don't think very quickly, and this seemed to exasperate him. He would say something, and I would say "What?" and he would start shouting. Morning after morning he used to make me cry at breakfast, and that seemed to exasperate him more. Well, quite suddenly one day about two weeks ago he changed completely. He became so sweet and kind and gentle that it took my breath away. I'm sure Peasemarch noticed it, for he was so often in the room when it happened. I mean, things like asking after my rheumatism and would I like a footstool and how nice I looked in that green dress of mine. He was a different man.'

'All to the good, I should have thought.'

'I thought so, too, at first. But as the days went by I began to get uneasy. I knew how overworked he always is, and I thought he must be going to have a nervous breakdown, if not something worse. Frederick,' her voice sank to a whisper, 'he sends me flowers! Every morning. I find them in my room.'

'Very civil. I see no objection to flowers in moderation.'

'But it's so *unnatural*. It alarmed me. I wrote to Sir Roderick Glossop about him. You know him?'

'The loony doctor? I should say so. What I could tell you about old Roddy Glossop!'

'He is a friend of the family, and I thought he would be able to advise me. But I didn't send the letter.'

'I'm glad you didn't,' said Lord Ickenham. His handsome face was grave. 'It would have been a floater of the worst description. There is nothing odd about this change in Beefy's attitude, my dear girl. I can give you the explanation in a word. Peasemarch.'

'Peasemarch?'

'He is behaving like this to conciliate Albert Peasemarch. An observant man, he noticed Albert Peasemarch's silent disapproval of the way he used to carry on, and realized that unless he speedily mended his ways, he would be a butler short, and nobody wants to lose a butler in these hard post-war days. As the fellow said—Ecclesiastes, was it?—I should have to check with Nannie Bruce—whoso findeth a butler findeth a good thing. I know that I would go to even greater lengths to retain the services of my Coggs.'

Phoebe's eyes were round. She looked like a white rabbit that is not abreast of things.

'You mean Peasemarch would have given notice?'

'Exactly. You wouldn't have seen him for dust.'

'But why?'

'Unable to stand the strain of watching you being put through the wringer each morning. No man likes to see a fourteen-stone Q.C. hammering the stuffing out of the woman he loves.'

'*Loves?*'

'Surely you must be aware by now that Albert Peasemarch worships the very ground you tread on?'

'But . . . but this is extraordinary!'

'I see nothing remarkable in it. When you don't sit up all night with sick cocker spaniels, you're a very attractive woman, my dear Phoebe.'

'But Peasemarch is a *butler*.'

'Ah, I see what you mean. You are thinking that you have never had a butler in love with you before. One gets new experiences. But Albert Peasemarch is only a synthetic butler. He is a man of property who took to buttling simply in order to be near you, to be able to exchange notes on your mutual rheumatism, to have you rub his chest with embrocation when he had influenza. Do you remember,' said Lord Ickenham, giving rein to his always rather vivid imagination, 'a day about two years ago when Beefy was standing you and me lunch at the Savoy Grill, and I nodded to a man at the next table?'

'No.'

Lord Ickenham was not surprised.

'That man,' he said, 'was Albert Peasemarch. He came to me later—he is an old friend of mine—and asked who you were. His manner was feverish, and it wasn't long before he was pouring out his soul to me. It was love, my dear Phoebe, love at first sight. How, he asked, could he get to know you? I offered to introduce him to Beefy, but he seemed to think that that wouldn't work. He said what he had seen of Beefy had not given him the impression of a man who would invite him to the home for long week-ends and generally give him the run of the place. I agreed with him. Beefy, when you introduce someone to him, is far too prone to say "Haryer, haryer," and then drop the party of the second part like a hot coal. We needed some mechanism whereby Albert Peasemarch could be constantly in your society, giving you the tender look and occasionally heaving the soft sigh, and to a man of my intelligence the solution was obvious. Who, I asked myself, is the Johnny who is always on the spot, the man who sticketh closer than a brother? The butler, I answered myself. Albert Peasemarch, I said, still addressing myself, must become Beefy's butler. No sooner—or not much sooner—said than done. A few simple lessons from Coggs and there he was, all ready to move in.'

Phoebe was still fluttering. The way the tip of her nose wiggled showed how greatly the story had affected her. She said she had never heard of such a thing, and Lord Ickenham agreed that the set-up was unusual.

'But romantic, don't you think?' he added. 'The sort of policy great lovers through the ages would have pursued, if they had happened to think of it. Hullo,' he said, breaking off. 'I'm afraid I must be leaving you, Phoebe.'

He had seen the station cab drive up to the front door and discharge Johnny Pearce from its interior.

'My godson has returned,' he explained. 'He went up to London to give his fiancée lunch, and I am anxious to learn how everything came out. The course of true love has not been running very smooth of late, I understand. Something of a rift within the lute, I gather, and you know what happens when rifts get into lutes. By and by they make the music mute and ever widening slowly silence all. I shall be glad to receive a reassuring bulletin.'

15

BESIDE Johnny Pearce, as he stood on the gravel drive, there was lying a battered suitcase. It signified, Lord Ickenham presumed, the advent of another paying guest, and he was delighted that business was booming so briskly. What with himself, this new arrival and the three vultures already in residence, Johnny in his capacity of jovial innkeeper was doing well. Though, now that he was in a position to study him closely, he had doubts as to whether 'jovial' was the right adjective. The young man's face, while not actually haggard, was definitely careworn. He looked like an innkeeper with a good deal on his mind, and when he spoke, his voice was toneless.

'Oh, hullo, Uncle Fred. I've just got back.'

'So I see. And you appear on your travels to have picked up some luggage. Whose suitcase is that?'

'It belongs to a bloke I shared the cab with. I dropped him at the Lodge. He wanted to see Bastable. Saxby he said his name was.'

'Saxby? Was he a fellow in the early forties with a jutting chin and a head like the dome of St Paul's, or a flattened-out septuagenarian who looked as if he had at one time been run over by a steam-roller? The latter? Then it must be Saxby senior, the father of the jutting chinner, I've met him at the Demosthenes Club. How did you get on with him?'

'Oh, all right. Odd sort of chap. Why did he ask me if I played the trombone?'

'One has to say something to keep the conversation going. Do you?'

'No.'

'Well, don't let yourself get an inferiority complex about it. Many of our most eminent public men don't play the trombone. Lord Beaverbrook, for one. Yes, that was old Saxby all right. I recognize his peculiar conversational methods. Every time I meet him, he asks me if I have seen Flannery lately. Who on earth Flannery is I have never been able to ascertain. When I reply that I have not, he says "Ah? And how *was* he?" The day old Saxby makes anything remotely resembling sense, they will set the church bells ringing and proclaim a national holiday. I wonder why he was going to see Beefy. Just a social call, I suppose. The question that intrigues one is why is he here at all. Is he staying with you?'

'Yes.'

'Good. Every little bit added to what you've got makes just a little bit more.'

'He may be staying some time. He's a bird-watcher, he tells me.'

'Indeed? I never saw that side of him. Our encounters have always taken place at the Demosthenes, where the birds are few and far between. I believe the committee is very strict about admitting them. Do you watch birds, Johnny?'

'No.'

'Nor I. If I meet one whose looks I like, I give it a nod and a wave of the hand, but I would never dream of prowling about and goggling at our feathered friends in the privacy of their homes. What a curse he must be to them. I can imagine nothing more unpleasant for a chaffinch or a reed-warbler than to get settled down for the evening with a good book and a pipe and then, just as it is saying to itself "This is the life," to look up and see old Saxby peering at it. When you reflect that strong men wilt when they meet that vague, fishy eye of his, you can imagine what its effect must be on a sensitive bird. But pigeon-holing old Saxby for the moment, what happened when you met Bunny? How was she? Gay? Sparkling?'

'Oh, yes.'

'Splendid. I was afraid that, with your relations a bit strained, she might have given you the Farthest North treatment or, as it is sometimes called, the ice-box formula. Cold. Aloof. The long silence and the face turned away to show only the profile. You relieve my mind considerably.'

'I wish someone would relieve mine.'

'Why, what's wrong? You say she was gay and sparkling.'

'Yes, but it wasn't me she was gay and sparkling with.'

Lord Ickenham frowned. His godson seemed to have dropped again into that habit of his of speaking in riddles, and it annoyed him.

'Don't be cryptic, my boy. Start at the beginning, and let your yea be yea and your nay be nay. You gave her lunch?'

'Yes, and she brought along a blighter called Norbury-Smith.'

Lord Ickenham was shocked and astounded.

'To a lovers' tryst? To what should have been a sacred reunion of two fond hearts after long parting? You amaze me. Did she offer any explanation of what she must have known was a social gaffe?'

'She said he had told her he was at school with me, and she was sure I would like to meet him again.'

'Good God! Smiling brightly as she spoke?'

'Yes, she was smiling quite a lot. Norbury-Smith!' said Johnny bitterly. 'A fellow I thought I'd seen the last of ten years ago. He's a stockbroker now, richer than blazes, and looks like a movie star.'

'Good heavens! Did their relations seem to you cordial?'

'She was all over him. They were prattling away like a couple of honeymooners.'

'Leaving you out of it?'

'I might as well have been painted on the back drop.'

Lord Ickenham drew a sharp breath. His face was grave.

'I don't like this, Johnny.'

'I didn't like it myself.'

'It's the Oh-well-if-you-don't-want-me-there-are-plenty-who-do formula, which too often means that the female of the species, having given the matter considered thought, has decided that she is about ready to call it a day. Do you know what I think, Johnny?'

'What?'

'You'd better marry that girl quick.'

'And bring her here with Nannie Bruce floating about the place like poison gas? We don't have to go into all that again, do we? I wouldn't play such a low trick on her.' Johnny paused, and eyed his companion sourly. 'What', he asked, 'are you grinning about?'

Lord Ickenham patted his arm in a godfatherly manner.

'If,' he said, 'you allude to the gentle smile which you see on my face—I doubt if somebody like Flaubert, with his passion for the right word, would call it a grin—I will tell you why I smile gently. I have high hopes that the dark menace of Nannie Bruce will shortly be removed.'

Johnny found himself unable to share this optimistic outlook.

'How can it be removed? I can't raise five hundred pounds.'

'You may not have to. You see that bicycle propped up near the back door,' said Lord Ickenham, pointing. 'Police Constable McMurdo's Arab steed. He's in the kitchen now, getting down to brass tacks with her.'

'It won't do any good.'

'I disagree with you. I anticipate solid results. I must mention that since I got here I have been seeing quite a bit of Officer McMurdo, and he has confided in me as in a sympathetic elder brother. He unloaded a police constable's unspotted heart on me, and I was shocked to learn on what mistaken lines he had been trying to overcome Nannie Bruce's sales-resistance. He had been arguing with her, Johnny, pleading with her, putting his trust in the honeyed word and the voice of reason. As if words, however honeyed, could melt the obstinacy of a woman whose mother, I am convinced, must have been frightened by a deaf adder. Action, Cyril, I told him—his name is Cyril—is what you need, and I urged him with all the vehemence at my disposal to cut the cackle and try the Ickenham System.'

'What's that?'

'It's a little thing I knocked together in my bachelor days. I won't go into the details now, but it has a good many points in common with all-in wrestling and osteopathy. I generally recommend it to diffident wooers, and it always works like magic. Up against it, the proudest beauty—not that that's a very good description of Nannie Bruce—collapses like a dying duck and recognizes the mastery of the dominant male.'

Johnny stared.

'You mean you told McMurdo to . . . *scrag* her?'

'You put it crudely, but yes, something on those lines. And, as I say, I anticipate the best results. At this very moment Nannie Bruce is probably looking up into Officer McMurdo's eyes and meekly murmuring "Yes, Cyril, dear," "Just as you say, Cyril, dear," "How right you are, Cyril, darling," as he imperiously sketches out his plans for hastening on the wedding ceremony. You might go and listen at the kitchen door and see how things are coming along.'

'I might, yes, but what I'm going to do is have a swim in the lake. I'm sweating at every pore.'

'Keep it clean, my boy. No need to stress the purely physical. Well, if you run into McMurdo, tell him I am anxious to receive his report and can be found in the hammock on the back lawn. Is that the evening paper you have there? I might just glance through it.'

'Before going to sleep?'

'The Ickenhams do not sleep. Anything of interest in it?'

'Only that movie thing.'

'To what movie thing do you allude?'

'About this chap Wisdom's book.'

'*Cocktail Time*?'

'Yes. Have you read it?'

'Every word. I thought it was extremely good.'

'It is. It's the sort of thing I should like to write, and I could do it on my head, only the trouble is that, once you start turning out thrillers, they won't take anything else from you. Odd, a fellow like Wisdom being able to do anything as good as that. He doesn't give one the impression of being very bright, do you think?'

'I agree with you. The book seemed to me the product of a much maturer mind. But you were saying something about a movie thing, whatever that is.'

'Oh, yes. Apparently all the studios in Hollywood are bidding frantically for the picture rights. According to the chap who does the movie stuff in that paper, the least Wisdom will get is a hundred and fifty thousand dollars. Oh, well, some people have all the luck,' said Johnny, and went off to take his swim.

The hammock to which Lord Ickenham had alluded was suspended between two trees in a shady nook some distance from the house, and it was in pensive mood that a few minutes later he lowered himself into it. His godson's words had opened up a new line of thought and, as so often happened to Johnny's Inspector Jervis, he saw all. The mystery of why there was this sudden muster of vultures at Hammer Hall had been solved. The motives of these vultures in seeking to secure the letter which was sewn into the lining of the coat he was wearing were crystal clear.

Obviously, with a hundred and fifty thousand dollars coming to the author of *Cocktail Time*, Cosmo Wisdom was not going to look favourably on the idea of writing a second letter to his Uncle Raymond, disclaiming the authorship of the book, and equally obviously he would strain every nerve to secure and destroy the letter he had already written. And the Carlisle duo would naturally strain every nerve to secure it first and start Sir Raymond and nephew bidding against each other for it. No wonder there was that coolness he had noticed between the vulture of the first part and the vultures of the second. With a hundred and fifty thousand dollars at stake, a coolness would have arisen between Damon and Pythias.

It was a mistake on Lord Ickenham's part at this point to close his eyes in order to brood more tensely on the problems this new development had raised, for if you close your eyes in a hammock on a warm summer evening, you are apt to doze off. He had told Johnny that the Ickenhams did not sleep, but there were occasions when they did, and this was one of them. A pleasant drowsiness stole over him. His eyes closed and his breathing took on a gentle whistling note.

It was the abrupt intrusion of a finger between his third and fourth ribs and the sound of a voice that said 'Hey!' that some little while later awakened him. Opening his eyes, he found that Gordon Carlisle was standing on one side of the hammock, his wife Gertie on the other, and he could not fail to notice that in the latter's shapely hand was one of those small but serviceable rubber instruments known as coshes.

She was swinging it negligently, as some dandy of the Regency period might have swung his clouded cane.

16

Although there was nothing in the unruffled calm of his manner to show it, Lord Ickenham, as he sat up and prepared to make the party go, was not at his brightest and happiest. He had that self-reproachful feeling of having been remiss which comes to Generals who wake up one morning to discover that they have carelessly allowed themselves to be outflanked. With conditions as they were at Hammer Hall, he should, he told himself, have known better than to loll in hammocks out of sight and earshot of friends and allies. The prudent man, aware that there are vultures in every nook and cranny of the country house he is visiting, watches his step. Failing to watch his, he had placed himself in the sort of position his godson Johnny's Inspector Jervis was always getting into. It was rarely in a Jonathan Pearce novel of suspense that Inspector Jervis did not sooner or later find himself seated on a keg of gunpowder with a lighted fuse attached to it or grappling in a cellar with one of those disagreeable individuals who are generally referred to as Things.

However, though recognizing that this was one of the times that try men's souls, he did his best to ease the strain.

'Well, well, well,' he said heartily, 'so there you are! I must have dropped off for a moment, I think. One is reminded of the experience of the late Abou ben Adhem, who, as you may recall, awoke one night from a deep dream of peace to find an angel at his bed-

side, writing in a book of gold. Must have given him a nasty start,
I have always thought.'

The interest of Oily and his bride in Abou ben Adhem appeared
to be slight. Neither showed any disposition to discuss this unusual
episode in his life. Mrs Carlisle, in particular, indicated unmistak-
ably that her thoughts were strictly on business.

'Shall I bust him one?' she said.

'Not yet,' said Oily.

'Quite right,' said Lord Ickenham cordially. 'There is, in my
opinion, far too much violence in the world today. I deprecate it.
Do you read Mickey Spillane?'

This attempt, too, to give the conversation a literary turn proved
abortive.

'Gimme,' said Oily. His manner was curt.

'I beg your pardon?'

'You heard. Remember making me turn out my pockets?'

'I don't like the word "making". There was no compulsion.'

'Oh, no? Well, there is now. Let's inspect what you've got in
your pockets, Inspector Jervis.'

'Why, of course, my dear fellow, of course,' said Lord Ickenham
with a cheerful willingness to oblige which should have lessened
the prevailing tension, if not removed it altogether, and in quick
succession produced a handkerchief, a cigarette case, a lighter,
the notebook in which he jotted down great thoughts when they
occurred to him, and a small button which had come off his shirt.
Oily regarded the collection with a jaundiced eye, and looked at his
wife reproachfully.

'He hasn't got it on him.'

Gertie, with her woman's intuition, was not so easily baffled.

'You poor simp, do you think he'd carry it around in his pocket?
It's sewn into his coat or sum'pn.'

This being actually the case, Lord Ickenham was conscious of
a passing regret that Gordon Carlisle had not selected a less intelligent mate. Had he led to the altar something more in the nature

of a dumb blonde, the situation would have been greatly eased. But he continued to do his best.

'What is it you are looking for?' he asked genially. 'Perhaps I can help you.'

'You know what I'm looking for,' said Oily. 'That letter.'

'Letter? Letter?' Lord Ickenham's face cleared. 'Oh, the *letter*? My dear fellow, why didn't you say so before? You don't suppose I would keep an important document like that on me? It is, of course, lodged at my banker's.'

'Oh, yeah?' said Oily.

'Oh, yeah?' said his wife, and it was abundantly evident that neither had that simple faith which we are assured is so much better than Norman blood. 'Oily!'

'Yes, sweetie?'

'Why *not* let me bust him one?'

It had become borne in on Lord Ickenham more and more that the situation in which his negligence had placed him was one of considerable embarrassment, and he was not finding it easy to think what to do next. Had he been able to rise to his feet, a knowledge of ju-jitsu, acquired in his younger days and, though a little rusty, still efficient, might have served him in good stead, but his chances of being allowed to exhibit this skill were, he realized, slight. Even under the most favourable conditions, a hammock is a difficult thing to get out of with any rapidity, and the conditions here were definitely unfavourable. It was impossible to ignore that cosh. So far, Gordon Carlisle had discouraged his one-tracked-minded wife's wistful yearning to bust him one with it, but were he to give the slightest indication of wishing to leave his little nest, he was convinced that the embargo would be lifted.

Like the youth who slew the Jabberwock, he paused awhile in thought. His problem, he could see, resembled that of his godson Johnny Pearce, in being undoubtedly one that presented certain features of interest, and he was conscious of feeling a little depressed. But it was not long before he was his old debonair self again, his apprehensions removed and the sun smiling through once more. Looking past his two companions, he had seen something that brought the roses back to his cheek and made him feel that, even though he be in a hammock, you cannot keep a good man down.

'I'll tell you—' he began.

Oily, his manner even curter than before, expressed a wish to be handed Lord Ickenham's coat.

'I'll tell you where you of the criminal classes, if you do not mind me so describing you, make your mistake, and a very serious mistake it is, too. You weave your plots and schemes, you spend good money on coshes, you tip-toe with them to people's bedsides, but there is something you omit. You don't allow for the United States Marines.'

'Gimme that coat.'

'Never mind my coat for the moment,' said Lord Ickenham. 'I want to tell you about the United States Marines. I don't know if you are familiar with the procedure where these fine fellows are concerned. To put it in a word, they arrive. The thing generally works out somewhat after this fashion. A bunch of bad men are beleaguering a bunch of good men in a stockade or an embassy or wherever it may be and seem to be getting along splendidly, and then suddenly the bottom drops out of everything and all is darkness, disillusionment and despair. Looking over their shoulders, they see the United States Marines arriving, and I don't suppose there is anything that makes bad men, when beleaguering someone, sicker. The joy goes out of their lives, the sun disappears behind the clouds, and with a muffled "Oh dear, oh dear, oh dear!" they slink away to their underground dens, feeling like thirty cents. The reason I bring this up,' said Lord Ickenham, hurrying his remarks to a conclusion, for he could see that his audience was becoming restive, 'is that, if you glance behind you, you will notice that the United States Marines are arriving now.'

And with a friendly finger he drew their attention to Police

Constable McMurdo, who, dressed in the authority of helmet and blue uniform, was plodding across the lawn toward them, the evening sun gleaming on his substantial official boots.

'I speak as a layman,' he said, 'but I believe the correct thing to do at a moment like this is to say "Cheese it, the cops!" and withdraw with all speed. What a fine, big fellow he is, is he not? Ah, Cyril, were you looking for me?'

'Yes, m'lord. Mr Pearce said I should find you here. But if your lordship is occupied—'

'No, it's quite all right,' said Lord Ickenham, sliding from the hammock. 'We had finished our little talk. I am sure Mr and Mrs Carlisle will excuse me. *Au revoir*, Mr Carlisle. Mrs Carlisle, I kiss your hand. At least, I don't, but you know what I mean. I am wholly at your disposal, Cyril.'

Police Constable McMurdo was a large man with an agreeable, if somewhat stolid and unintellectual face, heavily moustached toward the centre. He had a depressed and dejected look, and the cause of his mental distress was not far to seek, for while one of his cheeks was the normal pink of the rural constable, the other had taken on a bright scarlet hue, seeming to suggest that a woman's hand had recently landed on it like a ton of bricks. In his hot youth, Lord Ickenham, peering into the mirror, had sometimes seen his own cheek looking like that, and he needed no verbal report to tell him what must have happened at the late get-together in the kitchen.

'You bring bad news, I fear,' he said sympathetically, as they made their way to the house. 'The Ickenham System didn't work?'

'No, it didn't.'

Lord Ickenham nodded understandingly.

'It doesn't sometimes. One has to budget for the occasional failure. From the evidence submitted to my notice, I take it that she busted you one.'

'Rrrr!' said Officer McMurdo, with feeling. 'I thought my head had come off!'

'I am not surprised. These nannies pack a wicked punch. How did you leave things?'

'She said if I ever acted that way again, she'd never speak to me as long as she lived.'

'I wouldn't worry too much about that. She didn't break off relations?'

'She nearly broke me.'

'But not her troth. Excellent. I thought she wouldn't. Women try to kid us that they don't like ardour, but they do. I'll bet at this very moment she is pacing the kitchen floor, whispering "What a man!" and wishing you would play a return engagement. You wouldn't consider having another pop? Striking while the iron is hot, as it were?'

'I wouldn't, no.'

'Then we must think of some other way of achieving the happy ending. I will devote my best thought to your problem.'

And also, added Lord Ickenham to himself, to the problem of how to find a safe place to put that letter. The recent conference had left him convinced that the sooner such a place was found, the better. A far duller man than he would have been able to divine from the attitude of the Carlisle family that things were hotting up.

Not that he objected. He liked things to hot up.

17

OLD Mr Saxby, looking like something stationed in a corn field to discourage crows, stood on the lawn of Hammer Lodge, raking the countryside with his binoculars. At the moment when he re-enters this chronicle they were focused on the island in the middle of the lake.

The explanation of his presence in Dovetail Hammer, which Lord Ickenham had found mystifying, is a simple one. He was there at a woman's behest. Returning to the office after that brisk constitutional of his, he had been properly ticked off by Barbara Crowe for his uncouth behaviour to Cosmo Wisdom and sternly ordered by her to proceed without delay to Hammer Hall and apologize to him.

'No, a letter will *not* do,' said Barbara severely. 'Especially as you would be sure to forget to post it. You must go to him in person and grovel. Lick his shoes. Kiss the hem of his garment. Cosmo Wisdom has to be conciliated and sucked up to. He's a very important person.'

'He's a squirt.'

'A squirt maybe, but he wrote *Cocktail Time*, on its ten per cent of the proceeds of which the dear old agency expects to be able to afford an extra week at the seaside this year. So none of your larks, young Saxby. I shall want to hear on your return that he has taken you to his bosom.'

There was nothing Mr Saxby, whose view of Cosmo's bosom was a dim one, wanted less than to be taken to it, but he always did what Barbara Crowe told him to, even when it involved getting his hair cut, and he had set out obediently for Dovetail Hammer, consoling himself with the thought that a few days in the country, with plenty of birds to watch, would not be unpleasant. Nice, too, being next door to Bastable. He always enjoyed hobnobbing with Bastable.

Sir Raymond, who did not derive the same uplift from their hobnobbings, received him, when he was ushered into his presence by Albert Peasemarch, with a marked sinking sensation. Learning that his old clubmate was not proposing to make Hammer Lodge his headquarters but would be staying at the Hall, he brightened considerably, took him out on to the lawn to see the view and, finding that he had left his pipe behind, went back to fetch it. He now returned, and found the old gentleman, as has been stated, scrutinizing the island on the lake through his binoculars.

'Watching birds?' he asked, with the heartiness of a man assured that he is not going to have to put Howard Saxby senior up for an indefinite stay.

'Not so much birds,' said Mr Saxby, 'as that chap Scriventhorpe.'

'Chap who?'

'Scriventhorpe. Flannery's friend. I've met him with you at the club. I think you told me he was your son or your brother or something.'

Sir Raymond collected his wits, which, as so often happened when he was conversing with Howard Saxby senior, had been momentarily scattered.

'Do you by any chance mean Ickenham?'

'Didn't I say Ickenham?'

'You said Scriventhorpe.'

'Well, I meant Ickenham. Nice fellow. I don't wonder Flannery's fond of him. He's on that island over there.'

'Oh?' said Sir Raymond without enthusiasm. The only news

about his half-brother-in-law that would have brought a sparkle to his eyes would have been that he had fallen out of a boat and was going down for the third time.

'He's tacking to and fro,' proceeded Mr Saxby. 'Now he's crouching down. Seems to be looking for something. No, I see what he's doing. He's not looking for something, he's hiding something. He's got a paper of some kind in his hand, and he seems to be burying it.'

'What!'

'Odd,' said Mr Saxby. 'He jumped up just then and hurried off. Must have gone back to his boat. Yes, here he comes. You can see him rowing away.'

Sir Raymond had never expected that any observation of this clubmate of his would thrill him to the core, but that was what this one had done. He felt as if he had been reclining in an electric chair and some practical joker had turned on the juice.

The problem of what his relative by marriage had done with the fatal letter was one which for two weeks and more had never been out of Sir Raymond Bastable's thoughts. He had mused on it while shaving, while bathing, while breakfasting, while lunching, while taking his afternoon's exercise, while dining, while putting on his pyjamas of a night and while dropping off to sleep. The obvious solution, that Lord Ickenham had hidden it in his bedroom, he rejected. With determined bedroom searchers like Cosmo Wisdom and Mr and Mrs Gordon Carlisle on the premises, such a policy would be madness. He would have thought of some really ingenious place of concealment—a hollow tree, perhaps, or a crevice in some wall. That he would bury the document on an island, like a pirate of the Spanish Main disposing of his treasure, had never occurred to Sir Raymond. Yet to anyone familiar with Frederick Ickenham's boyish outlook on life, how perfectly in character it seemed.

Quivering, he grabbed at his companion's arm, and Mr Saxby quivered, too, for the grip of those fevered fingers had affected him like the bite of a horse. He also said 'Ouch!'

Sir Raymond had no time to waste listening to people saying 'Ouch!' He had seen Lord Ickenham bring his boat to shore, step out of it and disappear in the direction of the house, and he was feeling, as did Brutus, that there is a tide in the affairs of men, which, taken at the flood, leads on to fortune.

'Quick!' he cried.

'When you say "Quick!"' began Mr Saxby, but got no further, for he was being hurried to where the boat lay at a pace that made speech difficult for a man who was getting on in years. He could not remember having whizzed along like this, touching the ground only here and there, since the afternoon sixty-three years ago when, a boy of twelve, he had competed at a village sports meeting in the choirboys' hundred-yard race, open to all those whose voices had not broken by the second Sunday in Epiphany.

It was only natural, therefore, that as Sir Raymond bent to the oars, putting his back into it like a galley slave of the old school, silence should have prevailed in the boat. Mr Saxby was trying to recover his breath, and Sir Raymond was thinking.

The problem that confronted him, the one that so often bothers murderers, was what to do with the body—viz: Mr Saxby's. He had brought the old gentleman along because, having witnessed Lord Ickenham's activities, he would be able to indicate the spot where the treasure lay, but now he was asking himself if this had not been a mistake. There are men—the salt of the earth—who, if they see you searching islands on lakes, preserve a tactful silence and do not ask for explanations, but Mr Saxby, he was convinced, was not one of these. He belonged rather to the more numerous class who want to know what it is all about, and Sir Raymond had no desire for a co-worker of this description. Explanations would be foreign to his policy. By the time they reached their destination he had arrived at the conclusion that the less Mr Saxby saw of what was going on, the better.

'You stay in the boat,' he said, and Mr Saxby thought it a good idea. He was still in the process of trying to recover his breath, and was well content to be spared further exercise for the moment. His stamina was not what it had been in his choirboy days.

'Woof!' he said, meaning that he fully concurred, and Sir Raymond set out into the interior alone.

Alone, that is to say, except for the swan which was at the moment taking it easy in the undergrowth beside the bijou residence where its mate was nesting. It was unexpectedly meeting this swan that had caused Lord Ickenham to revise his intention of burying the letter on the island and take to his boat with all possible speed. The Ickenhams were brave, but they knew when and when not to be among those present.

For some minutes after his companion's departure Mr Saxby, whose breathing apparatus had now returned to normal, gave himself up to thought. But though nothing could be fraught with greater interest than a detailed list of the things he thought about, it is better perhaps to omit such a list and pass on to the moment when he felt restored enough to take up his binoculars again. It was as he scanned the mainland through these that he observed Cosmo Wisdom smoking a cigarette on the gravel outside the front door of the Hall, and the sight reminded him that he was a man with a mission. Long ere this, he felt guiltily, he should have been seeking the young squirt out and kissing the hem of his garment, in accordance with Barbara Crowe's directions.

Though what there was to kiss hems of garments about, he was thinking, as, having completely forgotten Sir Raymond Bastable's existence, he started to row ashore, was more than he could tell you. Young squirt barges in on a fellow while he is knitting his sock and needs every ounce of concentration for the successful turning of the heel. Fellow receives him with the utmost cordiality and civility, though most men, interrupted at such a moment, would have bitten his head off, and they chat pleasantly for a while of this and that. Finally, having threshed out all the matters under discussion, fellow bids squirt a courteous farewell, and goes for his brisk constitutional. Nothing wrong with that, surely? But

Barbara Crowe seemed to think there was, and women had to be humoured. As he rowed, he was throwing together in his mind a few graceful expressions of apology which he thought would meet the case.

These, a few minutes later, he delivered with an old-world charm. Their reception was what a dramatic critic would have called adequate. Cosmo did not take him to his bosom, but, the wound to his dignity apparently more or less healed, he offered him a cigarette, and they smoked in reasonable amity for a time, while Mr Saxby, always informative on his favourite subject, spoke at considerable length of birds he had watched. It was mid-way through a description of the peculiar behaviour of a sand martin he had once known in Norfolk—impossible to insert here owing to considerations of space—that he broke off suddenly and said:

'Bless my soul!'

'Now what?' said Cosmo rather sharply. He was finding Mr Saxby on sand martins a little trying.

'Exactly,' said Mr Saxby. 'What? You may well ask. There was something Barbara Crowe told me to tell you, and I've forgotten what it was. Now what could it have been? You don't happen to know, do you?'

At the name Barbara Crowe Cosmo had given a start. For the first time since their conversation had begun he was feeling that this Edwardian relic might be on the verge of saying something worth listening to.

'Was it about the movie end?' he said eagerly.

'The what?'

'Has there been another offer for the film rights of my book?'

Mr Saxby shook his head.

'No, it was nothing like that. Have you written a book?'

'I wrote *Cocktail Time*.'

'Never heard of it,' said Mr Saxby cordially. 'I'll tell you what I'll do. I'll go in and telephone her. She is sure to remember what it was. She has a memory like a steel trap.'

When he returned, he had a slip of paper in his hand, and was beaming.

'You were perfectly right,' he said. 'It *was* connected with what you call the movie end. I wrote it down, so that I should not forget it again. She said . . . Do you know Mrs Crowe?'

'I've met her.'

'Charming woman, though she bullies me unmercifully. Makes me get my hair cut. You don't know what the trouble was between her and your uncle, do you?'

'No.'

'They were engaged.'

'Yes.'

'She broke it off.'

'Yes.'

'Well, who can blame her? I wouldn't want to marry young Bastable myself.'

Cosmo spurned the gravel with an impatient foot.

'What did she *say*?'

'Ah, that we shall never know. What *do* women say on these occasions? Take back your ring and letters, do you think, or something of that sort?'

'About the movie end.'

'Oh, the movie end? Yes, as I told you, I have her very words here.' He peered at the paper. 'She said "Have you apologized?" and I said "Yes, I had apologized," and she said "Did he take you to his bosom?" and I said, "No, the young squirt did not take me to his bosom, but he gave me a cigarette," and she said "Well, tell him that Medulla-Oblongata-Glutz have offered a hundred and fifty thousand, and our man in Hollywood has gone back to Superba-Llewellyn to bump them up." Does that convey anything to you?'

Cosmo inhaled deeply.

'Yes,' he said. 'It does.'

And suddenly Mr Saxby, for all his fishy eye and flattened-out-by-a-steam-roller appearance, looked almost beautiful to him.

• • •

Sir Raymond Bastable, meanwhile, questing hither and thither like a Thurber bloodhound, had begun to regret that he had not availed himself of his shipmate's co-operation. Having no means of knowing whereabouts on this infernal island Mr Saxby had seen Lord Ickenham tacking to and fro and crouching down, he was in the position of one who hunts for pirate gold without the assistance of the yellowing map which says 'E. by N.20,' '16 paces S.' and all that sort of thing, and anyone who has ever hunted for pirate gold will tell you what a handicap this is. The yellowing map is of the essence.

The island was rather densely wooded—or perhaps under-growthed would be a better term—and was rich in spiky shrubs which caught at his ankles and insects which appeared to look on the back of his neck as the ideal rallying ground. 'Let's all go round to the back of Bastable's neck' seemed to be the cry in the insect world. He had become very hot and thirsty, and there was a hissing sound in his ears which he did not like. It suggested to him that his blood pressure was getting out of control. He was always a little nervous about his blood pressure.

It was as he straightened himself after his thirty-second attempt to find one of those spots, so common in fiction, where you can see, if you look closely, that the earth here has been recently disturbed, that he found he had wronged his blood pressure. This hissing sound had proceeded not from it but from the lips of a fine swan which had emerged from a bush behind him and was regarding him with unmistakable menace. There are moments when, meeting a swan, we say to ourselves that we have found a friend. This was not one of them. The chances of any fusion of soul between the bird and himself were, he could see at a glance, of the slightest.

It is always important at times like this to understand the other fellow's point of view, and the swan could certainly have made out a case for itself. With the little woman nesting in the vicinity and wanting to be alone with her eggs, it is not to be wondered at that it found intruders unwelcome. Already it had had to take a strong line with Lord Ickenham, and now, just as it was thinking that the evil had been stamped out, along came another human pest. It was enough to try the patience of any swan, and one feels that the verdict of history will be that in making hissing noises, staring bleakly, spreading its wings to their fullest extent and scrabbling the feet to indicate the impending frontal attack this one was perfectly justified. Swans, as every ornithologist knows, can be pushed only so far.

Sir Raymond, like Lord Ickenham, was not a pusillanimous man. If burglars had broken into Hammer Lodge, he would have sprung to the task of hitting them over the head with his niblick, and he had frequently looked traffic policemen in the eye and made them wilt. But the stoutest-hearted may well quail before an angry swan. It is possible that Sir Raymond, as he now started to withdraw, thought that he was doing so at a dignified walk, but actually he was running like a choirboy intent on winning the hundred yards dash. His one idea was to return as speedily as possible to the boat in which Mr Saxby was awaiting him.

Reaching the waterfront with something of the emotions of Xenophon's Ten Thousand when they won through to the sea, he was disconcerted to find that Mr Saxby was not awaiting him. Nor was there any boat. He saw what the poet Tennyson has described as the shining levels of the lake, but could detect nothing that would enable him to navigate them. And the hissing sound which he had wrongly attributed to his blood pressure was coming nearer all the time. The swan was not one of those swans that abandon a battle half fought. When it set its hand to the plough, it did not readily sheathe the sword. Casting a hasty glance behind him, Sir Raymond could see it arriving like a United States Marine.

It was a time for quick thinking, and he thought quickly. A split second later he was in the water, swimming strongly for the shore.

At the moment when he was making this dash for life, his sister Phoebe was up in her bedroom, trying her hair a new way.

It has so often been the chronicler's melancholy task to introduce this woman into his narrative in a state of agitation and tears
that he finds it pleasant now to be able to show her gay and happy.
Not even Sherlock Holmes, seeing her as she stood at her mirror,
would have been able to deduce that she had been up all night
with a sick cocker spaniel. Her eye was bright, her manner bumps-
a-daisy. She was humming a light air.

Nor is this to be wondered at. Lord Ickenham's sensational revelation of the fire that burned in the bosom of Albert Peasemarch
would alone have been enough to lift her to the heights, and on
top of that had come his comforting assurance that her brother
Raymond was not, as she had supposed, a candidate for the min-
istrations of Sir Roderick Glossop. Nothing, except possibly the
discovery that the ground on which she treads is worshipped by
a butler for whom she has long entertained feelings deeper and
warmer than those of ordinary friendship, can raise a woman's
spirits more than the knowledge that the brother who is the apple
of her eye is, in spite of appearances, in full possession of his marbles. One can understand Phoebe Wisdom humming light airs. A
weaker woman would have sung.

The mirror was in the window that looked over the lake and,
glancing past it as she turned to examine the new hair-do in profile, she found her eye attracted to something singular that was
going on in the water. A seal was there, swimming strongly for the
shore, and this surprised her, for she had not supposed that there
would be seals in an inland lake.

Nor were there. As she watched the creature emerge at journey's end, she saw that she had formed a wrong impression of its
species. It was, as Mr Saxby would have said, not so much a seal as
her brother Raymond. He was dressed, as always in the country, in
a sports coat, grey flannel trousers and a coloured shirt.

She stared, aghast. Her old fears had swept back over her. Do
men who have got all their marbles go swimming in lakes with
their clothes on? Very seldom, Phoebe felt, and feared the worst.

18

A T the hour of eight forty-five that night Lord Ickenham might have been observed—and was observed by Rupert Morrison, the landlord, licensed to sell ales, wines and spirits, who was polishing glasses behind the counter—sitting in the saloon bar of the village inn, the Beetle and Wedge, with a tankard of home-brew, watching television. Except for an occasional lecture by the vicar on his holiday in the Holy Land, illustrated with lantern slides, there was not a great deal of night life in Dovetail Hammer. The Beetle and Wedge's television set afforded the local pleasure-seekers about their only means of hitting the high spots after sundown.

The statement that Lord Ickenham was watching television is perhaps one calculated to mislead. His eyes, it is true, were directed at the screen, but what was going on there, apparently in a heavy snowstorm, made no impression on his mind. His thoughts were elsewhere. He was reviewing the current crisis in his affairs and turning stones and exploring avenues with a view to deciding how to act for the best.

Although it was his boast that the Ickenhams were not easily baffled, he could not conceal it from himself that the dislocation of his plans by the recent swan had left him in no slight quandary. With a bird as quick on the draw as that doing sentry-go there, burying the letter on the island in the lake was obviously not within the sphere of practical politics, and with two Carlisles and a Cosmo Wisdom prowling and prowling around in the manner popularized by the troops of Midian, any alternative place for its bestowal would have to be a very safe one. It is proof of the knottiness of the problem with which he was wrestling that in a moment of weakness he actually considered doing what he had tried to persuade the sceptical Carlisles that he had done and depositing the document with his bank.

A good deal shocked that he should even for an instant have contemplated a policy so tame and unworthy of an Ickenham, he turned his attention to the television screen. It might, he felt, enable him to come back to the thing with a fresh mind if he gave that mind a temporary rest.

They were doing one of those spy pictures tonight, a repeat performance, and he was interested to observe that by an odd coincidence the hero of it was in precisely the same dilemma as himself. Circumstances had placed this hero—D'Arcy Standish of the Foreign Office—in possession of papers which, if they fell into the hands of an unfriendly power, would make a third world war inevitable, and he was at the moment absolutely dashed if he could think how to hide them from the international spies who were surging around him, all right on their toes and up-and-coming. It was with a sympathetic eye that Lord Ickenham watched D'Arcy running about in circles and behaving generally like a cat on hot bricks. He knew just how the poor chap felt.

And then suddenly he started, violently, as if he had seen a swan entering the saloon bar, and sat up with a jerk, the home-brew trembling in his grasp.

'Egad!' he said.

'M'lord?' said Rupert Morrison.

'Nothing, my dear fellow,' said Lord Ickenham. 'Just Egad.'

As the saloon bar was open for saying Egad in at that hour, Mr Morrison made no further comment. He jerked a thumb at the screen.

'See what he's done?' he said, alluding to D'Arcy Standish. 'He wants to keep those papers safe from all those spies, so he's given 'em to his butler to take care of.'

Lord Ickenham said Yes, he had noticed.

'I call that clever.'

'Very clever.'

'Never occurs to 'em that the butler could have 'em,' proceeded Mr Morrison, who had seen the drama the previous week, 'so they keep after the fellow same as before. Thinking *he's* got 'em. See? But he hasn't. See?'

Lord Ickenham said he saw.

'They burgle his house and trap him in a ruined mill and chase him through the sewers,' Mr Morrison continued, giving the whole plot away, 'and all the time he hasn't got the papers, the butler's got 'em. Made me laugh, that did.'

'I'm not surprised. Have you a telephone here? I wonder if I might use it for a moment,' said Lord Ickenham.

Some minutes later, a fruity voice caressed his ear. Albert Peasemarch's mentor, Coggs, had advised making the telephone-answering voice as fruity as possible in the tradition of the great butlers of the past.

'Sir Raymond Bastable's residence. Sir Raymond's butler speaking.'

'*Not* the Albert Peasemarch there has been so much talk about?'

'Oh, good evening, Mr I. Do you wish to speak to Sir Raymond?'

'No, Bert, I wish to speak to you. I'm at the pub. Can you come here without delay?'

'Certainly, Mr I.'

'Fly like a youthful hart or roe over the hills where spices grow,' said Lord Ickenham, and presently the Beetle and Wedge's pictur-esque saloon bar was made additionally glamorous by the presence of Albert Peasemarch and his bowler hat. ('Always wear a bowler, chum. It's expected of you'—Coggs.)

'Bert,' said Lord Ickenham, when Rupert Morrison had supplied the ales he was licensed to sell and had withdrawn once more into the background, 'I hated to have to disturb your after-dinner sleep, but I need you in my business. You are probably familiar with the expression "Now is the time for all good men to come to the aid of the party." Well, this is where you do it. Let me start the conversational ball rolling by asking you a question. Do you take an active interest in world politics?'

Albert Peasemarch considered this.

'Not very active, Mr I. What with cleaning the silver and brushing the dog—'

'I know, I know. Your time is so full. Let me put it another way. You realize that there are such things as world politics and that a certain section of the community has the job of looking after them?'

'Oh, yes, Mr I. Diplomats they call them.'

'Diplomats is right. Well—can we be overheard?'

'Not unless someone's listening.'

'I'll whisper.'

'I'm a little deaf in the right ear.'

'Then I'll whisper into your left ear. Well, as I was about to say, the thing to bear in mind is that these diplomats can't get anywhere without papers. No, no,' said Lord Ickenham, as his old friend mentioned that he always read the *Daily Mirror* at breakfast, 'I don't mean that sort of paper, I mean documents. A diplomat without documents is licked from the start. He might just as well turn it up and go back to his crossword puzzle. And you know what I mean when I say documents.'

'Secret documents?'

'Exactly. You follow me like a bloodhound. A diplomat must have secret documents, and he gives these secret documents to trusted underlings to take care of, warning them on no account to let any international spies get their hooks on them. "Watch out for those international spies!" is the cry in what are called the chancelleries.'

This seemed reasonable to Albert Peasemarch.

'You mean if these spies got them, they would start creating?'

'Precisely. Throwing their weight about like nobody's business and making a third world war inevitable.'

'Coo! That would never do, would it?'

'I can imagine nothing more disagreeable. Remember those chilly nights in the Home Guard? I haven't been really warm since. You wouldn't want to go through all that again, would you?'

'I certainly wouldn't.'

'Nor I. Not even for the sake of hearing you sing Drake's Drum round the camp fire. Another beer, Bert?'

'Thank you, Mr I. Though I really shouldn't. I have to watch my figure.'

'If the document now in my possession falls into the hands of the gang that are after it, you won't have any figure to watch. It'll be distributed in little pieces over the countryside.'

To this Albert Peasemarch was prevented from replying immediately by the arrival of Mr Morrison, bringing up supplies. When the cup-bearer had retired and he was able to speak, he did so in the awed voice of a man who is wondering if he can believe his ears.

'What was that, Mr I? Did you say *you* had a document in your possession?'

'You bet I have, Bert. And it's a pippin.'

'But how——?'

'——did it come into my possession? Very simply. I'm not sure if I ever mentioned to you, when we were comrades of the Home Guard, that I was in the Secret Service. Did I?'

'Not that I can recall, Mr I.'

'Probably slipped my mind. Well, I am, and not long ago the head man sent for me. "Number X 3476," he said—the boys call me Number X 3476—"you see this document. Top secret, if ever there was one. Guard it day and night," he said, "and don't let those bounders get a smell of it." He was referring, of course, to the international spies.'

Albert Peasemarch drank beer like a man in a trance, if men in trances do drink beer.

'Cor lumme, stone the crows!' he said.

'You may well say "Cor lumme, stone the crows!" In fact, if anything, "Cor lumme, stone the crows" rather understates it.'

Albert Peasemarch drank some more beer, like another man in another trance. His voice, when he spoke, showed how deeply he was intrigued. Like so many of those with whom Lord Ickenham conversed, he was finding new horizons opening before him.

'These spies, Mr I. Are there many of them?'

'More than you could shake a stick at. Professor Moriarty, Doctor Fu Manchu and The Ace of Spades, to name but three. And every one of them the sort of chap who would drop cobras down your chimney or lace your beer with little-known Asiatic poisons as soon as look at you. And the worst of it is that they have got on to it that this document is in my possession, and it is only a question of time before they start chivvying me through the sewers.'

'You won't like that.'

'Exactly the feeling I had. And so, Bert,' said Lord Ickenham, getting down to the *res*, 'I have decided that the only thing to do is to pass the document on to you and let you take care of it.'

Albert Peasemarch was aware of a curious gulping sound. It reminded him of something. Then he knew what it reminded him of, the preliminary gurglings of the dog Benjy before reacting to that dose of mustard and water. It was only after listening to this odd sound for a moment or two that he realized that it was he who was making it.

'You see the devilish cleverness of the idea, Bert. The blighters will be non-plussed. When they chivvy me through the sewers, they'll just be chasing rainbows.'

'But, Mr I!'

A look compounded of astonishment and incredulity came into Lord Ickenham's face. It was as though he had been a father disappointed in a loved son or an uncle in a loved nephew.

'Bert! Your manner is strange. Don't tell me you are faltering? Don't tell me you are jibbing at taking on this simple assignment? No, no,' said Lord Ickenham, his face clearing. 'I know you better than that. We old Home Guarders don't draw back when we are asked to serve the country we love, do we? This is for England's sake, Bert, and I need scarcely tell you that England expects that every man will do his duty.'

Albert Peasemarch, having gulped again, more like the dog Benjy than ever, raised a point of order.

'But I don't want to be chased through sewers, Mr I.'

'You won't be. I'll attend to the sewer sequence. How on earth are they to know that you have got the thing?'

'You don't think they'll find out?'

'Not a chance. They aren't clairvoyant.'

That a struggle was going on in Albert Peasemarch's soul was plainly to be seen by anyone watching his moonlike face. Lord Ickenham could detect it with the naked eye, and he waited anxiously for the referee's decision. It came after a long pause in four words, spoken in a low, husky voice, similar in its intonation to a voice from the tomb.

'Very well, Mr I.'

'You'll do it? Splendid. Capital. Excellent. I knew you wouldn't fail me. Well, it's no good me giving you the thing now, for the very walls have eyes, so I'll tell you how we'll work it. Where's your bedroom?'

'It's off my pantry.'

'On the ground floor. Couldn't be better. I'll be outside your window at midnight on the dot. I will imitate the cry of the white owl—the white owl, remember, not the brown—and the moment you hear me hooting, you slip out and the document changes hands. It will be in a plain manilla envelope, carefully sealed. Guard it with your life, Bert.'

Albert Peasemarch's manner betrayed a momentary uneasiness.

'How do you mean, my life?'

'Just an expression. Well, that cleans it up, I think, does it not?

All you have to do is sit tight and say nothing. And now I ought to be leaving you. We must not be seen together. Hark!' said Lord Ickenham. 'Did you hear a low whistle? No? Then all is well. I thought for a moment those fellows might be lurking outside.'

Albert Peasemarch's uneasiness increased.

'You mean they're *here*, Mr I? Around these parts?'

'In dozens, my dear fellow, in positive droves. Dovetail Hammer has international spies the way other beauty spots have green fly and wasps. Still, it all adds to the spice of the thing, does it not?' said Lord Ickenham, and went out, leaving Albert Peasemarch staring with haggard eyes at the bottom of his empty tankard, a prey to the liveliest emotion.

Pongo Twistleton, had he been present, would have understood this emotion. He, too, had often experienced that stunned feeling, as if the solid earth beneath his feet had disintegrated, which was so apt to come to those who associated with the fifth Earl of Ickenham, when that fine old man was going good. And Pongo, in Albert Peasemarch's place, would have pursued precisely the same policy which now suggested itself to the latter.

'Another of the same, please, Mr M,' he said, and Rupert Morrison once more became the human St Bernard dog.

The results were instantaneous—indeed, magical would scarcely be too strong a word. Until now, the chronicler has merely hinted at the dynamic properties of the Beetle and Wedge homebrew. The time has come to pay it the marked tribute it deserves. It touched the spot. It had everything. It ran like fire through Albert Peasemarch's veins and made a new man of him. The careworn, timorous Albert Peasemarch ceased to be, and in his place there sat an Albert Peasemarch filled to the brim with the spirit of adventure. A man of regular habits, he would normally have shrunk from playing a stellar role in an E. Phillips Oppenheim story, as he appeared to be doing now, but with the home-brew lapping up against his back teeth he liked it. 'Bring on your ruddy spies!' about summed up his attitude.

He had had his tankard refilled for the fourth time and was telling himself militantly that any spies who attempted to get fresh with him would do so at their own risk, when the door of the saloon bar opened and Johnny Pearce and Cosmo Wisdom came in.

It was obvious at a glance that neither was in festive mood. Johnny was thinking hard thoughts about his old school-fellow, Norbury-Smith, whose attitude toward Belinda Farringdon at lunch had seemed to him far too closely modelled on that of a licentious clubman of the old silent films, and Cosmo was brooding on the letter, asking himself how it could be detached from Lord Ickenham's keeping and unable at the moment to see any means of achieving the happy ending. It was with a distrait listlessness that they put in their order for home-brew.

Rupert Morrison delivered the elixir, and looked regretfully at the television set, which was now deep in one of those parlour games designed for the feeble-minded trade. D'Arcy Standish had gone off the air ten minutes ago.

'You've missed the picture, Mr Pearce,' he said.

'Picture? What picture?'

'The spy picture that was on the TV just now. It's where this Foreign Office gentleman has these important papers,' began Mr Morrison, falling easily into his stride, 'and these spies are after them, so he gives them to his butler . . .'

'I saw it last week,' said Johnny. 'It was lousy. Absolute drivel,' he said, leaving no doubt as to how he felt about it. So much of his work had been turned down for television that he had become a stern critic of that medium.

'I do so agree with you, sir,' said Mr Morrison. Actually he had thoroughly enjoyed the picture and would gladly have sat through it a third time, but an innkeeper has to suppress his private feelings and remember that the customer is always right. 'Silly, I thought it. As if any gentleman would give an important paper to a butler to take care of. It just couldn't happen.'

'Oh, couldn't it?' said Albert Peasemarch, rising—a little

unsteadily—and regarding the speaker with a glazed but compelling eye.

It is only a man of exceptional self-restraint who is able to keep himself from putting people right when they begin talking ignorantly on subjects on which he happens to be well-informed, especially if he has just had four goes of the Beetle and Wedge home-brew. Knowing that these three were not international spies—in whose presence he would naturally have been more reticent—Albert Peasemarch had no compunction in intervening in the debate and speaking freely.

'Oh, couldn't it?' he said. 'Shows what a fat lot you know about it, Mr M. It may interest you to learn that a most important paper or document has been entrusted to me this very night by a gentleman who shall be nameless, with instructions to guard it with my life. And I'm a butler, aren't I? You should think before you speak, Mr M. I will now,' said Albert Peasemarch, with the air of a kindly uncle unbending at a children's party, 'sing Drake's Drum.'

And having done so, he slapped his bowler hat on his head and took his departure, walking with care, as if along a chalk line.

19

THE sun was high in the sky next day when Cosmo, approaching it by a circuitous route, for he had no desire to run into his Uncle Raymond, arrived at the back door of Hammer Lodge and walked in without going through the formality of ringing the bell. He was all eagerness for a word with Albert Peasemarch on a subject very near his heart.

It was the opinion of his late employer, J. P. Boots of Boots and Brewer, export and import merchants, an opinion he had often voiced fearlessly, that Cosmo Wisdom was about as much use to a business organization as a cold in the head, and in holding this view he was substantially correct. But a man may be a total loss at exporting and importing, and still have considerable native shrewdness. Though a broken reed in the eyes of J. P. Boots, Cosmo was quite capable of drawing conclusions and putting two and two together, and on the previous night he had done so. Where Johnny Pearce and Rupert Morrison, listening to Albert Peasemarch, had classified his observations as those of a butler who has had one over the eight, Cosmo had read between the lines of that powerful speech of his. He had divined its inner significance. The nameless gentleman was Lord Ickenham and the paper or document the fatal letter. It stuck out, he considered, a mile. As he hurried to Hammer Lodge, he did not actually say 'Yoicks!' and 'Tally ho!' but that was what he was thinking.

He found Albert Peasemarch in his pantry having his elevenses, two hard-boiled eggs and a bottle of beer. Butlers always like to keep their strength up with a little something in the middle of the morning, and at the moment of Cosmo's entry Albert Peasemarch was finding his in need of all the keeping up it could get. The one defect of the Beetle and Wedge's home-brew is that its stimulus, so powerful over a given period, does not last. Time marches on, and the swashbuckling feeling it induces wears off. Albert Pease-march, who on the previous night had gone out of the saloon bar like a lion, had come into his pantry this morning like a lamb, and a none too courageous lamb, at that. It is putting it crudely to say that he had cold feet, but the expression unquestionably covers the facts. He was all of a twitter and inclined to start at sudden noises. His reaction to the sudden noise of Cosmo's 'Good morning', spo-ken in his immediate rear, was to choke on a hard-boiled egg with a wordless cry and soar from his seat in the direction of the ceiling.

His relief on finding that it was not Professor Moriarty or The Ace of Spades who had spoken was extreme.

'Oh, it's you, Mr C,' he gasped, as his heart, which had crashed against his front teeth, returned slowly to its base.

'Just thought I'd look in for a chat,' said Cosmo. 'Do go on with your egg. Don't mind me.'

It was the beer rather than the egg that appealed to Albert Pease-march at the moment. He quaffed deeply, and Cosmo proceeded.

'You certainly pulled old Morrison's leg last night with that yarn of yours about the secret document,' he said, chuckling amusedly. 'He believed every word of it. Can you beat it? Never suspected for a moment that you were just kidding him,' said Cosmo, and broke into a jolly laugh. Very droll, he seemed to suggest, it had been, the whole thing.

There was a pause, and during that pause, though it lasted but an instant, Albert Peasemarch decided to tell all. He was in the overwrought state of mind that makes a man yearn for a confidant with whom he can share the burden that has been placed upon him, and surely Mr I would agree that it was perfectly all right letting Cosmo Wisdom, the child of his half-sister by marriage, in on the ground floor. If Cosmo had still had his little black moustache, he might have hesitated, but, as we have seen, the aesthetic authorities of Brixton prison had lost no time in shaving it off. Gazing into his now unblemished face, Albert Peasemarch could see no possible objection to cleansing his bosom of the perilous stuff which was weighing on his heart. If you cannot confide in the son of the woman you love, in whom can you confide?

'But I wasn't, Mr C.'

'Eh?'

'I wasn't kidding him.'

Cosmo's hand flew to the barren spot where his moustache had been. At times when he was dumbfounded he always twirled it. That he was dumbfounded now was plainly to be seen. He stared incredulously at Albert Peasemarch.

'Now you're pulling *my* leg.'

'No, really, Mr C.'

'You don't mean it's true?'

'Every word of it.'

'Well, I'm blowed!'

'It was like this, Mr C. His lordship sent for me—'

'His lordship?'

'Lord Ickenham, sir.'

'You don't mean he's mixed up in this?'

'It's his document I'm taking care of, the one that was entrusted to him by the head of the Secret Service, of which he is a member.'

'Old Ickenham's in the Secret Service?'

'He is, indeed.'

Cosmo nodded.

'By Jove, yes, so he is. I remember him telling me. One forgets these things. Let's have the whole story from start to finish.'

When Albert Peasemarch had concluded his narrative, Cosmo went through the motion of twirling his lost moustache again.

'I see,' he said slowly. 'So that's how it is. He's left you holding the baby.'

'Yes, sir.'

'It looks to me as if you were in a bit of a spot.'

Albert Peasemarch assented. That, he said, was how it looked to him, too.

'I don't suppose these international spies stick at much.'

'No, sir.'

'If they get on to it that you've got that document, the mildest thing they'll do is shove lighted matches between your toes.' Cosmo mused for a space. 'Look here,' he said, struck with a happy thought. 'Why don't you give it to *me*?'

Albert Peasemarch stared.

'You, sir?'

'It's the only way,' said Cosmo, becoming more and more enthusiastic about the idea. 'Put yourself in the place of these spies. They'll soon find out old Ickenham hasn't got this document, and then they'll start asking themselves what he's done with it, and it won't take them long to realize that he must have handed it on to someone. Then what'll they say? They'll say "To who?"'

'Whom,' murmured Albert Peasemarch mechanically. He was rather a purist. He shuddered a little, for those last words had reminded him of Lord Ickenham imitating the cry of the white owl.

'And they'll pretty soon answer that. They know you and he are friends.'

'Old comrades. Home Guard.'

'Exactly. It'll be obvious to them that he must have given the thing to you.'

Again Albert Peasemarch was reluctantly reminded of his old comrade giving his owl impersonation. He spoke with an increase of animation, for the scheme was beginning to appeal to him.

'I see what you mean, Mr C. They'd never suspect that you had it.'

'Of course they wouldn't. I hardly know old Ickenham. Is it

likely he'd give important documents to a fellow who's practically a stranger? Whatever this paper is, it will be as safe with me as if it were in the Bank of England.'

'It's certainly an idea, Mr C.'

'Where is the thing?'

'In my bedroom, sir.'

'The first place spies would look. Go and get it.'

Albert Peasemarch went and got it. But though Cosmo extended a hand invitingly, he did not immediately place the envelope in it. His air was that of a man who lets 'I dare not' wait upon 'I would', as so often happens with cats in adages.

'There's just one thing, Mr C. I must have his lordship's permission.'

'What!'

'Can't make a move like this without consulting his lordship. But it won't take a jiffy to step over to the Hall and get his okay. Five minutes at the outside,' said Albert Peasemarch, reaching for his bowler hat.

It sometimes happens at the Beetle and Wedge that a customer, demanding home-brew and licking his lips at the prospect of getting it, is informed by the voice of doom, speaking in the person of Rupert Morrison, that he has already had enough and cannot be served. On such occasions the customer has the feeling that the great globe itself has faded, leaving not a wrack behind, and that, as in the case of bad men interrupted in their activities by the United States Marines, all is darkness, disillusionment and despair. Such a feeling came to Cosmo Wisdom now. This unforeseen check, just as he had been congratulating himself on having fought the good fight and won it, induced a sudden giddiness and swimming of the head, so that his very vision was affected and he seemed to see two Albert Peasemarches with two round faces reaching for a brace of bowler hats.

Was there, he asked himself desperately, no way out, no means of persuading this man to skip the red tape?

There was. Beside the remains of the two hard-boiled eggs, which in that sudden spasm of spiritual anguish had seemed to him for an instant four hard-boiled eggs, there stood a pepper pot. To snatch this up and project its contents into Albert Peasemarch's face was with Cosmo the work of a moment. Then, leaving the suffering man to his sneezing, he shot out into the great open spaces, where he could be alone, in his pocket the only proof that existed that he was not the author of *Cocktail Time*, for the motion picture rights of which the Superba-Llewellyn studio would, he hoped, shortly be bumped up to an offer of two hundred thousand dollars.

But in assuming that in the great open spaces he would be alone, he was mistaken. Scarcely had he reached them, when a voice that might have been that of an ancient sheep spoke at his elbow.

'Well met by moonlight, proud Wisdom,' it bleated, and spinning on his axis he perceived old Mr Saxby.

'Oh, hullo,' he said, when able to articulate. 'Nice morning, isn't it? The sun and all that. Well, goodbye.'

'Let us not utter that sad word,' said Mr Saxby. 'Are you on your way to the Hall? I will walk with you.'

It was a pity that Cosmo had never taken any great interest in birds, for he was afforded now an admirable opportunity of adding to his information concerning their manners and habits. In considerable detail Mr Saxby spoke of hedge sparrows he had goggled at in their homes and meadow pipits he had surprised while bathing, and, had Cosmo been an ornithologist, he would have found the old gentleman's conversation absorbing. But, like so many of us, he could take meadow pipits or leave them alone, and it was with something of the feeling he had had when released from Brixton prison that at long last he saw the human porous plaster potter off on some business of his own.

It was in the hall of Johnny Pearce's ancestral home that this happened, and at the moment of Mr Saxby's departure he was standing beside one of the comfortable, if shabby, armchairs which were dotted about in it. Into this he now sank. The nervous strain to which he had been subjected, intensified by the society of the late bird *aficionado*, had left him dazed. So much so that it was several minutes before he realized that he ought not to be just sitting here like this, he should be acting. The letter was still in his pocket, undestroyed. He took it out, and removed its manilla wrapping. First and foremost on the agenda paper was the putting of it to the flames—not the tearing of it up and depositing it in the wastepaper basket, for a torn-up letter can be pieced together.

There was a table beside the chair, on it an ashtray and matches. He reached for these, and was in the very act of striking one, when he became aware of a wave of some exotic scent that seemed to proceed from behind him, the sort of scent affected by those mysterious veiled women who are always stealing Naval Treaties from Government officials in Whitehall. Turning sharply, he perceived Mrs Gordon Carlisle, and with considerable emotion noted that she was holding, and in the act of raising, one of those small but serviceable rubber instruments known as coshes. At her side, on his face the contented look of one who feels that his affairs are in excellent hands, stood her husband.

It was almost immediately after this that the roof fell in, and Cosmo knew no more. J. P. Boots, in his sardonic way, would have said that he had not known much even before that.

20

'NICE work, sweetie,' said Mr Carlisle, viewing the remains with satisfaction. 'Just behind the ear, that's the spot.'

'Never known it to fail,' said Gertie.

'He isn't dead, is he?'

'Oh, I shouldn't think so.'

'Just as well, maybe. Gimme the letter. And,' added Oily urgently, 'gimme that blackjack.'

'Eh?'

'Someone's coming. We've got to ditch them quick.'

'Slip 'em in your pocket.'

'And have them frisk me and find them there? Talk sense.'

'Yay, I see what you mean.' Gertie's eyes flickered about the hall. 'Look. Dump 'em in that thing over there.'

She alluded to the imitation walnut cabinet, the legacy of Johnny Pearce's Great-Uncle Walter, which had always so jarred on Lord Ickenham, and Oily approved of the suggestion. He darted across the hall, opened and slammed one of the drawers, dusted his hands and returned, just as Johnny appeared.

Johnny was on his way to get a breath of fresh air after a chat with Nannie Bruce about the new cook, concerning whose short-comings, more marked in her opinion even than those of the one who had held office two weeks previously, she had unburdened her mind in a speech containing at least three extracts from Ecclesiastes. He was in a sombre mood, having had his fill of Nannie Bruce, Ecclesiastes and paying guests, and the sight of one of these last apparently asleep in a chair would have left him uninterested, had not Cosmo at this moment slumped to the floor. A man who takes in paying guests can ignore them when they are vertical. When they become horizontal, he has to ask questions.

'What's all this?' he said, an observation which should more properly have been left to Police Constable McMurdo, who was down the passage, talking to Nannie. He had been hanging about outside the door of Johnny's study for some twenty minutes in the hope of finding an opportunity of pleading with her.

Gertie was swift to supply the desired information.

'Seems to me the guy's had some kind of a fit.'

Oily said that that was the way it looked to him, too.

'My husband and I was passing through on our way to our room, when he suddenly keeled over. With a groan.'

'More a gurgle, sweetie.'

'Well, with whatever it was. Could have been a death rattle, of course.'

Johnny frowned darkly. Life these days, he was thinking, was just one damn thing after another. First Nannie with her cooks and Ecclesiastes, then Norbury-Smith, from whom no good woman was safe, and now this groaning, gurgling or possibly death-rattling paying guest. Had even Job, whose troubles have received such wide publicity, ever had anything on this scale to cope with?

He raised his voice in a passionate bellow.

'Nannie!'

Nannie Bruce appeared, followed by Officer McMurdo, whose air was that of a police constable who has not been making much headway.

'Nannie, phone for Doctor Welsh. Tell him to come over right away. Mr Wisdom's had a fit or something. And for heaven's sake don't start yammering about what your biblical friend would have thought of the situation. Get a move on!'

Officer McMurdo looked at him with a wistful admiration. That was telling her, he felt. That was the way to talk to the other sex. Nannie Bruce, who did not hold this view, bridled.

'There is no necessity to shout at me, Master Jonathan, *nor* to make a mock of the holy scriptures. And I disagree with you when you say that Mr Wisdom has had a fit. Look at the way he's lying, with his legs straight out. My Uncle Charlie suffered from fits, and he used to curl up in a ball.' She went to where Cosmo lay, scrutinized him closely and ran an expert finger over his head. 'This man,' she said, 'has been struck with a blunt instrument!'

'What!'

'There's a lump behind his ear as big as a walnut. It's a matter for the police, such,' said Nannie Bruce, eyeing Officer McMurdo coldly, 'as they are. Still, when you say telephone for Doctor Welsh, that's sense. I'll go and do it at once.'

She departed on her errand with the dignity of a woman who does not intend to be ordered about but is willing to oblige, and long before she had disappeared Police Constable McMurdo's notebook was out and his pencil licked and poised.

'Ho!' he said. 'This throws a different light on the matter. I will now proceed to look into it. The great thing here is to ascertain who's responsible for this.'

'Ecclesiastes,' said Johnny bitterly, and Constable McMurdo's pencil leaped like a live thing. As far as was within the power of a man with a face like his, he was looking keen and alert. He eyed Johnny sharply.

'Have you evidence to support that charge, Mr Pearce?'

'No. It was just a suggestion.'

'I should like the address of the suspect Ecclesiastes.'

'I'm afraid I can't help you there.'

'Is he a juvenile delinquent?'

'More elderly than that, I should say.'

The constable pondered.

'I'm beginning to think you're right, sir. As I piece together the jig-saw puzzle, what happened was this. The gentleman was sitting here, dozing as the expression is, and the front door opens and in walks Ecclesiastes. To hit him on the napper with a blunt instrument, him being asleep, would be an easy task.'

Oily intervened in his suavest manner.

'I scarcely see how your theory can be correct, officer. My wife has told you that as we were passing through the hall, we saw Mr Wisdom—'

'Keel over,' said Gertie.

'Exactly. With a gurgle.'

'Or groan.'

'With a groan or gurgle.'

'Like as if somep'n had gone wrong with the works.'

'Precisely. You remember her mentioning it to you.'

'Not to me she didn't mention it.'

'Ah, no, it was to Mr Pearce before you came in. We both received the impression that he had had a fit.'

'Then why isn't he curled up in a ball?'

'There you take me into deep waters, constable.'

'And how do you account for the lump behind his ear, as big as a walnut?'

'That surely is very simply explained. He struck his head against the side of the chair as he was—'

'Keeling over,' said Gertie.

'As he was keeling over. It is far more probable—'

What was far more probable he did not get around to mentioning, for at this moment Cosmo Wisdom stirred, groaned (or gurgled), and sat up. He looked about him with what the poet has called a wild surmise, and said:

'Where am I?'

'Hammer Hall, Dovetail Hammer, Berks, sir,' Officer McMurdo informed him, and would have added the telephone number, if he had remembered it. 'If you'll just lie nice and quiet and relax, the doctor will be here in a moment. You've had some kind of fit or seizure, sir. This gentleman, Mr—'

'Carlisle.'

'This gentleman, Mr Carlisle, was passing through the hall, accompanied by Mrs Carlisle—'

The mention of that name brought memory flooding back to Cosmo. The past ceased to be wrapped in mist. He rose, clutched the chair with one hand, and with the forefinger of the other pointed accusingly.

'She hit me!'

'Sir?'

'That Carlisle woman. She hit me with a cosh. And,' said Cosmo, feeling feverishly through his pockets, 'she and that blasted husband of hers have stolen a very valuable paper from me. Grab them! Don't let them get away.'

Oily's eyebrows rose. He did not smile, of course, for the occasion was a serious one where levity would have been out of place, but his mouth twitched a little.

'Well, really, officer! One makes allowances for a sick man, but . . . well, really!'

Johnny Pearce's attention had been wandering. His thoughts had drifted back to that luncheon. Had he or had he not seen Norbury-Smith squeeze Belinda Farringdon's hand? At a certain point in the meal when Norbury-Smith's foot had collided with his under the table, had that foot's objective been Belinda Farringdon's shoe?

Aware now of raised voices, he came out of his reverie.

'What's the argument?' he enquired.

Constable McMurdo brought him abreast. This gentleman here, he said, had made a statement charging that lady there with having biffed him on the napper with a cosh. It did not, he added, seem plausible to *him*.

'Delicately nurtured female,' he explained.

Johnny could not quite see eye to eye with him in this view. In the stories he wrote you could never rule out females as suspects because they were delicately nurtured. Not once but on several occasions Inspector Jervis had been laid out cold by blondes of just that description. They waited till his back was turned and then let him have it with the butt end of a pistol or a paperweight. He looked at Gertie dubiously.

It was Oily who saw the way of proving his loved one's innocence.

'This is all very absurd,' he said in his gentlemanly way, 'but the thing can be settled, it seems to me, quite simply. If my wife struck Mr Wisdom with a . . . what was the word you used, officer?'

'Cosh, sir.'

'Thank you. I think you must mean what in my native country we call a blackjack. You know what a blackjack is, sweetie?'

'I've heard of 'em.'

'They are used a good deal by the criminal classes. Well, as I was saying, if my wife struck Mr Wisdom with an implement of this description, it is presumably either in her possession or mine. You will probably agree with me that Mrs Carlisle, wearing, as you see, Bermuda shorts and a shirt, would scarcely be able to conceal a weapon of any size on her person, so all that remains is for you to search me, officer. Frisk, is, I believe, the technical expression, is it not, ha, ha. Frisk me, constable, to the bone. You see,' he said, when the arm of the law had apologetically done so, 'not a thing! So we return to our original conclusion that Mr Wisdom had a fit.'

Police Constable McMurdo scratched his head.

'Why wasn't he curled up in a ball?'

'Ah, there, as I said before, you take me into deep waters. No doubt this gentleman will be able to tell you,' said Oily, as Nannie Bruce returned, ushering in Doctor Welsh with his black bag.

21

THE hall emptied soon after Doctor Welsh's arrival, like a theatre when the show is over. The doctor supported Oily's theory that Cosmo must have struck his head on the side of the chair, exercised his healing arts and, assisted by Johnny, helped the injured man to his room. Mr and Mrs Carlisle, confident that the walnut cabinet held their secret well, went up to theirs. When Lord Ickenham came in from the stroll he had been taking in the park, only Officer McMurdo was present. He was standing by the chair, eyeing it with professional intentness. Lord Ickenham greeted him with his customary geniality.

'Ah, Cyril, old friend. A very hearty good morning to you, my merry constable. Or,' he went on, peering more closely, 'are you so dashed merry? I don't believe you are. You seem to me to have a stern, official air, as if you had seen somebody moving pigs without a permit or failing to abate a smoky chimney. Has a crime wave broken out in these parts?'

Officer McMurdo was only too glad to confide in one for whose IQ he had a solid respect. What he was registering in his mind as the Wisdom case had left him puzzled.

'That's just what I'd like to ascertain, m'lord. Strange things have been happening at Hammer Hall. I still can't see why he wasn't curled up in a ball.'

'I beg your pardon? That one rather got past me.'

'Mr Wisdom, m'lord. When you have a fit, you curl up in a ball.'

'Oh, do you? Nice to know the etiquette. But what makes you think he had had a fit?'

'That's what the doctor said. He was lying on the floor with his legs straight out.'

'Was he, indeed? Quaint fellows, these doctors. Never know what they'll be up to next.'

'You misunderstand me, m'lord. It wasn't Doctor Welsh that was lying on the floor, it was Mr Wisdom. And Mr Carlisle made a statement that . . . I've got it all in my notebook . . . half a jiffy, yes, here we are . . . made a statement that he and Mrs Carlisle was passing through the hall and observed Mr Wisdom fall out of his chair and knock his head on the side of it, causing a lump behind the ear as big as a walnut. Some sort of a fit, they thought. But mark this, m'lord. On regaining consciousness, Mr Wisdom in his turn issued a statement, accusing Mrs Carlisle of striking him on the napper with a cosh.'

'What!'

'Yes, m'lord. Makes it sort of hard to sift the evidence and arrive at conclusions, don't it? If he'd been curled up in a ball, I'd say there was little credence to be attached to his words, but seeing that his legs was straight out, well, one sort of wonders if there might not be something in it. On the other hand, is it likely that a delicately nurtured female would go biffing—'

He broke off, and his face, which had been like that of a bloodhound on the trail, assumed the expression of a lovelorn sheep. Another delicately nurtured female, in the person of Nannie Bruce, had entered. She gave him a haughty look, and addressed Lord Ickenham.

'Your lordship is wanted on the telephone, m'lord. Sir Raymond Bastable from the Lodge. It's the third time this morning he's rung up, asking for your lordship.'

As Lord Ickenham went down the passage to Johnny's study, where the telephone was, he was conscious of a throbbing about

the temples and a dazed feeling usually induced only by the conversation of old Mr Saxby. Officer McMurdo's story had left him
bewildered. It was obvious to him, sifting, as the constable would
have said, the evidence, that for some reason Mrs Gordon Carlisle
had applied that cosh of hers to the skull of Cosmo Wisdom—
busted him one, as she would have put it—but why had she done
so? Because she disliked the young man? In a spirit of girlish exu-
berance? Or just because one had to do something to fill in the
time before lunch? Better, he felt, to dismiss the problem from
his thoughts and not try to fathom her mental processes. These
vultures acted according to no known laws.

Arrived in Johnny's sanctum, he took up the receiver, and
jumped several inches when a voice suggestive of a lion at feeding
time roared in his ear drum.

'Frederick! Where the devil have you been all this while?'

'Just out, Beefy,' said Lord Ickenham mildly. 'Roaming hither
and thither and enjoying the lovely sunshine. I hear you've been
trying to get me. What's your trouble?'

As far as could be gathered from aural evidence, Sir Raymond
appeared to be choking.

'I'll tell you what my trouble is! Do you know what I saw in the
paper this morning?'

'I think I can guess. It was in yesterday's evening paper.'

'About *Cocktail Time*? About these people offering a hundred
and fifty thousand for the picture rights?'

'Yes. It's a lot of money.'

'A lot of money! I should say it was a lot of money. And all going
into that blasted Cosmo's pocket unless you do the decent thing,
Frederick.'

'Spread sweetness and light, you mean? It is always my aim,
Beefy.'

'Then for God's sake give me that letter of his. It's the only proof
there is that I wrote the book. Frederick,' said Sir Raymond, and
his voice had taken on a pleading note, 'you can't hold out on me.

You must have heard from Phoebe by this time that my behaviour toward her these last two weeks has been . . . what's the word?'

'Angelic?'

'Yes, angelic. Ask Peasemarch if I've once so much as raised my voice to her. Ask anybody.'

'No need to institute enquiries, Beefy. It is all over Dovetail Hammer that your attitude where Phoebe is concerned has been that of one brushing flies off a sleeping Venus. Several people have told me that they mistook you in a dim light for the Chevalier Bayard.'

'Well, then?'

'But will this happy state of things last?'

'Of course it will.'

'I have your word for that as a man of honour and an old Oxford rugger blue?'

'Certainly. Wait a minute. Do you see what I've got here?'

'Sorry, Beefy, my vision's limited.'

'A bible, and I'm prepared to swear on it—'

'My dear old man, your word is enough. But aren't you forgetting something? How about your political career?'

'Damn my political career! I don't want a political career, I want a hundred and fifty thousand dollars.'

'All right, Beefy. You can relax. The money's yours. Go and fetch Albert Peasemarch and put him on the phone.'

'Do *what*?'

'So that I can tell him to hand that letter over to you. I had to put it in his charge, for bad men are after it and one never knows if the United States Marines won't sooner or later be caught asleep at the switch. Ring up again when you've got him. I don't want to sit here holding the instrument.'

Lord Ickenham hung up, and went back to the hall, hoping for further conversation with Officer McMurdo. But the constable had vanished, possibly to go about his professional duties but more probably to resume his wooing. The only occupant of the hall was old Mr Saxby, who was sitting in the chair recently vacated by Cosmo. He regarded Lord Ickenham with the eye of a benevolent codfish.

'Ah, Scriventhorpe,' he said. 'Nice to run into you. Have you seen Flannery lately?'

'I'm afraid I haven't.'

'Indeed? And how was he looking? Well, I hope? He suffers a little from sciatica. Is this your first visit to Hammer Hall?'

'No, I often come here. Johnny Pearce is my godson.'

'I used to be somebody's godson once, but many years ago. He has a nice place.'

'Very.'

'And some nice things. But I don't like that imitation walnut cabinet.'

'It's an eyesore, of course. Johnny's getting rid of it.'

'Very sensible of him. You remember what Flannery always says about fake antiques.'

Before Lord Ickenham was able to learn what that mystic man's views were on the subject indicated, Nannie Bruce appeared.

'Sir Raymond Bastable on the telephone, m'lord.'

'Oh, yes. Excuse me.'

'Certainly, certainly. Have you,' Mr Saxby asked Nannie Bruce, as Lord Ickenham left them, 'ever been to Jerusalem?'

'No, sir.'

'Ah. You must tell me all about it some time,' said Mr Saxby.

It is doubtful if even Miss Bruce's Uncle Charlie, at the peak of one of his celebrated fits, could have exhibited a greater agitation than did Sir Raymond Bastable when embarking on this second instalment of his telephone conversation with his half-brother-in-law. His visit to Albert Peasemarch's pantry, where that unfortunate stretcher-case was still sneezing, had left him—we must once more turn to Roget and his Thesaurus for assistance—unhappy, infelicitous, woebegone, dejected, heavy-laden, stricken and crushed. It is not easy for a man who is sneezing all the time to tell a story well, but Albert Peasemarch had told his well enough to enable Sir Raymond to grasp its import, and it had affected him like a bomb explosion. This, he said to Lord Ickenham, after he had informed him in a flood of molten words what he thought of his nephew Cosmo, was the end.

'The end,' he repeated, choking on the words. 'The young reptile must have burned the thing by now. Oh, hell and damnation!'

It was probably injudicious of Lord Ickenham to tell him at this moment not to worry, for the kindly advice, judging from the sounds proceeding from the Bastable end of the wire, seemed to have had the worst effects. But there were solid reasons for his doing so. In a flash he had divined the thought behind Mrs Gordon Carlisle's apparently inexplicable behaviour in busting Cosmo Wisdom one with her cosh. In supposing that she had merely been indulging some idle whim, busting just because it seemed a good idea to her at the time, he saw that he had done the woman an injustice. It was from the soundest business motives that she had raised that lump as big as a walnut behind Cosmo's ear.

'Listen,' he said, and started to place the facts before his relative by marriage, hampered a good deal at the outset by the latter's refusal to stop talking.

When he had finished, there was a pause of some moments, occupied by Sir Raymond in making a sort of gargling noise.

'You mean,' he said, becoming articulate, 'that that bounder Carlisle has got the letter?'

'Exactly. So now everything's fine.'

There was another pause. Sir Raymond appeared to be praying for strength.

'Fine?' he said, in a strange, low, husky voice. 'Did you say fine?'

'I did. He will be coming to see you about it shortly, I imagine, so what I want you to do, Beefy, is to step out into the garden and gather some frogs. About half a dozen. To put down the back of his neck,' explained Lord Ickenham. 'You remember what a sensitive skin he has. We grab him and decant the frogs. I shall be vastly surprised if after the third, or possibly fourth, frog has started to do the rock 'n roll on his epidermis, he is not all eagerness to transfer the letter to you. Years ago, when I was a child, a boy named Percy Wilberforce threatened that unless I gave him my all-day sucker, he would put frogs down my back. He got it F.O.B. in three seconds. Even then I was about as intrepid as they come, but I could not face the ordeal. And if an Ickenham weakened like that, is it likely that a Gordon Carlisle will prove more resolute? Off you go, Beefy, and start gathering. Put them in a paper bag,' said Lord Ickenham, and returned to the hall.

He found Mr Saxby pottering about in the vicinity of the walnut cabinet.

'Ah, Scriventhorpe. Back again? I've been having a look at this thing, and it's worse than I thought it was. It's a horrible bit of work. Flannery would hate it. I found something odd in one of the drawers,' said Mr Saxby. 'You don't happen to know what this is?'

Lord Ickenham looked at the object he was holding up, and started.

'It's a cosh.'

'Cosh, did you say?'

'That's right.'

'The word is new to me. What are its uses?'

'Delicately nurtured females bust people one with it.'

'Indeed? Most interesting. I must tell Flannery that when I see him. By the way,' Mr Saxby proceeded, 'I also found this letter addressed to Bastable.'

Lord Ickenham drew a deep breath, the sort of breath a gambler draws who has placed the last of his money on a number at the roulette table and sees it come up.

'May I look at it?' he said, his voice shaking a little. 'Thank you. Yes, you're quite right. It is addressed to Bastable. Perhaps I had better take charge of it. I shall be seeing him soon, and can give it to him. Curious it turning up in that cabinet.'

'A letter of Flannery's once turned up inside the Christmas turkey.'

'Indeed? Strange things happen in this disturbed post-war era, do they not? Rather a lesson to the dear old chap not to eat turkey. Excuse me,' said Lord Ickenham. 'I have to telephone.'

It was Phoebe who answered his ring.

'Oh, hullo, Phoebe,' he said. 'Is Raymond there?'

'He went out into the garden, Frederick. Shall I fetch him?'

'No, don't bother. Just give him a message. Tell him to stop gathering frogs.'

'Stop *what*?'

'Gathering frogs.'

'There must be something wrong with this wire. You sound as if you were telling me to tell Raymond to stop gathering frogs.'

'I am.'

'*Is* he gathering frogs?'

'He told me he was going to.'

'But *why* is he gathering frogs?'

'Ah, who can say? These eccentric barristers, you know. Probably just felt a sudden urge. Goodbye, Phoebe. Where are you at the moment?'

'I'm in Raymond's study.'

'Well, don't forget that Albert Peasemarch worships the very carpet you are standing on,' said Lord Ickenham.

He was humming a gay snatch of melody as he replaced the receiver, for there was no room for doubt in his mind that all things were working together for good. With the letter which had been leaping from vulture to vulture like the chamois of the Alps from crag to crag safely in his coat pocket, he was feeling at the top of his form. Something attempted, something done, had earned a mild cigar, and he was smoking it on the drive and thinking how pleasant it was to be away from Mr Saxby, when he found that he was not. The old gentleman came pottering along, having apparently popped up through a trap.

'Oh, Scriventhorpe.'

'Hullo, Saxby. I was just saying to myself how nice it would be if you were with me.'

'I have been looking for you, Scriventhorpe. I thought it would interest you to hear . . . A water ousel!'

'Worth hearing, are they, these water ousels?'

'There is a water ousel over there. I must go and look at it in a moment. What I started to say was that I thought it would interest you to hear that that beastly walnut cabinet has gone.'

'Has done what?'

'A couple of men came and took it away after you left. I understand it is to be put up for auction.'

Lord Ickenham started. One of those sudden inspirations of his had come to him.

'Put up for auction, eh?'

'So they told me. But I doubt if anyone in his senses would give more than a pound or two for it,' said Mr Saxby, and toddled away, binoculars in hand, to look at his water ousel.

As a rule, men whom old Mr Saxby relieved of his company were conscious of a wave of relief, coupled with a determination not to let him corner them again in a hurry, but Lord Ickenham hardly noticed that he had gone. His whole attention was riveted on a picture which had risen before his mind's eye, the picture of Beefy and Gordon Carlisle bidding furiously against each other for the imitation walnut cabinet, the proceeds of the winning bid to go to Jonathan Twistleton Pearce, that impoverished young man who had to have five hundred pounds in order to marry his Belinda. Knowing Beefy and knowing Gordon Carlisle—their deep purses and their iron resolve to get hold of the fateful letter—he was confident that considerably more than five hundred of the best and brightest would accrue to Jonathan Twistleton Pearce's bank account.

Though there are, of course, drawbacks to everything. In order to achieve this desirable end it would be necessary for him to depart a little from the truth and inform Beefy that the letter was in the cabinet, but he was a man who rather blithely departed from the truth when the occasion called. An altruist whose mission it is to spread sweetness and light is entitled to allow himself a certain licence.

22

THE auction sale was to be held in the village hall, a red-brick monstrosity erected in the eighties by the Victorian Pearce who had bought that walnut cabinet, and after lunch on the big day Lord Ickenham, in order to avoid old Mr Saxby, who was showing an increasing disposition to buttonhole him and talk about Flannery, had taken his cigar to his godson's study, feeling that there, if anywhere, a man might be safe. Johnny, his objective a heart-to-heart talk with Belinda Farringdon, had gone up to London in a car borrowed from Mr Morrison of the Beetle and Wedge, looking grim and resolute. It was his intention to take a firm line about this Norbury-Smith nonsense.

It was cool and peaceful in the study, with its french windows opening on the terrace, but on the fifth Earl's face, as he sat there, a frown might have been observed, as though sombre thoughts were troubling him. Nor would anyone who formed this impression have been in error. He was thinking of Beefy Bastable, that luckless toy of Fate who—for one of his wealth and determination could not fail to outbid Oily Carlisle at their coming contest— would shortly be parting with several hundred pounds for an imitation walnut cabinet worth perhaps fifty shillings.

Chatting with Oily while reclining in the hammock, Lord Ickenham, it will be recalled, had laid considerable stress on the spiritual agonies suffered by the dregs of society when they see the United States Marines arriving. Those of Sir Raymond on opening that cabinet and finding no letter in it would, he could not but feel, be even keener. There is a type of man who, however rich he be, has a sturdy distaste for paying out large sums of money for nothing, and it was to this section of humanity that the eminent barrister belonged. Lord Ickenham mourned in spirit for his old friend's distress. Too bad, he felt, that when you started spreading sweetness and light, you so often found that there was not enough to go round and that somebody had to be left out of the distribution.

On the other hand, if nobody was there to bid against Oily, carrying out the manoeuvre known to Barbara Crowe's man-in-Hollywood as bumping him up, the cabinet would be knocked down to that gentlemanly highbinder for about ten shillings, which would not greatly further the interests of a Jonathan Pearce who needed five hundred pounds. The occasion, in a word, was one of those, so common in this imperfect world, where someone has to get the short end of the stick, and only Beefy was available for the role. Lord Ickenham could see clearly enough that it was necessary to sacrifice Beefy for the good of the cause but that did not mean that he had to be happy about it.

To distract himself for a moment from his sad thoughts, he picked up the copy of that morning's *Daily Gazette* which Johnny had left lying on the floor beside his desk, and began to glance through it. It was a paper he had never much admired, and he was not surprised that he found little to intrigue him on pages one, two and three. But on page four the interest quickened. His attention was arrested by one of those large headlines in which this periodical specialized.

FRANK, FORTHRIGHT, FEARLESS

it said, and beneath this:

COCKTAIL TIME
Our Powerful New Serial
by
COSMO WISDOM
Begin It Today

There was also, inset, a photograph of Phoebe's ewe lamb, all shifty eyes and small black moustache, which might have been that of some prominent spiv who had been detained by the police for questioning in connection with the recent drug-ring raids.

'Cor lumme, stone the crows!' whispered Lord Ickenham, borrowing from Albert Peasemarch's non-copyright material. The scales had fallen from his eyes.

Until this moment it had never occurred to him to regard Cosmo Wisdom in the light of a potential bidder for the cabinet. He had supposed him to be, if not penniless, certainly several hundred poundsless. It was obvious that he must now revise this view. He knew little of the prices prevailing in the marts of literature, but it was to be presumed that for a serial as frank, forthright and fearless as *Cocktail Time* a paper like the *Gazette*, making more money than it knew what to do with and always on the look-out for a chance of giving it away to someone, would have loosened up on a pretty impressive scale. Cosmo, in other words, so recently a biter of ears for ten bobs to see him through till next Saturday, was plainly in the chips. If on this sunny summer afternoon his hip pocket was not filled to bursting with the right stuff, he, Lord Ickenham, would be dashed.

What, then, could be a happier thought than to substitute the opulent young man for Beefy?

And scarcely had he reached this most satisfactory solution of his problem when, glancing out of the french window, he saw the opulent young man in person. He was pacing the terrace with bent head and leaden feet, like a Volga boatman.

And if anyone might excusably have impersonated a Volga boatman, it was Cosmo Wisdom at this juncture. Behind the left ear of the head he was bending there was a large lump, extremely painful if he made any sudden movement, and this alone would have been enough to lower the *joie de vivre*. But far worse than physical distress was the mental anguish caused by the thought that the letter which meant everything to him was now in the custody of Oily Carlisle. It is scarcely to be wondered at that when he heard a voice call his name and, raising his bent head, saw Lord Ickenham beaming at him from the study window, his manner was not cordial. It was, indeed, rather like that of a timber wolf with its foot in a trap.

'Just come in here for a moment, will you, Cosmo? I want to speak to you.'

'What about?'

'Nothing that can be shouted from the house tops or yelled on terraces. I won't keep you long,' said Lord Ickenham as his young friend stepped through the french windows. 'It's about that letter.'

Cosmo's scowl darkened. He had no wish to talk about that letter.

'It is, is it?' he said unpleasantly. 'Well, you're wasting your time. I haven't got it.'

'I am aware of that. Mr Carlisle has it.'

'Curse him!'

'Certainly, if you wish. I don't like the fellow myself. We must baffle that man, Cosmo, before he can start throwing his weight about. You don't need to peer into any crystal ball to inform yourself of what the future holds in store, if this letter remains in his possession. Not much of that Hollywood largess of yours will be left after he has staked out his claim, for if ever a man believed in sharing the wealth, it is this same Carlisle. He must be foiled and frustrated.'

'A fat lot of good saying that,' said Cosmo, speaking even more unpleasantly than before. 'How the devil can I foil and frustrate him?'

'Listen attentively and I will tell you.'

The effect of Lord Ickenham's brief résumé of the position of affairs on Cosmo was to cause him to start convulsively. And as anything in the nature of a convulsive start makes a man who has recently been struck on the head by a woman's gentle cosh feel as if that head had a red-hot skewer thrust through it, he uttered a yelp of agony, like a Volga boatman stung by a wasp.

'I know, I know,' said Lord Ickenham, nodding sympathetically. 'The after effects of being bust one do linger, don't they? As a young man, in the course of a political argument in a Third Avenue saloon in New York, I was once struck squarely on the topknot by a pewter tankard in the capable hands of a gentleman of the name of Moriarty—no relation of the Professor, I believe—and it was days before I was my old bright self again.'

Cosmo was staring, open-mouthed.

'You mean the letter's in that cabinet?'

'Carlisle certainly put it there.'

'How do you know?'

'I have my ways of getting to know things.'

'And it's up for auction?'

'Precisely.'

'I'll go and bid for it!'

'Exactly what I was about to suggest. You will, of course, have to be prepared to bid high. Carlisle is not going to let the thing go without a struggle. But, what with this serial and everything, I imagine that you are rolling in money these days, and a few hundred pounds here and there mean nothing to you. How is your voice?'

'Eh?'

'Say "Mi-mi". Excellent,' said Lord Ickenham. 'Like a silver bell. The auctioneer will hear your every word. So off you go. Bid till your eyes bubble, my boy, and may heaven speed your efforts.'

And now, he was saying to himself, as Cosmo hurried away and a distant howl told that he had incautiously jerked his head again, to find some simple ruse which would remove Beefy from the centre of things. The village hall must not see Beefy this summer afternoon.

It was seldom that Lord Ickenham sought for inspiration in vain. Why, of course, he was thinking a few moments later. Yes, that would do it. How simple these things always were, if you just sat back and closed your eyes and let the little grey cells take over. It needed but a quick telephone call to Albert Peasemarch, instructing him to lock Beefy up in the wine cellar, and the situation would be stabilized.

He was about to reach for the instrument, glowing as men do when their brains are working well, when it rang its bell at him in the abrupt way telephones have. He took up the receiver.

'Hullo?' he said.

It was Phoebe who replied. As nearly always, she appeared agitated.

23

'OH, Frederick!' she said, panting like a white rabbit heated in the chase.

'Hullo, Phoebe, my dear,' said Lord Ickenham. 'What's the matter? You seem upset.'

There was a brief pause while she seemed to contemplate the adjective, weighing it as Roget might have done if someone had suggested admitting it into his Thesaurus.

'Well, not upset exactly. But I don't know if I am standing on my head or my heels.'

'Sift the evidence. At which end of you is the ceiling?'

'Oh, don't be silly, Frederick. You know what I mean. Oh dear, I do hope Cossie will approve of this step I'm taking. I mean, it isn't as if I were a young girl. I'm nearly fifty, Frederick. He may think it odd.'

'That you are joining the chorus at the Hippodrome?'

'Whatever are you talking about?'

'Isn't that what you are trying to tell me?'

'Of course it isn't. I'm going to marry again.'

The receiver jumped in Lord Ickenham's right hand, the cigar in his left. This was big stuff. Any popular daily paper would have used it without hesitation as its front page feature story.

'Bert?' he exclaimed. 'Has Bert at last cast off his iron restraint and spoken? Are you going to be Lady Peasemarch?'

'Mrs Peasemarch.'

'For a while, no doubt, yes. But a man of Bert's abilities is bound to get knighted sooner or later. My dear Phoebe, this is news to warm the cockles of the heart. They don't come any truer and stauncher than Bert. You know what Ecclesiastes said about him? He said . . . No, sorry, it's gone for the moment, but it was something very flattering. There's only one thing you have to watch out for with Albert Peasemarch, the Drake's Drum side of him. Be careful that he doesn't sing it during the wedding ceremony.'

'What, dear?'

'I was saying that if, as you stand at the altar, Bert starts singing Drake's Drum, give him a nudge.'

'We are going to be married at a registrar's.'

'Oh, then that's all right. These registrars are good sports. Yours will probably join in the chorus. What does Raymond think of the proposed union?'

'We haven't told him yet. Albert thought it would be better if he finished his month first.'

'Very sensible. It will save Beefy a lot of embarrassment. It's always difficult for a man to be really at his ease with his butler, if he knows the latter is engaged to be married to his sister. A certain constraint when Bert was handing the potatoes would be inevitable. But aren't we skipping some of the early chapters? Tell me how it all happened. Be frank, forthright and fearless.'

'Well—'

'Yes?'

'I was trying to think where to begin. Well, I had gone to Albert's pantry to talk to him about poor little Benjy, who is ever so much better, you will be glad to hear. Albert says his nose is quite cold.'

'I remember it used to get very cold in our Home Guard days.'

'What, dear?'

'You were saying that Albert Peasemarch's nose was cold.'

'No, no, Benjy's.'

'Oh, Benjy's? Well, that's fine, isn't it?'

'And then we got talking, and something Albert said made me think of Raymond. I don't mean I've ever *not* thought of Raymond, but this something Albert said reminded me of what you had said the other day, about him not having got all his marbles.'

'I said he *had* got all his marbles.'

'Oh, did you? I thought you said he hadn't, and it worried me terribly. Thinking of George Winstanley, you know. Because Raymond has been behaving so very oddly this last week or two. I don't mean so much giving me flowers and asking after my rheumatism, but I do think it was strange of him to go swimming in the lake with all his clothes on.'

'Did he do that?'

'I saw him from my window.'

'According to Shakespeare, Julius Caesar used to swim with all his clothes on.'

'But he didn't gather frogs.'

'No, you have a point there. One finds it very difficult to see why Beefy should have wanted to gather frogs. Puzzled me a good deal, that.'

'You must admit that I had enough to worry me.'

'Oh, quite.'

'It seemed to me so dreadfully sad.'

'I don't wonder.'

'And I couldn't help it. I broke down and sobbed. And the next thing I knew, Albert was striding up to me and seizing me by the wrist and pulling me about till I felt quite giddy. And then he said "My mate!" and clasped me to him and—'

'Showered burning kisses on your upturned face?'

'Yes. He told me later that something seemed to snap in him.'

'I believe that often happens. Well, I couldn't be more pleased about this, Phoebe. You have done wisely in linking your lot with Bert's. Instinct told you you were on a good thing, and you very sensibly pushed it along. The ideal husband. Where is Bert, by the way? In his pantry?'

'I think so. He was giving Benjy beef extract.'

'Will you bring him to the phone. I would have speech with him.'

'You want to congratulate him?'

'That, of course. But there is also a little business matter I would like to discuss with him. Just one of those things that crop up from time to time. Oh, Bert,' said Lord Ickenham some moments later, 'I've been hearing the great news. Felicitations by the jugful, my old comrade, and a million wishes for your future happiness. Very interesting to learn that yet another success has to be chalked up to the Ickenham System. It seldom fails, if you remember to waggle with sufficient vigour, as I understand you did. The preliminary waggle is everything. That was probably where Cyril McMurdo went wrong. Well, I suppose you're walking on air and strewing roses from your bowler hat?'

'I do feel extremely grateful for my good fortune, Mr I.'

'I bet you do. There's nothing like getting married. It's the only life, as Brigham Young and King Solomon would tell you, if they were still with us. And now here's something I was wanting to ask you. I wonder if plighting your troth has affected you as plighting mine many years ago affected me. I remember that I was filled with a sort of yeasty benevolence that embraced the whole human race. I wanted to go about doing acts of kindness to everybody I met. Do you feel the same?'

'Oh yes, Mr I. I feel just like that.'

'Splendid! Because there's a little routine job I would like you to do for me. Will your future wife be on the premises during the next hour or so?'

'I shouldn't think so, Mr I. She went off to this sale in the village hall, and wasn't expecting to get back too soon.'

'Excellent. Then there will be no one to hear his cries.'

'Cries, Mr I?'

'The big chief's. I want you to lock him up in the wine cellar, Bert, and I imagine he'll shout a good deal. You know how people do, when you lock them in wine cellars.'

It seemed to be Lord Ickenham's fate these days to extract from those with whom he conversed on the telephone what Mr and Mrs Carlisle called groans or gurgles, though for the sound that now came over the wire a precisian might have preferred the term 'gulp'. Whatever its correct classification, it indicated plainly that his words had made a deep impression on Albert Peasemarch. In the manner in which he spoke there was more than a suggestion of Phoebe Wisdom at her most emotional.

'Do *what* to Sir Raymond, did you say, Mr I?'

'Lock him in the wine cellar. I wouldn't call him Sir Raymond, though, now that you are linked to him in such sentimental bonds. It's time you were thinking of him as Ray or Beefy. Well, that's all, Bert. Carry on.'

'But, Mr I!'

Lord Ickenham frowned. Wasted, of course, on a Peasemarch who could not see him.

'You have a rather annoying habit, Bert, when I ask you to do some perfectly simple thing for me, of saying "But, Mr I",' he said, a little stiffly. 'It's just a mannerism, I know, but I wish you wouldn't. What's on your mind?'

'Well, the question it occurred to me to ask was—'

'Yes?'

'*Why* do you want me to lock Sir Raymond in the wine cellar?'

Lord Ickenham clicked his tongue.

'Never mind why. You know as well as I do that the Secret Service can't give reasons for every move it makes. If I were to tell you why, and it got about through some incautious word of yours, a third world war would be inevitable. And I seem to remember you saying that you were opposed to the idea of a third world war.'

'Oh, I am, Mr I. I wouldn't like it at all. But—'

'That word again!'

'But what I was going to say was How do I go about it?'

'My dear fellow, there are a hundred ways of luring a man into a wine cellar. Tell him you would like his opinion on the last lot of claret. Ask him to come and inspect the ginger ale, because you're afraid the moths have been at it. That part of the thing presents no difficulty. And the locking-in will be equally simple. You just shimmer off while his back is turned and twiddle the key. A child of four could do it. A child of three,' said Lord Ickenham, correcting himself. 'Drake would have done it without missing a drum beat. Snap into it, Bert, and give me a ring when you're through.'

It was some ten minutes later that the telephone bell rang. When Albert Peasemarch spoke, it was in the subdued voice of a nervous novice who had just done his first murder.

'Everything has been attended to, Mr I.'

'He's in storage?'

'Yes, Mr I.'

'Capital! I knew I could rely on you not to bungle it. We of the Home Guard don't bungle. It wasn't so hard, was it?'

'Not hard, no—'

'But it has taken it out of you a little, no doubt,' said Lord Ickenham sympathetically. 'Your pulse is high, your breathing is stertorous and there are floating spots before your eyes. Well, go and lie down and have a nice nap.'

Albert Peasemarch coughed.

'What I was thinking I'd do, Mr I, was take the bus to Reading and catch the train to London, and spend the next week or two there. I would prefer not to encounter Sir Raymond until some little time has elapsed.'

'From what you were able to gather through the closed door, he seemed annoyed, did he?'

'Yes, Mr I.'

'I can't imagine why. I know dozens of men who would think it heaven to be locked in a wine cellar. Still, no doubt you're right. Time, the great healer, and all that sort of thing. Then this is goodbye for the moment, Bert. A thousand thanks. I will see that word of what you have done reaches the proper quarter. And if you're in London long enough, I'll look you up and we'll have a night out together.'

Well pleased, Lord Ickenham replaced the receiver and went on to the terrace. He had been there a few minutes, finishing his cigar and enjoying the peace of the summer afternoon, when a car came by and drew up at the front door. Fearing that this might be the County paying a formal call, he had recoiled a step and was preparing to make a dive for safety, when the occupant of the car alighted, and he saw that it was Barbara Crowe.

24

Lord Ickenham would probably have been deeply offended if he had been told that in any circumstances his mind could run on parallel lines with that of Cosmo Wisdom, a young man whose intelligence he heartily despised, but it is undoubtedly the fact that the sight of Barbara Crowe set him thinking, as Cosmo had done, what a consummate ass Raymond Bastable had been to let this woman go. In her sports dress, with the little green hat that went with it, she was looking more attractive than ever, and nothing could have been more warming to the heart than the smile she gave him as he hailed her.

'Why, Freddie,' she said, 'what on earth are you doing here?'

'I am staying with Johnny Pearce, my godson, while my wife is in Scotland. She wanted me to go with her, but I would have none of it. So, having some foolish prejudice against letting me run loose, as she calls it, in London, she dumped me on Johnny. But what brings you to these parts?'

'I've come to see Cosmo Wisdom about making some appearances on television. And Howard Saxby junior wants me to bring Howard Saxby senior back. He's afraid he'll fall into the lake or something. This place of your godson's is a kind of pub, isn't it?'

'Johnny takes in paying guests, yes.'

'I'd better book a room.'

'Plenty of time. I want to talk to you, Barbara. Let us go and

seat ourselves under yonder tree. What I was hoping when I saw
you get out of that car,' said Lord Ickenham, having settled her in a
deck chair and dropping into one himself, 'was that you had come
to see Beefy Bastable.'

Barbara Crowe started.

'Raymond? What do you mean? Is he here?'

'Not actually in Johnny's dosshouse. He lives at the Lodge
across the park. We might look in on him later. Not just now, for I
know he will be occupied for the next hour or so, but after you have
had a wash and brush-up.'

Barbara's cheerful face lost some of its cheerfulness.

'This is a bit awkward.'

'Why?'

'He'll think I'm pursuing him.'

'Of course he will, and a very good thing, too. It will give him
the encouragement he sorely needs. He'll say to himself, "Well,
dash my buttons, I thought I'd lost her, but if she comes legging it
after me like this, things don't look so sticky after all." It will make
his day. And from that to restoring relations to their old footing will
be but a step. Why,' asked Lord Ickenham, 'do you laugh in that
hollow, hacking way?'

'Well, don't you think it's funny?'

'Not in the least. What's funny?'

'The idea you seem to have that Raymond still cares for me.'

'My dear girl, he's potty about you.'

'What nonsense! He's never been near me or phoned me or
written to me since . . . it happened.'

'Of course he hasn't. You don't realize what a sensitive plant
Beefy is. You see him in court ripping the stuffing out of witnesses,
and you say to yourself, "H'm! A tough guy!" little knowing that
at heart he is . . . what are those things that shrink? . . . violets,
that's the word I was after . . . little knowing that at heart he is a
shrinking violet. He's not a coarse-fibred chap like me. Every time
my Jane broke our engagement, I hounded her with brutal threats

till she mended it again, but Beefy would never do that. Delicacy is his dish. He would assume that when you gave him the old heave-ho, it meant that you didn't want to have any more to do with him, and, though it was agony, he kept away. He should have known that little or no importance is to be attached to these lovers' tiffs. That hacking laugh again! What amuses you?'

'Your calling it a tiff.'

'I believe that is the expression commonly used. If it wasn't a tiff, what was it?'

'A terrific row. A pitched battle, which culminated in my calling him a pompous old stuffed shirt.'

'I wouldn't have thought Beefy would have objected to that. He must know that he is a pompous old stuffed shirt.'

Barbara Crowe blazed into sudden fury.

'He isn't anything of the sort! He's a lamb.'

'A *what?*'

'He's the most wonderful man there ever was.'

'That is your considered opinion?'

'Yes, Frederick Altamont Cornwallis Twistleton, that is my considered opinion.'

Lord Ickenham gave a satisfied nod.

'So, as I suspected, the flame of love still burns! It does, does it not?'

'Yes, it does.'

'One word from him, and you would follow him to the ends of the earth?'

'Yes, I would.'

'Well, he won't be going there, not at the moment, anyway. My dear Barbara, this is extremely gratifying. If that's how things are at your end, we ought to be able to fix this up in no time in a manner agreeable to all parties. I wasn't sure how you felt. I knew, of course, that Beefy loved you. That habit of his, when he thinks he is alone, of burying his face in his hands and muttering "Barbara! Barbara."'

'He always called me "Baby".'

Lord Ickenham started.

'*Beefy* did?'

'Yes.'

'You're sure?'

'Quite sure.'

'Well, you know best. I wouldn't have thought . . . but that is neither here nor there. Then no doubt it was "Baby! Baby!" that he was muttering. It doesn't really matter. The salient point is that he muttered. Well, I must say everything looks pretty smooth now.'

'Does it?'

'Surely? Here, as I see it, are two sundered hearts it will be very simple to bring together.'

'Not so simple as you think.'

'What seems to be the difficulty?'

'The difficulty, my dear Freddie, is that he is determined that Phoebe shall share our little nest, and I'm equally determined that she shan't. That's the real rock we split on.'

'He wanted Phoebe to live with you?'

'Yes. There's a parsimonious streak in Raymond. I suppose it comes from having been so hard up when he was starting at the Bar. He was desperately hard up, you know, before he got going. When I suggested that our married life would run much more smoothly if he gave Phoebe a couple of thousand a year and told her to go off and take a flat in Kensington, or a villa in Bournemouth or whatever she fancied, he said he couldn't possibly afford it. And, as they say, one word led to another. Do you ever lose your temper, Freddie?'

'Very seldom. I'm the equable type.'

'I wish I were. When moved, I spit and scratch. He kept saying things like "We must be practical" and "Women never realize that men are not made of money", and I couldn't take it. That was when I called him a pompous old stuffed shirt. Yes?' said Barbara coldly. 'Why are *you* laughing in that hollow, hacking way?'

'I doubt if those are the right adjectives to describe my little ripple of mirth. They suggest gloom and bitterness, and I am anything but gloomy and bitter. I laughed—musically and with an infectious lilt—because it always entertains me to see people creating, as Albert Peasemarch would say, when there is no necessity.'

'No necessity?'

'None whatever.'

'God bless you, Frederick Ickenham. And who is Albert Peasemarch?'

'An intimate friend of mine. To tell you all about him—his career, his adventures by flood and field, his favourite breakfast food and so on—would take too long. What will probably interest you most is the fact that he will very shortly be marrying Phoebe.'

'What!'

'Yes. They fixed it up this afternoon. The expression you are probably groping for,' suggested Lord Ickenham, seeing that his companion was struggling to find speech, 'is "Cor lumme, stone the crows!"—It is the one Bert Peasemarch uses when in the grip of some powerful emotion.'

Barbara found speech.

'He's marrying *Phoebe?*'

'This surprises you?'

'Well, it isn't everybody who would want to marry Phoebe, is it? Who is this humble hero?'

'Beefy's butler. Or perhaps, after what he was saying to me on the telephone just now, I should put an "ex" before the word.'

'Phoebe's marrying a *butler?*'

'Somebody's got to, or the race of butlers would die out. And Bert will be a notable improvement on the late Algernon Wisdom. You spoke?'

'I said, "Quick, Freddie—your handkerchief!"'

'Cold in the head?'

'Crying. Tears of joy. Oh, Freddie!'

'I thought you might possibly be pleased about it.'

'Pleased! Why, this solves everything.'

'Things have a way of getting solved when an Ickenham takes a hand in them.'

'You mean, you worked it?'

'I think something I said to Phoebe, some casual remark about Albert Peasemarch worshipping the ground she trod on, may have been not without its influence.'

'Freddie, I'm going to kiss you.'

'There is nothing I would enjoy more, but if you will glance over your shoulder, you will see that we are about to have Howard Saxby senior with us. This frequently happens here. Whatever Hammer Hall's shortcomings, there is never any stint of Howard Saxby senior. I have been wondering what has been keeping him away. It is not often that he denies one his society for such a lengthy period. Hullo, Saxby.'

'Ah, Scriventhorpe.'

'Cigarette?'

'No, thank you,' said Mr Saxby, taking needles and a ball of wool from his pocket. 'I would prefer to knit. I'm roughing out a sweater for my little grandson. An ambitious project, but I think something ought to come of it!'

'That's the spirit. Here's Barbara Crowe.'

'So I see. It's an extraordinary thing. I was saying to myself, as I came up, "That woman has quite a look of Barbara Crowe." I understand now why there was such a resemblance. What are you doing here, Barbara?'

'I've come to take you home, young Saxby.'

'I don't want to go home.'

'Howard junior says you must.'

'Then I suppose I'll have to. When did you arrive?'

'About ten minutes ago.'

'I am sorry I was not here to greet you. I have been down at the village hall, watching that sale. You should have been there, Scriventhorpe. That cabinet . . .'

Lord Ickenham sat up alertly.

'How much did it fetch?'

'I wish you would not bark at me like that,' said Mr Saxby a little peevishly. 'You've made me drop a stitch. I was telling you about the sale, was I not? It was replete with interest. You have often accused me, Barbara,' Mr Saxby proceeded, 'of being eccentric, and there may be something in the charge, for others have told me the same. But real eccentricity, eccentricity in the fullest sense of the term, flourishes only in Dovetail Hammer. I must begin by saying—you will forgive me, Scriventhorpe, for going over ground which is already familiar to you—that there was recently on these premises an imitation walnut cabinet which was an offence to the eye and worth at the most a few pounds. It was included in this sale of which I speak, and judge of my astonishment—'

'How much did it fetch?' said Lord Ickenham.

Mr Saxby gave him a cold look.

'And judge of my astonishment when, after several other objects of equal horror had been put up and knocked down for a few shillings, this cabinet was displayed, and I heard a voice say "Fifty pounds".'

'Ha!'

'I wish you wouldn't say "Ha!" in that abrupt way. I've dropped another stitch. It was the voice of that American fellow who is staying at the Hall. Carstairs is, I think, the name.'

'Carlisle.'

'Indeed? Flannery knows a man named Carlisle. You've probably heard him speak of him. A most interesting life he has had, Flannery says, with curious things constantly happening to him. He was once bitten by a rabbit.'

'You don't say?'

'So Flannery assures me. An angora. It turned on him and sank its teeth in his wrist while he was offering it a carrot.'

'Probably on a diet,' said Lord Ickenham, and Mr Saxby agreed that this might have been so.

'But we must not allow ourselves to get mixed up,' he proceeded. 'It was not that Carlisle, the one who was bitten by a rabbit, who said "Fifty pounds", but this other Carlisle, who is staying at the Hall and has never, to the best of my knowledge, been bitten by a rabbit. He said "Fifty pounds", and I was still gasping with astonishment, when another voice said "A hundred". It was that young fellow who was in my office the other day, Barbara, the squirt, the one you sent me here to apologize to. Though what there was to apologize about . . . However, what is his name? I've forgotten.'

'Cosmo Wisdom.'

'Ah, yes. Connected somehow with the motion picture industry. Well, he said "A hundred pounds"!'

'And to cut a long story short,' said Lord Ickenham.

Mr Saxby never cut long stories short.

'I could scarcely credit my senses. I must emphasize once again that this beastly cabinet would have been dear at five pounds. Sometimes you will see an imitation walnut cabinet that looks reasonably attractive. Some quite good work done in that line, if you know where to find it. But this one had no redeeming features. And yet these two eccentrics persisted in bidding against each other for it, and might have gone on for ever, had not a peculiar interruption occurred. I don't know if either of you are acquainted with Bastable's sister?'

'We know her well,' said Barbara. 'Do get on, young Saxby. Phoebe Wisdom is Freddie's wife's half-sister.'

'Is that so? Who is Freddie?'

'This is Freddie.'

'Oh, really? Did you say Wisdom?'

'Yes.'

'Related in any way to the squirt?'

'His mother.'

'Then I understand everything. She was saving him from himself.'

'Doing what?'

'Preventing him throwing away his money on a cabinet no man

of discernment would willingly have been found dead in a ditch with. For as the bidding reached a certain point—'

'What point?' asked Lord Ickenham.

'—this woman, bathed in tears, approached the squirt, accompanied by the village policeman, and after, so I gathered from her manner, pleading with him and trying in vain to use a mother's influence to stop him making a fool of himself signalled to the policeman to lead him away, which he did. So Carstairs got the cabinet.'

'How much for?' said Lord Ickenham.

'Well,' said Mr Saxby, rising, 'I think I will go and take a bath. I got very warm and sticky in that village hall. There was practically no ventilation.'

'Hi!' cried Lord Ickenham.

'You were calling me?' said Mr Saxby, turning.

'How much did Carlisle pay for the cabinet?'

'Oh, didn't I tell you that?' said Mr Saxby. 'I fully intended to. Five hundred pounds.'

He pottered away, and Lord Ickenham expended his breath in a deep sigh of satisfaction. Barbara Crowe shot an enquiring look at him.

'Why are you so interested in this cabinet, Freddie?'

'It belonged to my godson, who was in urgent need of five hundred pounds. Now he's got it.'

'Was it really worth nothing?'

'Practically nothing.'

'Then why did Cosmo Wisdom and that other man bid like that for it?'

'It's a long story.'

'Your stories are never too long.'

'Bless my soul, I remember my niece Valerie saying that to me once. But she spoke with a nasty tinkle in her voice. It was on the occasion when she found me at Blandings castle, posing—from the best motives—as Sir Roderick Glossop. Did I ever tell you about that?'

COCKTAIL TIME · 201

'No. And you can save up these reminiscences of your disreputable past for another time. What I want to hear now is about this cabinet. Don't ramble off on to other subjects like old Mr Saxby.'

'I see. You would like it short and crisp. You would wish me, as I was saying to Johnny the other day, to let my Yea be Yea and my Nay be Nay?'

'I would.'

'Then here it comes,' said Lord Ickenham.

It was, as he had predicted, a long story, but it gripped his audience throughout. There was no wandering of attention on Barbara Crowe's part to damp a raconteur's spirits. At each successive twist and turn of the plot her eyes seemed to grow wider. It was some moments after he had finished before she spoke. When she did, it was with a wealth of feeling.

'Cor lumme, stone the crows!' she said.

'I was expecting you to say that,' said Lord Ickenham. 'I must remember, by the way, to ask Albert Peasemarch what the meaning of the expression is. What crows? And why stone them? I have met men who, when moved, have said "Cor chase my Aunt Fanny up a gum tree!", which seems to me equally cryptic. However, this is not the time to go into all that. I anticipated that you would react impressively to my revelation, for it is of course a sensational tale. Are you feeling faint?'

'Not faint, no, but I think I'm entitled to gasp a bit.'

'Or gurgle. Quite.'

'Fancy Toots writing that book! I wouldn't have thought he had it in him.'

Lord Ickenham clicked his tongue.

'Haven't you been listening? I said the author of *Cocktail Time* was Raymond Bastable.'

'I used to call him Toots.'

'You did?'

'I did.'

'How perfectly foul! And he used to call you Baby?'

'He did.'

'How utterly loathsome! It makes one realize that half the world never knows how the other half lives. Well, you'll soon be calling him that revolting name again. If, that is to say, what I have told you has not killed your love.'

'What do you mean?'

'Lots of people recoil in horror from *Cocktail Time*. The bishop did. So did Phoebe. So, according to Beefy, did about fifty-seven publishers before he finally landed it with the Tomkins people. It doesn't diminish your love for him to know that he is capable of writing a book like that?'

'It does not. If anything was needed to deepen my love for Beefy, as you call him—'

'Better than calling him Toots.'

'—it is the discovery that he has a hundred and fifty thousand dollars coming to him from the movie sale of the first thing he ever wrote. Golly! Think what we'll get for the next one!'

'You feel there will be a next one?'

'Of course there will. I'll see to that. I'm going to make him give up the Bar—I've always hated him being a barrister—and concentrate on his writing. We'll live in the country, where he can breathe decent air and not ruin his lungs by sitting all day in stuffy courts. Have you ever been in the Old Bailey?'

'Once or twice.'

'I believe you can cut the atmosphere there with a spoon. They carve it up in slices and sell it as rat poison. And living in the country, he'll get his golf every day and bring his weight down. He had put on weight terribly the last time I saw him. I suppose he's worse than ever now.'

'He is far from streamlined.'

'I'll adjust that,' said Barbara grimly. 'Do you know when I first saw Raymond? When I was ten. One of my uncles took me to see the Oxford and Cambridge match, and there he was, looking like a Greek god. My uncle introduced me to him after the game, and I got his autograph and fell in love with him there and then. Gosh, he was terrific!'

'You plan to pare him down to the Beefy of thirty years ago?'

'Well, not quite that, perhaps, but some of that too, too solid flesh is certainly going to melt. And now,' said Barbara, rising from her deck chair, 'I think I'll follow our Mr Saxby's excellent example and have a bath. What's the procedure about clocking in here? Do I see your godson and haggle about terms?'

'He's gone to London. You conduct the negotiations with his old nurse. And I'd better come and help you through the ordeal. She's rather formidable.'

If there was a touch of smugness in Lord Ickenham's demeanour as he returned to his deck chair after piloting Barbara Crowe through her interview with Nannie Bruce, it would have been a stern judge who would not have agreed that that smugness was excusable. He had set out for Dovetail Hammer with the intention of spreading sweetness and light among the residents of that inland Garden of Eden, and in not one but several quarters he had spread it like a sower going forth sowing. Thanks to his efforts, Barbara would get her Toots, and Beefy would get his Baby, plus all that lovely cash from the cornucopias of Hollywood. Johnny had got his five hundred pounds, Albert Peasemarch his Phoebe, and it would not be long presumably before Cyril McMurdo got his Nannie Bruce. It was true that both Mr and Mrs Carlisle were at the moment probably feeling a little short of sweetness and light, but, as has already been pointed out, there is seldom enough of that commodity to go round. No doubt in due season they would be able to console themselves with the thought that money is not everything and that disappointments such as they had suffered are sent to us to make us more spiritual.

After perhaps half an hour had elapsed, his meditations were interrupted by the arrival of Johnny Pearce, who approached him on foot, having returned his borrowed car to the Beetle and Wedge. His manner, Lord Ickenham was amused to see, was gloomy. He would soon, as Barbara had put it, adjust that.

'Hullo, Johnny.'

'Hullo, Uncle Fred.'

'Back again?'

'Yes, I'm back.'

'Everything all right?'

'Well, yes and no.'

Lord Ickenham frowned. His objection to his godson's habit of talking in riddles has already been touched on.

'What do you mean, Yes and No? Did you square things with Bunny?'

'Oh, yes. We're getting married next week. At the registrar's.'

'Business is certainly brisk in the registraring industry these days. And I suppose you're asking yourself what the harvest will be when she settles down here with Nannie?'

'Yes, that's what's worrying me.'

'It need worry you no longer, my dear boy. Do you know what happened at that sale this afternoon? You will scarcely credit it, but that cabinet of yours fetched five hundred pounds.'

Johnny collapsed into the deck chair in which Barbara Crowe had sat.

'What!' he gasped. 'You're kidding!'

'Not at all. That was the final bid, five hundred pounds. Going, going, gone, and knocked down to Mr Gordon Carlisle. So all you have to do now is go to Nannie . . . Why', asked Lord Ickenham, breaking off and regarding his godson with amazement, 'aren't you skipping like the high hills? Well, I suppose you could hardly do that, sitting in a deck chair, but why aren't you raising your eyes thankfully to heaven and giving three rousing cheers?'

It was some moments before Johnny was able to speak.

'I'll tell you why I'm not giving three rousing cheers,' he said, and laughed in a way which Lord Ickenham recognized as hol-

low and hacking. 'That sale was the vicar's jumble sale. I contrib-
uted the cabinet to it, glad to get rid of the beastly thing. So not
a penny of the five hundred quid comes to me. It will be applied
to the renovation and repair of the church heating system, which,
I understand,' said Johnny, with another hollow, hacking laugh,
'needs a new boiler.'

25

Mr Saxby, feeling greatly refreshed after his bath, came out into the cool evening air and started to toddle across the park. He had decided not to resume the knitting of his grandson's sweater, which could very well wait till the quiet period after dinner, but to stroll over to Hammer Lodge and tell his friend Bastable about the auction sale. It would, he thought, interest him. For though Bastable had probably never seen that cabinet, whose peculiar foulness was the point of his story, he was convinced that he could describe it sufficiently vividly to make him appreciate the drama of what had occurred.

Nothing happened when he reached the Lodge and rang the front door bell. The butler appeared to be away from his post, down at the Beetle and Wedge perhaps or possibly out having a round of golf. But things like that never deterred Mr Saxby. The door being open, he walked in, and having done so, raised his voice and bleated:

'Bastable! BASTable!'

And from somewhere in the distance there came an answering shout. It seemed to proceed from the depths of the house, as though the shouter were in the cellar. Very strange, Mr Saxby felt. What would Bastable be doing in a cellar? And then the obvious solution presented itself. He was having a look at his wine. The

good man loves his wine, and it is only natural that he should go
down from time to time to see that all is well with it.

'Bastable,' he said, arriving at the cellar door.

'Who's that?' a muffled voice replied.

'Saxby.'

'Thank God! Let me out!'

'Do what?'

'Let me *out*.'

'But why don't you *come* out?'

'The door's locked.'

'Unlock it.'

'The key's on your side.'

'You're perfectly correct. So it is.'

'Well, turn it, man, turn it.'

Mr Saxby turned it, and there emerged an incandescent figure
at the sight of which Albert Peasemarch, had he been present,
would have trembled like one stricken with an ague. Lord Ickenham had spoken of men of his acquaintance who would thoroughly have enjoyed being locked up in a wine cellar. Sir Raymond
Bastable did not belong to this convivial class. He was, as Gordon
Carlisle had put it, when speaking of his wife Gertie, vexed.

'Where's Peasemarch?' he said, glaring about him with reddened eyes.

'Who?'

'Peasemarch.'

'I don't think I know him. Nice fellow?'

Sir Raymond continued to glare to left and right, as if expecting
something to materialize out of thin air. As the missing member of
his staff did not so materialize, he glared at Mr Saxby.

'How did you get in?'

'I walked in.'

'He didn't let you in?'

'Who didn't?'

Sir Raymond tried another approach.

'Did you see a round little bounder with a face like a suet pudding?'

'Not to my recollection. Who is this round bounder?'

'My butler. Peasemarch. I want to murder him.'

'Oh, really? Why is that?'

'He locked me in that damned cellar.'

'Locked you in the cellar?' bleated Mr Saxby, toiling in the rear as his companion, snorting with visible emotion, led the way to his study. 'Are you sure?'

'Of course I'm sure,' said Sir Raymond, sinking into an armchair and reaching for his pipe. 'I've been there for hours, with nothing to smoke. A-a-a-ah!' he said, puffing out a great cloud.

Tobacco rarely fails to soothe, but you have to give it time. The mixture of Sir Raymond's choice was slow in producing any beneficent effects. As he finished his first pipeful and prepared to light a second, his eyes were still aflame and those emotional snorts continued to proceed from him like minute guns. In a voice which would have been more musical if he had not been shouting all the afternoon, he sketched out the plans he had formed for dealing with Albert Peasemarch, should fate eventually throw them together again.

'I shall strangle him very slowly with my bare hands,' he said, rolling the words round his tongue as if they were vintage port. 'I shall kick his spine up through that beastly bowler hat he wears. I shall twist his head off at the roots. He got me to that cellar saying he wanted me to look at the last lot of claret, and when I went over to look at it, he nipped out, locking the door behind him.'

It was a simple tale, simply told, but it gripped Mr Saxby from the start. He uttered a curious high cry which he had probably picked up from some wild duck of his acquaintance.

'How extremely odd. I have never heard of a butler locking anyone in a wine cellar. I knew one once, many years ago, who kept tropical fish, but that', said Mr Saxby, who could reason clearly when he gave his mind to it, 'is not, of course, quite the same thing. Do you know what I think, Bastable? Do you know the conviction that recent happenings in Dovetail Hammer have forced on me? It is that there is something in the air here that breeds eccentricity. You see it on all sides. Take the auction sale this afternoon.'

It was agony to Sir Raymond to be reminded of the auction sale, and once again there surged up in him a passionate desire to twist Albert Peasemarch's head off at the roots. But curiosity overcame his reluctance to speak of it.

'What happened?' he asked huskily.

Mr Saxby slid into his narrative with the polished ease of one who even at the Demosthenes, where the species abounds, was regarded as something unusual in the way of club bores. Members who could sit without flinching through Sir Roderick Glossop's stories about his patients or old Mr Lucas-Gore's anecdotes of Henry James, paled beneath their tan when Howard Saxby senior started to tell the tale.

'I must begin by saying,' he began by saying, 'that at Hammer Hall, where, as you know, I am now residing, though my son tells me I must return home, so I shall shortly be leaving, and sorry to go, I assure you, for apart from your delightful society, Bastable, there is a wealth of bird life in these parts which an ornithologist like myself finds richly rewarding—'

'Get on,' said Sir Raymond.

Mr Saxby looked surprised. He had supposed that he was getting on.

'At Hammer Hall, as I was about to say,' he resumed, 'there is—or was—an imitation walnut cabinet, the property of my host Mr Pearce . . . Do you know Mr Pearce?'

'Slightly.'

'Well, this imitation walnut cabinet belonged to him, and it stood in the hall, facing you as you entered through the front door. I stress this, because it was impossible, as you went in and out, not to see the beastly thing, and it had given me some bad moments.

I want to impress upon you, Bastable, that this loathsome cabinet was entirely worthless, for that is the core and centre of my story. This afternoon I was relieved to hear that it was being included in the auction sale which was held at the village hall, for words cannot tell you the effect which the sight of that revolting object had on a sensitive eye. It was—'

'I know all about the cabinet,' said Sir Raymond. 'Get on.'

'You do bustle me so, my dear fellow. Men at the club do the same thing, I never know why. Well, this cabinet came up for auction, and judge of my amazement when I heard Carlisle—not the Carlisle who was bitten by an angora rabbit but the one who is staying at the Hall—bid fifty pounds. But more was to come. The next moment, a squirt of the name of Cosmo Wisdom, whom you have probably not met, had bid a hundred. And so it went on. A cabinet, I must again emphasize, of no value whatsoever. Can you wonder that I say that the air of Dovetail Hammer breeds eccentricity? Are you in pain, Bastable?'

Sir Raymond was, and he had been unable to check a groan. The way the story appeared to be heading, it looked to him as though the blow-out or punch of it was going to be that his frightful nephew had won the cabinet, which would be the end of all things.

'Get on,' he said dully.

'How you do keep saying "Get on"! But I think I see what is in your mind. You want to know how it all ended. Well, I always think it spoils a good story to hurry it, but if you must have it in a nutshell, what happened was that just as Carlisle bid five hundred pounds, the squirt's mother with the assistance of the village policeman removed him from the scene, so the distressing cabinet was knocked down to Carlisle at that figure.'

Sir Raymond puffed out a relieved cloud of smoke. Everything was . . . well, not perhaps all right, but much more nearly all right than it might have been. He knew Gordon Carlisle to be a man who had his price. That price would undoubtedly be stiff, but to secure

Cosmo's letter he was prepared to pay stiffly. Yes, things, he felt, looked reasonably bright.

'So Carlisle got the cabinet?'

'I told you he did,' said Mr Saxby. 'But when you say "So Carlisle got the cabinet?" as if that were the important thing, it seems to me that you are missing the whole point of my story. It is immaterial which of the two eccentrics made the higher bid, what is so extraordinary is that they were bidding at all in fifties and hundreds for this entirely worthless object. It bears out what I was saying to Barbara Crowe just now—'

Sir Raymond sat up with a jerk. His pipe fell from his mouth in a shower of sparks. Mr Saxby regarded it with a shake of the head.

'That's how fires get started,' he said reprovingly.

'Barbara Crowe?'

'Though Boy Scouts start them, I believe, by rubbing two sticks together. How, I have never been able to understand. Why two sticks, rubbed together, should—'

'Is Barbara Crowe *here?*'

'She was when I went to take my bath. Looking very well, I thought.'

As Sir Raymond picked up his pipe, strange emotions were stirring within him—exultation one of them, tenderness another. There could be only one reason for Barbara's arrival in Dovetail Hammer. She had come to see him, to try to effect a reconciliation. She was, in short, making what is known as the first move, and it touched him deeply that anyone as proud as she could have brought herself to do it. All the old love, so long kept in storage, as if it had been something Albert Peasemarch had locked up in a wine cellar, came popping out as good as new, and in spite of the presence in it of men like Gordon Carlisle and his nephew Cosmo the world seemed to him a very pleasant world indeed.

That strange tenderness grew. He could see now how wrong had been the stand he had taken about Phoebe sharing their home. Of course a bride would not want her home shared by any-one, let alone a woman like his sister Phoebe. Wincing a little, he resolved that, even if it meant paying out the two thousand pounds a year she had mentioned, Barbara must be alone with him in their little nest.

He had just reached this admirable decision, when Lord Icken-ham came in through the french windows, and paused, momen-tarily disconcerted, at the sight of Mr Saxby. He had come to talk to Sir Raymond privately, and there was nothing in Howard Saxby senior's manner to suggest that he did not intend to remain rooted to the spot for hours.

But he had always been a quick thinker. There were ways of removing this adhesive old gentleman, and it took him but an instant to select the one he knew could not fail.

'Oh, there you are, Saxby,' he said. 'I was looking for you. Flan-nery wants to see you.'

Mr Saxby gave an interested bleat.

'Flannery? Is he here?'

'Just arrived.'

'Why didn't you bring him along?'

'He said he wanted to see you on some private matter.'

'It must be something to do with those Amalgamated Rubber shares.'

Sir Raymond, who had been daydreaming about little nests, came out of his reverie.

'Who's Flannery?'

'He's on the stock exchange. He looks after my investments.'

'They could be in no safer hands,' said Lord Ickenham, with a curious little thrill of satisfaction as he realized that the mists had at last cleared away and he now knew who Flannery was. 'I wouldn't keep him waiting, Beefy,' he went on, as Mr Saxby ambled off, making remarkably good time for a man of his years, 'I come bearing news which will, unless I am greatly mistaken, send you gambolling about the house and grounds like a lamb in

springtime. But before going into that,' he said, cocking an interested eyebrow, 'I would like, if I may do so without giving offence,
to comment on your personal appearance. Possibly it is my imagination, but you give me the idea of being a bit more dusty than
usual. Have you been rolling in something, or do you always have
cobwebs in your hair?'

A cloud marred the sunniness of Sir Raymond's mood. This
reminder that he was sharing the same planet with Albert Peasemarch caused a purple flush to spread over his face.

'You'd have cobwebs in your hair, if you'd been in a cellar all the
afternoon,' he said warmly. 'Do you know where Peasemarch is?'

'I was chatting with him on the phone not long ago, and he told
me he was going to London for a week or two, presumably to stay
with his sister, who has a house at East Dulwich. I was surprised
at his leaving you so suddenly. No unpleasantness, I trust?'

Sir Raymond breathed heavily.

'He locked me in the cellar, if you call that unpleasantness.'

Lord Ickenham seemed staggered, as a man might well be at
hearing such sensational words.

'Locked you in the cellar?'

'The wine cellar. If Saxby hadn't come along, I'd be there still.
The man's insane.'

'One of the mad Peasemarches, you think? I'm not so sure. I
admit that his behaviour was peculiar, but I believe I can understand it. Owing to a singular piece of good fortune which has just
befallen him, Albert Peasemarch is a bit above himself this afternoon. Needing an outlet for his high spirits and feeling that he
had to do something by way of expressing himself, he chose this
unusual course. Where you or I in similar circumstances would
have opened a bottle of champagne or gone about giving small boys
sixpences, Peasemarch locked you in the cellar. It's just a matter
of how these things happen to take you. I suppose he thought you
would laugh as heartily as he at the amusing little affair.'

'Well, he was wrong,' said Sir Raymond, still breathing heavily. 'If Peasemarch were here and I could get my hands on him, I would take him apart, limb by limb, and dance on his fragments.'

Lord Ickenham nodded.

'Yes, I can see your side of the thing. Well, when I meet him, I will let him know that you are displeased, and you will certainly get a letter of apology from him, for there is good stuff in Albert Peasemarch and no one is quicker than he to admit it when he knows he has acted mistakenly. But we must not waste precious moments talking of Albert Peasemarch, for there are other and far more important matters that call for our attention. Prepare yourself for a surprise, Beefy. Barbara Crowe is here.'

'It isn't a surprise.'

'You knew?'

'Saxby told me.'

'And what steps do you propose to take?'

'I'm going to tell her I've been a fool.'

'Doesn't she know?'

'And I'm going to marry her, if she'll still have me.'

'Oh, she'll have you, all right. I could tell that by the way, every time I mentioned your name, she buried her face in her hands and murmured "Toots! Toots!"'

'She did?' said Sir Raymond, much moved.

'Brokenly,' Lord Ickenham assured him.

'You know what the trouble was,' said Sir Raymond, removing a cobweb from his left eyebrow. 'She didn't want Phoebe living with us.'

'Very naturally.'

'Yes, I see that now. I'm going to give her two thousand pounds a year and tell her to go off and take a flat somewhere.'

'A sound and generous decision.'

'Or do you think she might settle for fifteen hundred?' said Sir Raymond wistfully.

Lord Ickenham considered the question.

'If I were you, Beefy, I would cross that bridge when you come to it. For all you know, Phoebe may be getting married herself.'

Sir Raymond stared.

'Phoebe?'

'Yes.'

'My sister Phoebe?'

'Stranger things have happened.'

For an instant it seemed that Sir Raymond was about to say 'Name three', but he merely gave a grunt and brushed away another cobweb. Lord Ickenham studied him with a thoughtful eye. He was debating within himself whether or not this was a suitable moment to reveal to the barrister-novelist that he was about to become allied by marriage to the East Dulwich Peasemarches. He decided that it was not. It is only an exceptionally mild and easy-tempered man who can receive with equanimity the news that his sister will shortly be taking for better or for worse a butler who has recently locked him in the wine cellar. Apprised of the impending union, it seemed highly probable to Lord Ickenham that Sir Raymond Bastable would follow in the footsteps of Nannie Bruce's Uncle Charlie and curl up in a ball. He turned to another matter, one to which ever since his momentous talk with Johnny Pearce he had been devoting his powerful mind.

'Well, I'm delighted, my dear fellow, that all is well again between you and Barbara,' he said. 'If there is one thing that braces me up, it is to see two sundered hearts come together, whether it be in springtime or somewhat later in the year. Oh, blessings on the falling out that all the more endears, as the fellow said. But there's one thing you must budget for, Beefy, when you marry Barbara, and this may come as something of a shock to you. You will have to be prepared to start work on another book.'

'What!'

'Well, of course.'

'But I can't.'

'You'll have to. If you think you can write a novel and sell it for a hundred and fifty thousand dollars and marry a literary agent and not have her make you sit down on your trouser seat and write another, you sadly underestimate the determination and will to win of literary agents. You won't have a moment's peace till you take pen in hand.'

Sir Raymond's lower jaw had fallen to its fullest extent. He stared into the future and was appalled by what he saw.

'But I can't, I tell you! It nearly killed me, writing *Cocktail Time*. You haven't any conception what it means to sweat your way through one of these damned books. I daresay it's all right for fellows who are used to it, but for somebody like myself . . . I'd much rather be torn to pieces with red-hot pincers.'

Lord Ickenham nodded.

'I thought that might possibly be your attitude. But I see a way out of the difficulty. Ever hear of Dumas?'

'Who?'

'Alexandre Dumas. *The Three Musketeers. Count of Monte Cristo.*'

'Oh, Dumas? Yes, of course. Everybody's read Dumas.'

'You're wrong. They just think they have. What they were really getting was the output of his corps of industrious assistants. He was in rather the same position as you. He wanted the money, as much of it as he could gouge out of the reading public, but he strongly objected to having to turn out the stuff. So he assigned the rough spadework—the writing of his books—to others.'

Hope leaped into Sir Raymond's haggard eyes. There flooded over him a relief similar to that which he had experienced when hearing Mr Saxby's voice outside the cellar door. It was as though spiritual United States Marines had arrived.

'You mean I could get someone else to write the infernal thing?'

'Exactly. And who more suitable than my godson, Johnny Pearce?'

'Why, of course! He's an author, isn't he?'

'Been one for years.'

'Would he do it?'

'Nothing would please him more. Like Dumas, he needs the money. Fifty-fifty would be a fair arrangement, I think?'

'Yes, that seems reasonable.'

'And of course he would have to have something down in advance. A refresher you call it at the Bar, don't you? Five hundred pounds suggests itself as a suitable figure. Just step to your desk, Beefy, and write him a cheque for that amount.'

Sir Raymond stared.

'You want me to give him five hundred pounds?'

'In advance of royalties.'

'I'm not going to give him any five hundred pounds.'

'Then I, on my side, am not going to give you that letter of young Cosmo's. I quite forgot to mention, Beefy, that shortly after our Mr Carlisle placed it in the cabinet, I found and removed it. I have it in my pocket now,' said Lord Ickenham, producing it. 'And if', he added, noting that his companion had begun to stir in his chair and seemed to be gathering himself for a spring, 'you are thinking of rising and busting me one and choking it out of me, let me mention that I have a rudimentary knowledge of ju-jitsu, amply sufficient to enable me to tie you into a lover's knot which it would take you hours and hours to get out of. Five hundred pounds, Beefy, payable to Jonathan Twistleton Pearce.'

There was a silence, during which a man might have uttered the words 'Jonathan Twistleton Pearce' ten or perhaps twelve times, speaking slowly. Then Sir Raymond heaved himself up. His manner was not blithe. Roget, asked to describe it, would have selected some term such as 'resigned' or 'nonresisting' or possibly 'down on his marrowbones (*slang*)', but it was plain, when he spoke, that he had made his decision.

'How do you spell Pearce?' he said. 'P-e-a-r-c-e or P-i-e-r-c-e?'

218 · P. G. WODEHOUSE

The shadows were lengthening across the grass as Ickenham started to saunter back through the park to Hammer Hall, the cheque in his pocket which would bring wedding bells to Belinda Farringdon, his godson Johnny, Nannie Bruce and Officer Cyril McMurdo—unless, of course, they were all going to be married at the registrar's, in which event there would be no bells. It was one of those perfect days which come from three to five, times in an English summer. The setting sun reddened the waters of the lake, westward the sky was ablaze with green and gold and amethyst and purple, and somewhere a bird, probably an intimate friend of Mr Saxby's, was singing its evensong before knocking off for the night.

Everywhere was peace and gentle stillness, and it made Lord Ickenham think how jolly it would be to be in London.

He had become a little tired of country life. Well enough in its way, of course, but dull . . . humdrum . . . nothing ever happening. What he needed to tone up his system was a night out in the pleasure-seeking section of the metropolis in the society of some congenial companion.

Not his nephew Pongo. You couldn't dig Pongo out nowadays. Marriage had turned him into a sober citizen out of tune with the hopes and dreams of a man who liked his evenings lively. Ichabod was the word that sprang to the lips when the mind dwelt on Pongo Twistleton, and for a moment, looking back on the days when a telephone call had always been enough to bring his nephew out with, as the expression is, a whoop and a holler, Lord Ickenham was conscious of a slight depression.

Then he was his bright self again. He had remembered that in his little red book in his bedroom at the Hall he had the address of Albert Peasemarch.

What pleasanter than to go to Chatsworth, Mafeking Road,

East Dulwich, imitate the cry of the white owl, tell Albert Pease-march to put on his bowler hat, and, having checked that bowler hat in the cloakroom of some gay restaurant, to plunge with him into London's glittering night life?

Which, he was convinced, would have much to offer to two young fellows up from the country.

UNCLE FRED RETURNS
"TO SPREAD SWEETNESS AND LIGHT" . . .

UNCLE DYNAMITE

In which Pongo Twistleton smashes a prized bust of his lady love's father. Uncle Fred must come clean up the mess.

SERVICE WITH A SMILE

In which Uncle Fred returns to Blandings Castle to relieve Lord Emsworth of his many woes: a nagging secretary, prankster Church Lads, and a plot to thieve his prize-winning sow.

YOUNG MEN IN SPATS

In which Uncle Fred makes his memorable first appearance among a collection of short stories about the Drones Club.

UNCLE FRED IN THE SPRINGTIME

In which Uncle Fred is called on to prevent a pignapping, bring together two young lovers, and diagnose the ailments of the upper class.